I'M WAITING

I'M WAITING

SAMMY REESE

1974
DOUBLEDAY & COMPANY, INC.
Garden City, New York

All of the characters in this book
are fictitious, and any resemblance
to actual persons, living or dead,
is purely coincidental.

First Edition

ISBN: 0-385-08527-3
Library of Congress Catalog Card Number 73–10816
Copyright © 1974 by Sam Reese
All Rights Reserved
Printed in the United States of America

FOR . . .

      ELOISE ANDREWS

      WINIFRED HALL

      CHILES HARRIS

I'M WAITING

CHAPTER ONE

Charles's office was in the rear administrative area of the building. He neither liked nor disliked his job. In fact, he felt nothing about it. It was simply where he worked. Had always worked. Since high school. Always. When possible he ignored the others who worked there, for isolation was necessary to him. It left him time to think, time to dream. To plan.

Kneeling in the hallway outside his office, he carefully loaded the books that were stacked there onto a cart. He seemed to devote total concentration to his work, double-checking each volume with a master list of new publications. But he was not concentrating on the books at all.

He heard someone enter the hall at the far end but did not turn. From the sound of her steps, he knew that it was Miss Murray. It was. And he knew that she would turn into her office. She did. Then, continuing his work, he waited for what he knew would follow.

And of course he was right.

Charles could hear the high, sharp voice coming from the cubicle at the end of the hall. "You girls might as well take your break now." The typewriters stopped. "Remember fifteen minutes. Not twenty-five."

After a moment the two secretaries, Jeanette and Carol, both in their twenties but still pathetically girlish in behavior, came into the hall and walked toward Charles. Facing away from them, he closed his eyes and could see them more clearly than if he had been openly studying them. They were utterly usual young women; pretty, affected, physical monuments to the terminal quality of youth. Charles bent farther over his work, smiling, as in fantasy he watched them. He could see the vapid, whining older women that they would become and his smile turned inward, warmed him, for he knew them to be incapable of seeing this most obvious truth; the truth of age that would eventually wither and cripple them. It was just the kind of minor flight that colored his day with the ghost of enjoyment.

Miss Murray called again, too sweetly, "Last time you were gone for twenty-five minutes, Jeanette."

Charles smiled, just as he knew that in her office, Miss Murray was smiling.

The girls paused. Jeanette started to answer; but Carol stopped her with a look and they continued on toward the water fountain, Jeanette speaking quietly through clenched teeth, "If she keeps that up, I just don't know how long I'll be able to stand it."

Carol glanced back toward the office, fearful that Miss Murray would be watching. She wasn't. Nudging Jeanette, she warned, "Shhh."

"I mean it. I can't take this much longer. There's lots of jobs in this town, and this one doesn't pay that good anyway."

There was contagion in Jeanette's minor rebellion. After a second reassuring glance backward to the empty hallway, Carol offered a whispered, conspiratorial, "I didn't even get my last increase."

Charles, sensing the girls' nearness, shifted his body so that he and the books almost completely blocked the hallway. The girls held no deep interest for him, but he wanted to present them with a dilemma. In order to get past, they would have to brush against him. He knew how distasteful they would find that for both of them had attempted mild flirtations with him as most of the girls did when they first came to work there. He remembered with pleasure that his response had been a frustrating and unique experience for these two, for immediately it had been obvious that in their own eyes they were attractive, special, sure of their power to please. He had refused to return their looks, or even to speak, and this had so stunned them both that they still bore the grudge.

The two young women stopped behind him. Jeanette was the more disgusted of the two. "Charles," she said, her voice brimming with distaste, "we know you know we're here. And you can just damn well move!"

Cool and disinterested, he continued working. "In a minute."

In no mood to wait, they brushed past; and, as they went by, he watched their silken legs; still youthful, the texture smooth, beautifully pale. He smiled as they continued on without looking back;

wanted to laugh for he could see them old, the skin of those firm, youthful legs withered, loose and blue-veined.

Jeanette had always been the victim of immediate fury and, as her mother had long ago promised that it would, it had "blighted her life." The frustration of the last few minutes now began to take over. "Do you mean to tell me that Miss Murray would not okay your increase?"

"Exactly what I mean," Carol intoned, propping her ring-cluttered hand on her spreading hip.

"She's afraid one day one of us'll take her job." Now at the water fountain Jeanette took a drink, the fury continuing to build. For a moment she had almost turned it toward Charles, but Miss Murray had first call. "I feel like quitting."

Carol stopped mid-drink. "Jeanette!"

"I do. Serve her right if we all just up and quit."

Charles, quietly pushing the cart before him, came up behind them. Unaware that he was there, they continued blocking the narrow hall. At the last minute, without slowing, he gave warning. "Clear."

They just had time to press against the books as he went by, his arms brushing against their bodies.

It was not a good day for Jeanette. "Why don't you just knock us down next time!"

Charles continued walking without looking back. Expertly, he maneuvered the book-laden cart into his office.

After exchanging a look of silent disgust, the girls moved on to the Coke machine. Jeanette slammed in a quarter and watched as the cup filled with brown bubbles, thoughts of Miss Murray still charging through her. "She's jealous 'cause we can do her job better than she can; that's what it is." As her anger built, her voice became louder.

Again Carol glanced backward. "Hush. She'll hear you."

Jeanette gave the machine a shake and began hitting it. "This damn thing has my change." After a final violent rattling, the red and white monster coughed up the dime. "And anyway, I don't care if she does hear." She moved on to the candy machine.

Carol followed closely, whispering, "I'm sure she did. Loud as you were talking. I'm sure she did hear you."

Sobered by that frightening possibility, Jeanette paused before feeding the dime into the Baby Ruth slot, her concern suddenly real. "Do you think that she did?" She needed the job, certainly did not want to lose it. What would she do if they fired her? What would she do? "Carol." She was trembling. "Do you think so? . . . Do you?"

But Carol, her smile grown malicious, only laughed and shrugged.

In his office Charles could hear the inane chatter, the petty rivalries, the endless replaying of what he had heard for so many years. The room was small and, although incredibly crowded with stacks of books, there was some visible order. His office he liked neat.

Seated at his work table, a makeshift plywood affair that he had constructed himself more than twenty years before, he was marking the new books with an ink stamp. LOS ANGELES PUBLIC LIBRARY. He worked methodically with what appeared to be total concentration. An observer would find it almost impossible to believe that he was not thinking of his job at all, that what he was doing was the result of habit so long established that it left his mind free to rove as it would.

He placed the stamp exactly and neatly on the page, marking first the inside cover; then the catalog pocket, page 99, 199, 299 and on to the end. Then to the next book. His glasses gave him an intellectual, rather interesting look; and as he brushed his hair back from his forehead, and reached for a few dry-roasted peanuts, he seemed a calm, relaxed man.

His eyes warm and pleasant, he relived very slowly, completely, the sight of those legs as they had brushed past him, the feel of those bodies against his arms. From memory he moved to fantasy. And then he began to plan in such a quiet way that even he was not aware yet that the plan had begun.

In what appeared to be monotony but to him was not, the early afternoon went.

A faint ringing was heard. From beneath the mound of books Charles unearthed an alarm clock. It was three. His work day was ended. He turned off the alarm, closed the ink pad in its case so that the moisture would not evaporate, cleaned the stamp, rose, and put on his jacket. All his movements were precise, expected. At the doorway he snapped off the light but did not immediately go into the hall. He stood for a moment in the comfort of the shadows, a nice-looking, somewhat haggard man going into middle age. As he leaned against the doorframe, his weariness seemed to grow. But it was not that. Something was happening within him. Something unexpected. His mind was giving way to a hidden need. He walked into the hall wondering if this would be one of the days that it happened. Perhaps it would.

Driving was an escape for him. The other cars, people walking, the constant noise, the occasional glances that strangers gave. It was pleasing. And through it all, he was aware of power. Behind the wheel the choice was his. His movements as he drove were slow and deliberate. Almost as though he had a foreknowledge of the ever-changing patterns of traffic. He was aware of how easily he could alter the pattern. Stop. Turn. And it would all be changed—the pattern of movement that surrounded him. The choice was his.

But it was a puzzle, for in some things choice did not exist. At times an inner need dictated certain actions; and as he drove he felt himself going into that world . . . beyond choice. This would be one of the days that it happened. He could feel it. The pleasure of anticipation was building, lifting him, taking him away from the expected.

No longer was he on his way home.

Always when this began to happen, there was that short time, no longer than a breath, when he was sure that he could stop it. But of course he could not. Immediately the thought passed. The decision was firm. He was on his way.

His car was in the left lane, signaling for a turn. Abruptly he cut through the traffic and turned right, the plan now clear in his mind.

He was on his way to a strange apartment, one that he had never entered before. It belonged to a girl he had never met. By accident he had seen her one day. And had followed her.

Soon he would see her again.

And she would see him for the first time. He would be there. Waiting when she came home. He leaned forward into the warmth of the thought. He would be there in the room with her. And she would be unaware.

"Jane." He whispered her name. It was a nice name. And he smiled as he drove.

CHAPTER TWO

"Los Angeles?" Jane Atkins absent-mindedly straightened the sweaters on the counter and looked toward the other salesgirl, smiling. "Love it. Absolutely." She appeared relaxed and confident. And why not? She was obviously bright and attractive, an admirable, outgoing young girl who seemed totally at ease with her generation.

But she was not. She was seldom at ease in any area of life. Insecurity was her companion in whatever she did but she covered it so completely that few had ever suspected that she was not totally confident. Through years of discipline and training she had learned to hide her fears, conceal them beneath an outward display of friendly concern for others. She was never confident, never pleased with herself, never free of those endless doubts that would enable her to say, "So what?" or "Who cares?" or "It doesn't matter what they think." For to her it did matter. All of her life she had desperately cared. She was afraid of the mysterious "them"; was convinced that they would not like her, that they would talk about her, watch when she walked away, laugh and whisper.

Her parents remarked about how she had changed, how shy she "used to be." Even they did not suspect the constant fears that were hers. And so when she had left home ("Great things. We expect great things."), everyone in Porterton was sure that the Atkins girl would "show those folks in Hollywood how it oughta be done." She was nineteen and a very beautiful girl. Quiet and friendly, with a "great" voice . . . ("Better than Mama Cass, that's how good.")

She had been in Los Angeles for almost a year, and in that time had more or less mastered the terrifying prospect of living alone. In fact, she had grown to like it. The only time that she felt free and secure was the time when she returned to her apartment, closed the door and locked it. Then she was safe. Safe. It was to her a solemn word and with it the tensions of the day disappeared. Alone she felt an assurance that was not possible when she was with others.

Her career in the frantic California world of music was nonexistent. This she kept secret from her parents. Her letters to them concerning her theatrical endeavors were a deceptive fabric of half truths, half lies. It was true that she had left demonstration records at the various companies. But she had not expected immediate acceptance and she was shamed by the secret relief that her failure brought.

She worked in a dress shop on the Sunset Strip, Estelle's Mod. Owned by a middle-aged businesswoman, the store was what it was expected to be—forward-looking, but considered by the California extremists in fashion to be conservative. It was a successful shop, at least for the season, and Jane had the qualities that Estelle appreciated in her salesgirls—she was attractive, polite, and friendly to the customers. The other young girl who worked there was not as much to Estelle's liking. Rita. Estelle did not like the name. It had a sound of challenge. There was something selfish and offhand about her that Estelle found offensive, but the customers seemed pleased enough and that was, after all, the only thing that mattered.

"There's something here on this rack." It was late in the afternoon and Estelle was busy with the only customer in the shop. She rummaged through the half-priced suits, having exhausted the possibilities in the more expensive things. As always she felt a deep need to make the sale. The thought of losing it was a true offense to her, and she had to struggle to keep the casual façade that her customers liked. "A pants suit. Little on the conservative side. But it has a flair."

In the quietness of the store there was the drone of hushed conversation between the two girls, and Estelle longed to tell them to shut up. Their chatter was annoying. She was paying them to work and there they were, standing and talking. Paying them to talk, to just stand around and do nothing. It was definitely offensive. For a moment Estelle almost lost her easy attitude. Then, just in time, she found the pants suit that she was looking for. "Here." She took it down and started her pitch. This was the part that she liked. She would make the sale. She felt it. She smiled. "Don't you love it?"

The boredom of late afternoon had settled over Rita and Jane as it did every day when the clock was edging toward freedom. Rita lounged against the counter, smoking as she twirled a pencil in her frizzy hair. (Her hair had always been her problem and now she was deeply thankful that the Afro had made its way into the white world.) "I don't know," she said. "L.A.'s as good as any other town, I guess."

Jane continued folding the sweaters. "Sometimes I wish I'd gone to New York instead. You just don't know what to do." This was a lie. Los Angeles was terrifying enough. But New York . . . The thought chilled her.

Rita ground out the cigarette. "I think New Orleans sounds fun." She yawned and twirled the pencil, thankful that the endless day at last was ending.

In the front of the shop another customer had entered and, unnoticed by either of the girls, was looking through the blouses. Estelle, peeved that neither employee was watchful enough to notice something as inescapable as a customer, called to them casually, but with an edge, "There's a customer, girls."

Jane smiled as she went forward. "Can I help you?" And with the smile she was a beautiful girl, unaware that at that moment a man she did not know was thinking of her, waiting for her.

Charles drove slowly. There was little traffic in the Beachwood area above Hollywood. The section was liberally sprinkled with medium-rent apartment houses, each with its own palm tree, some with two. He turned onto Franklin Avenue, a somewhat busier thoroughfare, and parked. With very deliberate actions, he put on the hand brake, removed the key, took a last drag from his cigarette and flipped it illegally into the street. Then he got out of the car and slowly walked up Beachwood Drive, an attractive man taking a pleasant stroll on an uneventful Tuesday.

The afternoon was usual and a usual quiet hovered over the street. Two boys pedaled past, racing and calling to each other as their bikes sped along. Their voices receded and the silence returned as Charles approached an apartment house. After the slightest hesitation, a glance backward along the deserted sidewalk, he went up the steps and into the building.

He appeared relaxed. Almost casual. More so, in fact, than in the library. But the excitement was building and he had to struggle for control. He was not fearful that he would be caught. He felt instead a kind of desperation that he would be interrupted. That had happened before—on two occasions—and it had left him shaken and haunted. He had no regrets for his past actions. No guilt. But to be interrupted . . . That was his fear. And so his tension built.

Quickly he checked for her name on the mailboxes. There it was.

He reached out and lightly touched the card. *JANE ATKINS— APT. 207.* He almost smiled as he went into the building.

As he was about to press the elevator button, he heard it descending. He turned and hurried up the stairs, disappearing as the doors slid open and two teen-age girls got off. Both were rather short but that is where the resemblance ended. Elizabeth Mitchell was very thin and intense. (She had been smoking for two years and now, at sixteen, she was fearful for her health and was desperately trying to give it up.)

Sue Laughton was a very heavy little girl with a ponderous attitude and a round, puffball face. "Do you have the list?" she cried as she tried to catch up with her friend.

Without bothering to answer, Elizabeth held it aloft and hurried through the doorway.

"Well, wait," Sue whined, waddling after Elizabeth, panting with the exertion of it.

In the upstairs hallway, Charles expertly jimmied the door to 207 and quickly stepped inside.

Safe.

This was one of the best times.

Safe.

He was in.

And he was safe. He took a deep breath. It would all go right. He knew it . . . But if she did not come in alone . . . Quickly he dismissed it, leaving the thought unfinished. She would be alone. She had to be.

He leaned against the door and only then did he allow himself the pleasure of trembling. He was in. In. He looked about the small neat apartment. It was as he had thought it would be. One bedroom. And orderly. A little too orderly, and distinctly feminine. Almost disturbingly so. The curtains were frilly with a homemade look and the pillows on the sofa, ruffled. It was immediately obvious that she had taken great care in decorating the small ugly rooms. Even the magazines on the coffee table were "displayed," neatly stacked on each side of the plastic flower arrangement. Like a dentist's office, he thought.

Charles moved slowly through the quietness, studying each small detail with great care, for he knew that in the days to come he would

need these impressions. Of course then all of it would be clouded
with the softness of dream memory. But it was that, the remembered
images, the shadowed impressions, that would lead him to new
fantasies.

He was in.

It was the initial moment of violation and he loved it, trembled
with it. Someone's secret and private world had been broken into.
That, combined with the deathlike quiet, colored the moment with
disquiet. And it pleased him. He smiled. It was a good beginning.

He lit a cigarette and relaxed, the sure fantasy of what would
soon happen blending into memory, swirling about him like the
smoke.

Charles emptied the ashes into his coat pocket and with his handkerchief carefully cleaned the ashtray. There was an upright piano
in the corner. A singer? It was possible. A tape recorder rested on a
small table nearby. Then he noticed the sheets of music paper with
penciled arrangements. Yes. Either a singer or composer. Perhaps
both. It was the only note of disorder in the room.

He glanced into the efficiency kitchen, neat, frilly; the curtains,
bright and flowery; the backs of the straight chairs covered in the
same material. Abruptly he turned and went to the bedroom.

There the blinds were pulled and the half light that filtered
through created a softness that was mournful, for the colors were
somber. It was unlike the rest of the apartment. The room was more
comfortable. There were no frills or ruffles, no Easter egg colors. It
was a room that someone lived in and it was a relief after the cloying
neatness of the rest of the apartment.

In the corner there was a sewing machine and, on a card table,
pieces of material pinned to a pattern. Over the cluttered dressing
table was a large mirror with a jumble of snapshots and photographs
stuck around the edges. Other pictures were beneath the glass that
protected the top of the table.

Charles sat before the mirror and studied the snapshots. He remained there for a long time without moving.

Jane . . .

A beautiful girl.

From a high school graduation picture she smiled at him. Very
beautiful.

Without moving his eyes from the picture, he took a knife from his pocket and, with a satisfying click, he laid it on the glass.

The day was ending and Estelle stood by the door waiting for the two girls to leave. This was the time that she looked forward to, even on the worst days—this half hour or so when she was alone and went over the receipts, counted the money, studied the checks, the charge slips. Profit. She loved it.

She watched the girls as Rita struggled into her poncho, talking as usual. About some man. As they drew near, Estelle was tempted to have a few words with them about the customer they had failed to notice, but Rita's non-stop girl talk made it clumsy. What the hell. Hurry and leave, she thought. Just leave.

Jane was listening to Rita's endless chattering. Or was she? Estelle was never quite sure.

Almost at the door, Rita paused and lit a cigarette. "He kept pressuring me. Pressuring me 'til finally I just said, Look, Gordon. This is a first date."

"Good night, Estelle." Jane smiled as they passed.

Rita smiled as well, or rather grimaced. "Night."

Then they were outside and Rita breathed the air of freedom. She hated work.

"What did Gordon say?" Jane's question was meaningless for she did not care what any of the endless string of Gordons had said or not said. But it was expected and always Jane accommodated.

"The usual." Rita fished in her shoulder bag for the keys to the MG, found them. "We're down here." Together they walked to the car. "About how with certain people . . ."

As the glib voice droned on, Jane seemed to be listening but she wasn't. Quickly she moved to the outside so that when she turned to Rita her face would be away from the passing cars. She would never become accustomed to the way people stared at each other in Los Angeles. There was something frightening about it; the speed of the cars as they whipped around one another, the drivers all the while cruising the sidewalks—some for pickups, some simply for the pleasure of looking.

During the weeks when she had ridden the bus, before Rita had come to work in the shop, Jane had found the end of the day a torment. Cars would stop while she was waiting for the bus, men

would call to her. Some of them old men. Forty. Even older. Older
even than her own parents. It was unbelievable. In front of everybody. It didn't matter how many people were waiting there with her.
Still the men would call. The boldness of it always amazed her.
Some of the other girls found it flattering, would wave and laugh,
sometimes even accept a ride. But to Jane it was never flattering. She
hated it; and if Rita had not come to work at the shop with her car—
that wonderful car that closed her in and kept her safe—then Jane
would have quit her job and looked for work in a quieter area.

Rita continued talking and laughing, jangling the keys, taking
deep puffs on her cigarette. Jane walked beside her, never looking to
the street. She either held her head down letting her hair cover as
much of her face as possible or, as she was doing then, turned away
from the traffic.

At last they were at the car.

Safe, Jane thought.

Safe.

Charles was fascinated by the pictures around the mirror which
bore witness to Jane's small-town beginning. There was a vaguely
cheap, almost embarrassing quality about them and that was what he
loved. The complete lack of glamour, the rawness of them. Perfect.
She was perfect for him. Even the seediness of her parents was right.
The house she had grown up in, cheap, the paint peeling.

She was perfect.

If most of the pictures were studied carefully, Jane's discomfort
became obvious. The smile was what gave her away. Always smiling.
And always the same smile. A kind of desperate plea for something.

Even Jane did not know what the smile meant. She had always
smiled. ("The most beautiful smile, baby," her mother said.)

After she had been in Los Angeles for only a few weeks, her
mother had sent the pictures and Jane had startled herself by crying
when she saw what the manila envelope contained. Immediately she
had put them around her bedroom mirror. Just as they had been at
home. And they gave her comfort. When bad thoughts came, on
lonesome days, sometimes at night while she was brushing her hair,
she would study the pictures and they would warm her. She looked

on them as happy memories although she did not appear truly happy in any of them.

Charles leaned forward and looked closely at one of the pictures of Jane and her parents. They were standing before a weathered frame house. The mother, plump and smiling, had her head tilted at just the wrong angle so that the sun caught her glasses and flares of light streaked across her face. The father, sleeves rolled up and beginning to bald, was standing a little apart from them.

And Jane was smiling.

She was perfect.

The only thing that annoyed him was that he almost liked her. Certainly more than he had liked the others. Would that ruin it? He did not know. He knew only that there was something touching about her—her neatness, her desire to make the place "nice," her vanity, the plastic flowers, cheap frills and ruffles.

He heard the hum of the elevator and was immediately alert. Quickly and silently he moved to the closet, concealed himself and listened. He heard the elevator stop, the door slide open, someone get off. There were soft footsteps in the corridor. He waited but the sound went past; listened as someone entered the apartment next door.

He came back into the room and slowly, methodically he undressed, carefully folding each garment as he took it off.

He closed his eyes and could see her moving toward him; graceful, unaware.

Rita's car wove through the traffic and, with the movement, Jane relaxed. As soon as she could afford it, she definitely would buy a car. A Volkswagen perhaps. But not a convertible. That was the only thing that she did not like about Rita's car. She could not understand why anyone would want a convertible.

Rita continued to talk as she swerved around and between the other cars. "Anyway, I'm going out with Gordon again tonight."

There was no consistency to Rita. Or if there was, Jane had never been able to find it. It was impossible for her to understand why anyone would go out with someone she did not like. "Why?" she asked. Coming from her, it was an unusual question and immediately she was sorry that she had asked it.

Rita hated direct questions about herself, especially those to which she did not know the answer. Abruptly, she turned into the parking lot of a Safeway market. "Stop for groceries?"

Charles stood by the window from which he would be able to see her as she approached the building. It wasn't often that a setup was so perfect. Peering through the blinds, he called back memories of other times, other girls. He could see their faces, follow them in fantasy as they moved about those other rooms. Unaware, all of them.

Some movement in the street shattered his thoughts. A car had stopped and she was there. He watched, frozen, his pale eyes intense. Just right. "Come on home," he whispered. She was perfect.

Double-parked in front of the building, Rita let the motor idle. She hated to be alone and so she prolonged every meeting, no matter how trivial. She smiled. "Gordon's got a cousin."

Jane, familiar with the lengthy farewells, picked up her groceries. "Some other time."

"From Stockton." The smile faded, replaced by a more truthful plea. "Come on, Jane . . . Really." She turned away. "I hate going out with Gordon all by myself."

Touched by the change, Jane for a moment considered the possibility of going. "I don't know . . ."

Immediately Rita pulled the car into a No PARKING area and hopped out. "I'll come up. We'll grab your things and you can change at my place."

Jane hesitated, undecided. "Wait. I don't . . ."

But Rita was ready for the negative, had grown to expect it and she hurried on, enthusiastic over the prospect of a foursome. Her smile became a promise of good times about to be shared. "He's nice. Good-looking. We ran into him that night. Really. He's something."

But it was too late. Jane was glad to be home. To be safe. "I have to work. I'd like to go. Honestly. But . . ."

It was incredible to Rita that anyone would prefer staying at home when she could have an evening out. An evening with almost anyone would be better than sitting alone. Blind dates had always appealed to her and she could not understand why everyone did not feel the excitement that they held. She would not let go. "He's handsome, Jane. Handsome." Again she smiled, this time with soft insinuation. "And you know when I say handsome . . . The nicest face. And quiet. You know? It's right there. Everything. I mean it. Tall. Rangy. They grow 'em nice in Stockton."

Jane laughed. She could not help it. Rita's endless fascination with men was infectious. "You make it sound good. Very good. But I have too much to do."

Rita was quiet for a moment. Another battle lost. "Sure?"

"That's what I came to Los Angeles for."

With a shrug Rita got back into the car. "All right . . ." The reminder that it was "career" that had brought Jane to Hollywood always surprised her. "But think what you might be missing." She beeped the horn as the car started away.

"See you tomorrow." Jane waved, and adjusting the bag of groceries, walked toward the building.

Moving back from the window, Charles shifted the blind slightly so that every detail in the room would be exactly as he had found it. He grabbed the knife from the dresser and, taking his clothes with him, closed himself in the closet. The door was left slightly ajar—just enough so that he could see without being seen.

He was unaware that he had left a cigarette burning in the ashtray on the windowsill.

Jane waited for the elevator. In one respect she was sorry that she had not gone with Rita. Not because she wanted to go, but because she felt guilty about constantly turning the invitations down. The next time she would accept. Definitely.

The elevator door opened and she got on, grateful for the security of the small enclosed space. Almost home.

She got off on the second floor, walked down the hallway, put the key in the lock. Home. She began to relax.

From the closet, Charles listened. Now he knew that it would all go well. She was alone. He heard the front door close. She was in the apartment. Scratch of metal on metal; the door was double-locked. And he smiled. Locked in. He enjoyed the thought.

The smile disappeared. He froze. On the far side of the room, he saw the smoke from his forgotten cigarette idly curling and rising in the stillness.

She was moving about. He could hear her. But where? He was not sure. His field of vision was limited to the bedroom. He was afraid to take a chance but he knew that he must. Then he heard it, a familiar sound, and he knew it would be all right. The refrigerator door had been opened.

Charles hurried to the window, took the cigarette and ashtray back to the closet with him. He tried to stop trembling but could not. Stupid. Never had he done anything so stupid before. Never. Almost ruined it. Everything. And all because of something so stupid. He fought to control his breathing. But it was not ruined. Everything was all right. It would be fine. Smooth. Right. Like the others.

He listened and the usual sounds of a girl putting groceries away, touched him, warmed him, filled him with pleasure.

Then he took a woman's stocking from the pocket of his jacket and as he pulled it over his face, he enjoyed the feeling of closeness, the anonymity it gave. There was excitement in that for the material clung and distorted with the smothering breathlessness of the womb. He opened his lips wide and with the knife, made a large slit in the mesh. He worked his lips and tongue free.

He was ready. The indescribable pleasure of the final waiting began.

". . . ninety-eight . . . ninety-nine . . . one hundred." Jane dropped the hairbrush onto the dresser top and took a deep breath.

Home.

She pulled her slip over her head and dropped it on the bed beside her skirt and blouse, wrapped her terrycloth robe about her.

Home. She almost smiled with it.

From the next apartment the sound of a television set just turned on came through the thin walls. The voice of the Six O'clock News was low in volume, but still it could be heard. Jane turned on her bedside Sony to compete with the melodious drone of Walter Cronkite. She gathered up her clothes, moved toward the closet.

Charles tensed. She was more beautiful than he had thought. He stepped back a little. Her robe was loosely tied and there was a gracefulness to her movements that he had not noticed before. She was almost with him. He watched as she reached out to open the door. Then the telephone rang and when she turned away, Charles leaned his forehead against the coolness of the shadowed wall. He was shaking but it was all right. He caught his breath, tried to stop the trembling. It would be all right. Better this way really. The longer he waited, the better it finally would be.

"Hello."

The professional machine-like voice of long distance greeted her. "I have a collect call for anyone from Mrs. Laura Atkins in Porterton, California. Will you accept the charges?"

Her mother. Of course she would accept. She always accepted the calls and always in the next few days her mother's letter would contain three or four neatly folded dollar bills. More than enough to repay her. It was ridiculous. The minor deceptions. Jane had lived with those games always, at least for as long as she could remember and she was sure that they must have been there before she was born. Why must everything be kept from her father? Why couldn't he be told about the calls? It seemed such a useless deception. Jane promised herself that she would not mention her father, knowing very well that her mother would. She always did. Taking a Kent from the package on the dresser, she lit up. "Mama?"

Laura Atkins sat at her kitchen table, her heavy, aging face tense. She would never be totally at ease with long distance and was aware of it. It was, she supposed, a hangover from that fabled, long-ago depression that she had known as a child, the years that had driven her, her parents, and brothers from Kansas to California. The memory of that had never left her, the humiliation of it. She still saw herself as ragged, would always remember the way that they were stared at as their old Ford chugged and sputtered through those dusty Western towns of hard-faced people.

"Mama, are you there?"

Love touched the woman, filled her as she heard her daughter's voice on the other end of the line. "Sorry I had to make it collect," she said.

"That doesn't matter." Jane looked about for the ashtray, smiling over the fact that the conversation always started this way. Always.

"Of course I'll send it to you, but still I wish I didn't have to do it this way."

The ashtray.

Jane was mildly puzzled. Where was the ashtray?

"I didn't interrupt you? I mean you're not busy? Your music or anything?" Laura always asked questions in the negative, a habit that greatly annoyed her husband but when he complained she found it difficult to understand what he meant and so she continued to do it. "I can call back tomorrow if you're working." In this she was serious for her daughter's career was of foremost importance to her. Every night her prayers were filled with gratefulness for her only child and for that child's future. Another hangover from those depression years—the future was everything.

"No. I'm glad you called. I just got home."

"I'll send the money for it. I'll put it in an envelope first thing tomorrow so that it'll get there by . . ."

"It's two or three dollars. What difference does it make?"

Every time Laura heard a statement like that, it surprised her. She would never become accustomed to it. What difference does two or three dollars make? A lot of difference. But she did not go into it for she knew that others did not want to hear it, that her daughter did not really understand it. "Is everything all right?"

"Great."

Great. There was something about that word. It had become an almost vacant thing, meaningless. She was not satisfied. "You're sure?"

Jane juggled the receiver between her shoulder and ear as she reached for the other ashtray which was on the sewing table. "Mother. Everything is fine."

Laura was aware that her negative expectations were an aggravation but she could not control them. "You're sure? You would tell me?"

"Of course I would." The ashtray almost within her grasp, she dropped the telephone. "Damn." She grabbed the ashtray (an abalone shell from Catalina) and retrieved the receiver. "Mama."

"What happened?"

"Dropped the stupid phone." Again she settled herself in front of the mirror. "Couldn't find the ashtray." She glanced among the bottles and boxes on the dresser top. "It's always right here." But it wasn't.

Laura had begged her daughter to stop smoking. It would ruin her voice. Destroy her health. Bring on cancer. Emphysema. Laura had watched her baby brother die with it. Young. In his thirties. For months he had wheezed and gasped for breath while they watched. Not pretty. Her daughter's smoking was true anguish for her. "You're still smoking?"

"What?"

"You smoke too much."

"I know I do."

"You promised you'd try to quit."

"I did try."

"You just don't know what that can do to you . . ."

Jane had heard it a thousand times. Ten thousand. "Mother. I promised I'd quit and I did. For six nerve-shrieking days I walked around this place like a zombie and then I . . ." Having methodically looked everywhere on the dresser top, she was disturbed. "Where the hell is that ashtray?"

Laura realized that she had stayed with the subject of smoking long enough, perhaps too long. "The reason I wanted to call . . ."

"No. Wait." Jane was standing. "This is where I keep it. Right here on . . ."

"I wanted to remind you . . ."

"The ashtray, where is it?"

"Remind you about your father's birthday."

"What?"

"Tom's birthday. You didn't forget?"

Jane turned from the dresser and sat on the bed. "Of course I didn't forget." And the ashtray was forgotten. "It's the first of the week, the fourteenth. And I've already sent him a sweater." She looked to one of the pictures of her parents which was wedged along the side of the mirror, moved toward it and for a moment studied her father. "Is he fifty-one or fifty-two?"

"Fifty-two years old. Isn't that unbelievable? Tom is fifty-two and I'm forty-eight. That's what I really find unbelievable. Fat and forty-eight." She laughed a little self-consciously as she always did when she made a negative joke about herself. "Goes fast."

And with that sound of laughter, Jane was aware of how much she loved her mother, how much she missed her. She could see her as she must be—sitting at the kitchen table, a pad before her. And on the pad, Jane's telephone number. Long distance was serious business and so she always had the number before her, recited the digits slowly to the operator without ever taking her eyes from the pad, careful not to make a mistake.

"It does go fast, Mama."

Laura laughed, no hint of apology about it this time. The thought of her daughter having any conception of age or time was amusing to her.

"No. I'm beginning to feel it myself." Jane listened to her mother's laughter. "All right, go ahead. Make fun. But I am." The laughter warmed her and suddenly she wanted everything right between them, all of them. "I don't suppose Dad's there?"

This was the subject most painful to Laura, her daughter's disagreement with Tom. "Not yet . . . But Jane, I wish you'd make it up with him. I do. Pray for it every night. If only you'd try."

"Why doesn't he try?"

"Round and round the mulberry bush."

"Something like that . . . Give it up, Mama. We just can't get along. Who knows why?" It was true that she did not understand it, any more than her father did. Or her mother. It was something that had happened slowly over so many years that they had all lost touch with the beginning and now knew only that they were caught in the hopeless circle of unforgiving.

"So awful. The things you said to him before you left." Laura shuddered with the memory of it; that morning almost a year before when Jane was leaving, her suitcases packed and waiting, her new coat—such an expensive coat, so carefully chosen—folded casually over the back of the davenport. And it had started again, the endless petty arguments. She had prayed that they could avoid it, that the departure would go smoothly. But that prayer, like so many others, had gone unanswered and they had said it all, her husband shouting, trembling with it; Jane speaking the terrible words so quietly. The things they had said to each other, unforgivable things. "The awful things you said to him."

"I didn't mean those things, Mama. He knows that."

"Why don't you tell him?"

It was hopeless and Jane was suddenly weary. "And what about the things he said to me? You don't think about those, do you?"

"Round robin, huh? Another mulberry bush. There's no end."

"That's right."

Laura knew that her husband would never be the one to ask forgiveness, that if it were ever smoothed over, it would have to start with Jane. "But why must it be like that? That's what I can't understand. If only you'd call him. On his birthday. You could call him. Or maybe even come home. It's a Sunday. You wouldn't have to take time off from your job or anything. And I'd pay for the ticket. I've saved a little . . ."

So that's why she had called. Jane knew that her mother would never give up, that it was not possible for her to do that. She wanted to give some of the reasons that made it impossible for her to go home. Her father was only one of them. She put out the cigarette, so caught by the jumble of images and ghosts the words had awakened that she no longer thought of the missing ashtray. "It's no use, Mother."

"If only someone would explain it to me."

"It's not difficult to understand. We . . ." She stopped herself, knowing that if she went on she would again say things that should not be said. "Oh, never mind. You always take up for . . ." No. She would not go on with it. "Why am I even talking about it? The truth is, I don't really care any more." But as she said it she knew it was not true. "No. That's not right. I do care . . . I do and I don't. Something." She could not talk about it any longer. "Listen. This is costing a fortune and it's leading nowhere. Just over the same old endless roads. You called to remind me about his birthday, right?"

Laura hated for the visit to end. She had not meant for it to go as it had, and now it was too late. "Right."

"I'm reminded."

"I'll send the money for the call. They're going to give me the charges after we finish."

"I told you not to worry about that." But she knew that her mother did worry about money, that nothing could cure that concern.

"You should have it by Thursday. Maybe tomorrow if I mail it tonight."

Then Jane knew that after dinner her mother would make a special trip to the corner mailbox to send the neatly folded dollar bills. She was embarrassed by it, mildly guilt-stricken that Laura was always the one who had to place the calls. It was touching, all of it. And she was ashamed. She knew the pleasure that it would give if some afternoon on her coffee break, she would be the one to call. It was something that she had meant to do for a long time but had never quite gotten around to it. "Two dollars more or less is not going to make one bit of difference."

Immediately Laura took up that gauntlet. "That, my dear, is something no one can ever be sure of."

The predictability of her mother's reaction relaxed her. She started to prolong the moment but changed her mind. "Oh, to hell with it . . ."

"Have to hang up now," her mother said. "You're right. The bill will be terrible. And Jane. You shouldn't swear so much. It's not becoming. Bye."

"Goodbye, I love . . ." It was too late. Laura was no longer there to hear but Jane was still so filled with love that she spoke her feelings aloud as she placed the receiver in its cradle. "I love you."

Once more she looked at her parents' picture. Her mother was right. There should not be bad feelings. How had it started? That was one of the things that she could never remember.

She shivered with loneliness and caught her breath. Perhaps she would go home on Sunday after all.

At the kitchen table Jane stirred the black coffee and sipped it, knowing that two hundred miles up the coast and a little inland, her mother was doing the same. As she sat there, it came over her, a great longing for home. Yes. Definitely. She would definitely go home on Sunday. Perhaps Saturday afternoon. Slowly she relaxed as she planned the trip.

Charles fingered his knife, the darkness of the closet comforting him. Leaning against the cool wall, he relaxed into the pleasure of the moment. She was the best. Of them all, the very best. And as always, he loved the thought that she did not know that he was there.

He could hear her moving about the kitchen and he knew that she would come back—perhaps soon, perhaps not for hours. But time was no longer important. Waiting was pleasure, part of the whole thing, a necessary part.

Again he allowed his mind to float into memory, starting with the names. Alice Tresler. Dodie Shaeffer. Isobel Grove. Norma . . . Norma Morgan. He went on through the list and each name brought back a memory so clear that even the smallest detail was there.

The reverie faded as he heard her soft footsteps on the carpet. He held the knife firmly and peered through the crack in the door. She stood for a moment, her back to him. Then she saw the clothes on the bed, put the coffee cup down and scooped up the skirt and blouse. Slowly she moved toward the closet.

Charles wondered what she was thinking. Everything that had gone before faded and that moment became the true beginning. Now there was no memory and he knew that this was what he had waited for.

She opened the door, unaware.

That was the pleasure of it. Unaware.

She gasped. And from there it was fast, much too fast. Always, those moments were too jumbled to recall clearly.

In the confusion, he covered her mouth with one hand and with the other, held the knife against her throat. Still Jane struggled but she knew that it was useless. They both knew it.

He forced her onto the bed and, kneeling beside her, took the knife away from her throat. She did not move. He watched her for a moment, surprised that he had so quickly gained control. Almost too quickly. He did not know that her life for more years than she could remember had been a long expectation of defeat and now that it had come she could no longer fight. She had felt his strength and was immediately lost. He could see it in her eyes, her will to fight fading into sorrow. He heard the muffled sound of her crying and, pressing his hand harder against her mouth, leaned close to her and whispered a jumble of words, verbal pictures of fantasy. He could feel her fighting for control.

She would be easy . Too easy.

"That's right. That's it. Now I'm going to move my hand." He held the knife so that she could see it. "But before I do . . ." He touched the tip of steel lightly against her throat, felt her draw away. He applied the least bit of pressure and carefully drew the knife across her skin, leaving a thin crimson thread. "Like a razor . . ." Then he kissed her throat and ran his tongue along the cut. When he looked up, he saw that her eyes were tightly closed, felt the muscles of her jaw tense. He pressed his fingers against the shallow wound. "Ssst . . . Like that."

She opened her eyes and he slowly leaned forward and kissed her, could feel her tremble. Very carefully he studied her face, his vision blurred by the stocking. "Those eyes would close," he whispered and almost smiled. "And what would you see then?" He lay beside her and rested his chin on her forehead, smoothed her hair with his hand. "I'm not bad under this. Not bad at all . . . Gray eyes. They're nice . . . Like to see my eyes?"

She tried to turn her head away but he forced her to face him and after a moment he kissed her again. It was a soft kiss, gentle. And he whispered to her so quietly that she could hardly hear him. "Are my lips bad? . . . Are they? . . . They're not bad." He kissed her throat, again ran his tongue along the cut and when she shivered he rested his head there in the curve of her neck. "I love that." And again words poured from him, words that he was unaware he was speaking. This is what he would do to her. And this. And this and this. He pulled her closer so that he could feel the length of her as he pressed against her. Again she tried to turn away.

"No." He touched her temple with the knife, turning her face back to him. His voice was a quiet command. "I want you to watch me." He eased the tip of the blade into her cheek and a red dot appeared. "Open your eyes." And when she did the tears brimmed over and mingled with the blood on her cheek.

A terrible quiet settled through her mind and she took refuge behind it, unaware that she was crying. *I'm going to die.* The thought so stunned her that she could only repeat it over and over in the new quietness that her mind had become.

He was too close. She could feel him pressing against her. She wanted to scream but could not. Wanted to fight. To scream and scream, never stop screaming. But she could not. She could only wait, her fear surrounded by silence.

Her tears did not surprise Charles. He had expected them. He brushed his cheek against her face. "Might as well stop that. It won't work." He tightened the pressure of his hand over her mouth and brought the point of the knife back to her throat. "Going to stop?"

She nodded.

"Are you?"

Again she promised with a nod of her head.

"All right . . . I'm going to take my hand away. And if you scream . . . If you make a sound . . ." With the knife, he gave a slight pressure. "Then the evening would be over. And that wouldn't be too good, would it? For you or me." The desperation in her eyes reassured him and slowly he took his hand away, still ready with the knife in case he had misjudged her.

He kissed her and as he did, he began to tremble.

Urgently, Jane wanted to turn away but was afraid that she would do something wrong. That was her first concern, that she not do anything wrong. "Oh, God," she whispered. "Please . . ." And the whisper was a prayer.

"Sssh . . ." Charles eased the tip of the knife down from her neck.

"Please don't hurt me."

He pressed himself against her and she wanted to fight but was afraid. "No," she whispered, turning her face away. She wanted to

scream but she knew that she must keep control, must not do anything that would make him kill her. For there was a part of her that
did not truly believe that she was going to die.

"Afraid?" His voice was soft, almost kind.

She felt the control she had sought so desperately going but she
knew that somehow she must keep it. She must. She willed herself
not to surrender to the panic that was building.

"Are you? . . . Answer me." Still quiet, but the ghost of kindness
gone. "Are you afraid?"

She nodded.

"Say it," he whispered.

"Please." She must not let go. She sensed that that was the secret.
That if only she could hold on, not let go, it would be all right.

"Are you?" He kissed her.

"Don't."

"Afraid? . . . Say it!"

"Yes."

"Yes, what?"

Why did he insist? She could not hold on much longer, could feel
herself going and was terrified of what would follow. "Oh, God. I
am afraid . . . Don't hurt me."

"Show me. Show me how afraid." This was what he wanted, the
moment he waited for. And always it was different. "Show me." His
voice was as soft as a child's and his lips trembled on hers. "You are
afraid. You are." He knew that she would scream and he was ready.

With his encouragement, her fear was released and that in turn
released him. She screamed and as the sound of her terror filled the
room, he stabbed her. Clamping his hand over her mouth, struggling
with her as she fought for breath, for life; he drove the knife into
her again and again, slicing and tearing. And as she violently con-
vulsed in pain and terror, the room was filled with inhuman
sounds—muted, desperate.

Then her hands fell away. And she was still.

His fury going, Charles rested his head against her forehead, his
eyes tightly closed, his jaw clenched. And as it was ending for him
he kissed her and ripped the knife across her abdomen.

Slowly he became aware of the soft sounds of the room; the quiet
music from the radio, distant traffic, and from the next apartment,
the low hum of a television set.

But there was something else. Charles sat up. In the stillness, he felt that someone was listening.

The muffled sound of the television set abruptly stopped. From the apartment next door, Charles heard footsteps. Then quietness.

He was right.

Someone was listening.

He was sure of it.

Then there was a light knock on the wall and a voice called softly, "Jane."

The room was quiet. Too quiet.

"Jane. Are you there?"

CHAPTER THREE

"Jane." Mildred Hirsch waited but there was no answer.

She was an inquisitive neighbor and, aware that her curiosity was aggravating to others, she tried to control it. For a moment she listened, her ear against the wall; but there was only the sound of Jane's radio, playing softly.

Still Mildred was not satisfied.

She had heard something.

Of that she was certain.

Some muffled sounds.

Something.

Obviously Jane was there. But if she was there . . . if everything was all right, then why didn't she answer? Mildred hated being a nuisance and she understood that a young woman Jane's age needed privacy. She turned away, trying to dismiss it. But she could not.

She had heard something and she could not rationalize it away.

As a rule Mildred did not like young people. A quiet woman edging into her sixties, she had had her fill of the "now" generation and considered the majority of them "jerks, sullen jerks, and pot heads—spoiled and selfish—and I wouldn't give you fifteen cents for a baker's dozen of them." She was bored and impatient with the whole drug culture "scene" that had swept through the country. But Jane was different. Immediately Mildred had recognized it. Jane was likable. Admirable. And slowly the older woman's long-neglected maternal instincts had been awakened. Finally she had gone so far as to establish a correspondence with Jane's mother. But she had taken great care not to intrude. She remembered from her own youth how irritating older people could be and so she tried never to be burdensome.

She stood close to the wall, listening.

Someone was moving about in there.

It was not something that she heard. Rather it was something that she felt.

She knocked on the wall. "Jane. Are you all right?"

She waited, breathless, convinced that someone was there beyond the wall, listening.

Slowly, Mildred backed away . . . She was trembling . . . She could hardly breathe.

Someone was there.

And something was wrong.

She hurried from her apartment out into the hall.

Something was definitely wrong.

Charles finished buttoning his shirt, tucked it into his trousers and checked the room, making sure that he had left nothing. He wiped the knife on the bedspread and put it in his pocket.

He steadied the miniature camera and took a series of pictures, moving slowly about the bed. And as the shutter clicked, he smiled. She was nice. Very nice.

Silently he hurried into the living room. Perfect. But as he reached for the doorknob, there was a knock.

He stepped back.

"Jane!" Mildred tried the door but it was locked. For a moment she was quiet, her mind bordering on confusion. She was certain that someone was beyond the door. "Jane. Are you all right? . . . If you are, just answer."

She tried to fight the panic but it was useless. She was convinced that something had happened. If not, then why the silence?

Slowly she started back to her apartment. Then stopped. "Something is wrong." She whispered the words aloud. "Wrong." She turned, knowing that she was making a fool of herself, that everyone in the building would be talking about the "old maid" in 209, laughing and making insulting jokes. But she no longer cared. An inner urgency had driven the situation beyond her control and she hurried down the hallway to the manager's apartment, no longer caring what others might think.

Aware of every sound, Charles was careful to remain quiet. He listened as the woman's footsteps faded. Then, in the distance, he heard her knocking urgently and calling.

"Mr. Chambliss." Mildred waited in the hall outside the manager's apartment. Again she knocked, impatient now that she had committed herself. "Mr. Chambliss."

The door was opened by a disgruntled, slightly groggy man in his early fifties. His open irritation grew when he saw that the source of the unexpected disturbance was Mildred Hirsch. While she explained the reasons for her concern, Mr. Chambliss turned back into the room to quiet the yapping of his cocker spaniel.

Mildred followed him into the apartment. ". . . Of course I know that it sounds foolish . . ."

The manager searched his desk for the key, his face weary with forbearance.

"But . . . Well, if you had been there . . ."

Charles eased the door open. The woman's voice had diminished to an almost indiscernible hum. He felt sure that she must have gone into an apartment at the far end of the hall. Quickly, without looking in the direction of the voices, he hurried across the hall and down the stairs.

Free.

No one had seen him. He reached the lobby and, careful not to run, made his way to the entrance.

Free.

His breath caught with excitement. Luck was with him. As always.

It was over and no one had seen him. Just as on those other days, the ones that had gone before, he left as quietly as though nothing had happened. There was no one in the lobby. No one in any of the buildings had ever seen him. No one on the street had ever noticed him.

Free. He was free.

As he reached out to open the door to the street, he stopped.

There on the other side of the glass, a young girl was facing him, her eyes looking directly into his. Frozen for a moment, he stared at her and she did not look away. Unlike so many youngsters, her gaze was direct and she was neither embarrassed nor disinterested. With a coolness that was jarring, her eyes held his.

Then Charles hurried through the doorway, brushing past her. On the steps there was another young girl but he turned his face away and did not look at her.

She had seen him. The first girl. She had looked directly at him. That was not startling in itself. It was the other part of it that puzzled him. As he moved along the sidewalk, he tried to understand it. Still he could see himself . . . standing in the light, there at the door. It seemed that he had stood there an eternity. Waiting. But for what? And why? There was no explanation.

He had looked at the girl and she had looked at him for an endless moment. He had not even attempted to cover his face. Or turn away.

Why?

Then he was at the car, the keys in his hand. But the excitement that he usually felt was missing.

He stood by the car, the traffic speeding past, and relived the moment at the doorway.

How long had he stood there?

And why?

"Come on, Sue. These thing's weigh a ton." Elizabeth Mitchell's arms were aching with the weight of the grocery bags as she held the door for her friend.

Sue Laughton took a deep breath as she lumbered heavily up the steps and into the building. No one understood. Elizabeth was her best friend. Her very best friend. Ever. Would always be her best friend. For all the rest of her life. Always. And even Elizabeth did not understand. Sue was convinced that no thin person could possibly know what it was like for a fat person. In the lobby she paused again. "Looks like that man could at least have held the door for us."

Elizabeth pressed the elevator button. "Handsome is as handsome does."

This captured Sue's devotion to daydreaming, for physical beauty was a source of endless interest to her. Especially the beauty of men.

She knew that men were not supposed to be considered beautiful but she considered them so. She could study their faces for hours. Could, in fact, while away any random Monday afternoon or Thursday or any other day leafing through magazines, memorizing the faces of men in the advertisements. This was, for her, not an erotic adventure. It was romance, as innocent and passing as touching fingertips.

The beauty of men—their lips and arms, their shoulders and hands. Their necks, their incredible muscular, sun-darkened necks. She never tired of that. Their eyes. The beautiful quietness of their eyes.

And Elizabeth felt as she did.

That was the miracle of their friendship. When the Mitchells had moved into the apartment across the hall, Sue had been very careful not to appear too eager for friendship. Always, that ruined it. And so their acquaintance had started slowly, in a guarded way. That suited them for they were both rather covered.

Then one day when they were walking home from school, just the two of them, Elizabeth had very casually opened the door to the most staggering friendship. Near the corner of Argyle and Franklin they had passed two motorcycle policemen who were parked at the curb; and as though it were the most natural thing in the world, Elizabeth had voiced Sue's deepest, most secret thoughts. "Look, Sue," she had said, nodding to the policemen. "Aren't they beautiful?"

The openness of it had stunned Sue. Elizabeth had stopped and looked directly at the two officers. She had made no attempt to cover her actions—no side glances, no giggling and turning away. Sue had stood beside her while together they studied the beautiful, quiet men.

Finally one of the policemen had turned and asked if they needed something. In humiliation Sue had looked away. But Elizabeth had not been at all embarrassed. "We just wanted to look at you," she had said. And that simple declaration of truth had made her the most important person in Sue's overweight life. When the two men had smiled and asked "What's the verdict?" the girls had answered in unison, "It's yes!"

And their schoolbooks suddenly lighter, they had walked on, enjoying the laughter of the two young policemen.

The elevator door slid closed. "Was he really handsome?" Sue asked, wanting an exact impression of the man who had passed them. "He turned away as he came toward me."

Elizabeth thought for a moment. "Well . . . an uncle. Or maybe a brother a lot older than you are. Handsome in a way, nice eyes . . . Sensational eyes."

As they emerged from the elevator, Mildred Hirsch was walking down the hall a little ahead of Mr. Chambliss, her voice impatient, urging him on. "She screamed. I heard her."

The teen-agers stopped, recognizing the concern in the older woman's voice. Elizabeth took the lead, as usual. "What is it?"

"I heard something." Almost at Jane's apartment, Mildred stopped, shaken by the sight of the open door. She turned to the others, her fear seeming exaggerated, even foolish to them. "It was locked. The door. Just a second ago. I tried the knob." From the threshold she called into the apartment. "Jane." Mildred's voice was now so filled with fear that her concern became a contagion which infected the group.

Cautiously, Mr. Chambliss stepped into the living room, closely followed by Mildred. Then after a moment of hesitation, a look exchanged, Elizabeth and Sue went in.

The manager forced himself to assume a voice of unconcern. "Miss Atkins." He hated entering a tenant's apartment uninvited.

"Jane," Mildred called softly. But there was no answer.

In the silence the young girls unconsciously drew closer together. Mr. Chambliss turned and went into the kitchen. Hesitantly, Mildred went toward the bedroom. At the doorway she stopped suddenly and gasped.

Elizabeth and Sue came up behind her. Over her shoulder they saw the bed. They saw Jane's body and were frozen by the terror of it, for it did not look like a human thing, twisted and tangled as it was in the blood-soaked spread—like some animal, slashed and ripped, its intestines tumbled out and lying there, waiting to be gutted and cleaned by a butcher. *By a butcher. A butcher.* The thought caught and held in Elizabeth's mind and over the thought she saw the eyes that she had seen through the glass of the door. The pale eyes. *A butcher.*

They turned away.

But not quickly enough.

They had seen. And in that fraction of a moment, the image of

the aftermath of violence was so harshly impressed on their minds
that they would never forget it.

Gutted by a butcher. The thought ran with Elizabeth as she
hurried into the hall. It surrounded her and she could not escape it.
Sue grabbed her hand and they looked at each other. But they could
see only Jane. Jane and the spread that was twisted beneath her.

And the pale eyes.

CHAPTER FOUR

Lieutenant Ben Hamilton had already left his office when the call
came through to Homicide. One of the younger men from the department caught him in the parking lot. For a moment he stood there
in the twilight, unable to move, his memory jarred by unbidden images of other victims. This was what he had been expecting for over
six weeks and now that it had come, Ben was filled with frustration.
It was not often that he felt on the verge of losing control, for the
forty-two years of his life had been a tedious training ground for that
quality.

Control. The early years spent with his father had conditioned
him for it. His mother had died when he was small and he did not
remember her. It was his father who dominated the memories of his
childhood. He had been a ranch hand; still was, Ben supposed, although it had been over six years since Ben had heard from him.
The letters came back marked *Address Unknown* and always the
words touched him although he did not want them to.

Perhaps the old man was dead. Sometimes at night Ben would
dream that he was, and he would awaken from that fear cold and
shaken. He would see the weathered body lying alone in some hidden gully in the Sangre de Cristos and memories would fill the
room. It was this dependency, this concern for his father, that most
disturbed Ben. He did not want to care, considered it weakness. But
he awakened, shaking and longing like a child to turn on the light
and banish whatever ghosts might be hiding in the shadows; he
knew that he did care, that he was in bondage forever to feelings
that he neither understood nor respected. For he did not respect his
father, did not want to like him, to need him.

At times months would go by without any reminder of the dream. He would almost forget it. Then he would awaken, his face damp, his breath short and for a few moments he would be a child again with no control, no confidence, understanding only that he was afraid. *Address Unknown.* The words would come to him and he would turn on the lamp, light a Lucky and, like the smoke, slowly drift in the stillness away from that part of himself that he did not understand until once more he was in control.

Control.

He curved onto the Hollywood Freeway; and as he joined the flow of traffic, he felt the excitement building, the frustration.

Control. That was foremost. Without it everything would fall away. Without it there would be no Law and Ben's respect for the Law was total. He cursed his misfortune at not having been born a hundred years earlier when Lawmen had the power, the strength to function independently and immediately without the encumbrance of contemporary refinements.

America. That was his concern and it was always with him. In the last decade he had seen everything in the country begin to fly apart as though some mysterious, unnamed disease had infected what was most important to him. He was in mourning, believing that his country had passed the zenith; that quietly—without anyone realizing it—America had tipped to the far side of the hill; and that slowly everyone was losing sight of what it had all been about.

To him, his was a nation of laws that had degenerated into a nation of opportunists using Law to evade the Law. Self. That was the four-letter word that he considered the cause of the fall. He knew that the politicians cared only for self, for maintaining their own power. He had seen them operate, was familiar with the deals that were made, the lies that they used for ladders.

But still, for people who did not have full power, there was Law. And Ben was a Lawman. He lived it. He knew that he and his fellow officers were despised but that did not bother him. Hostility was a definite quality that he could deal with and, in a way, he enjoyed it. He liked for someone to turn to him and say, "What the hell do you mean by that?" because always he knew exactly what he meant, always had the facts and statistics to back up his beliefs. He loved a good fight; whether physical, verbal, or a combination of the two. And always while he fought he was aware of a second battle—a struggle within himself for control.

Control. He had structured his life around that necessity.

As his car smoothly flowed from lane to lane in the ordered confusion of the freeway, he tried to stifle his frustration. His raw, handsome face remained calm; his hands, steady. He was completely familiar with the series of murders, had memorized every fact, knew the victims so well that they seemed a living part of his past. In Homicide they were known as Hamilton's girls, Ben was so completely dominated by the case.

Without ever having entered this latest apartment, Ben could see it. And the victim—he could see her as well. Blond. Young. Pretty. He knew that all of those words would apply and that the struggle of such a hard death would have left a terrible distortion of what she had been.

Control. He swerved his car along the curving off-ramp at Gower and headed for Beachwood.

"Same man?" Ben took a report form from one of the uniformed policemen.

"Looks like it."

While the Homicide photographer's bulbs flashed, Ben studied the position of the body, then glanced over the report. He was jolted by one of the notations of the investigating officer. There was a possibility that the murderer had been seen by two teen-age girls. Trying to conceal his excitement, he turned to the young officer who was silently following him about the apartment. "These girls live in the building?"

"Yes, sir."

"Let's go."

And he went with the tension of a boy on the first day of hunting season.

Avis Mitchell hovered nervously over her daughter while the officer asked his endless questions. Always she had been unsure of her maternal duties. She wanted to be a good mother, had always wanted to, but had never understood exactly how to go about it. Now this had happened. Elizabeth had been in the room when that girl's body had been discovered. Elizabeth and Sue both. And they had most likely come face to face with the murderer when he was leaving the building. Face to face. Avis shuddered at the effectiveness of the cliché and took another Butisol to calm her nerves though she knew that it would not help.

She felt that she should protect her child. But how? It was done. And to further complicate matters, she felt some undefined responsibility toward Sue whose mother had not yet returned from work. The strain of it was almost too much. And interwoven through the entire nightmare situation was the rising antagonism that she felt toward the policeman who was questioning the children. She did not like him. The way he stood, the tilt of his head, the strength of his hands—everything about him offended her. He was handsome of course, in a rough way, and that was another thing she did not like; he was too handsome. He seemed arrogant and overconfident, exactly the kind of man her husband had been. It was for those very reasons that she had divorced him.

Again she tried to interrupt but the detective's look was a warning that she understood. It was the exact look that her husband had given her so many times and she despised it. She had not wanted the children questioned so soon. It was obvious that they were too upset; but the detective had brushed her complaints aside, and after that the interview had become a verbal match between the two of them while the girls looked on in confusion.

Ben wanted to slam the woman against the wall, have her booked. But of course he could not. It was, after all, her apartment. Lack of co-operation from the public was even more disgusting to Ben than overt criminal behavior. He found it impossible to understand.

"I just think that it would be much better if we postponed the whole thing," Avis said, forcing a smile.

Control. Control. With controlled anger, Ben turned to Sue.

"You understand." Avis's smile became a whisper of victory. But the smile quickly faded for Ben did not look at her.

"All right, Sue," he said. "Now I'm just asking for your impression. You've said that you can't be specific. Well, don't worry about that, about being exactly right. Just describe the man you saw as best you can."

Sue sighed with frustration knowing that she would make a wonderful witness if only she had seen the man. But she had not. He had hurried past, his face turned away, and she had not seen him clearly enough to describe him in any detail at all. This she did not want to confess. It seemed to her a failure and so she took refuge in evasion. "It was so quick."

Again Avis Mitchell broke in, a triumphant edge to her quiet voice. "You can see that the girls are upset and I think . . ." Smiling, she left the sentence unfinished.

Sue wished that Elizabeth's mother would shut up. The whole thing was exciting and she did not want it to end. "I didn't see him as good as Elizabeth did."

Ben glanced over his notes. The interview had been completely unsatisfactory. Control. He was good at it. "All right. Now . . ."

Sue whispered to Elizabeth, "He was facing you."

Immediately Ben turned to Elizabeth and fired his question. "How tall?"

"Tall." Elizabeth's answer was as immediate as the question.

In the uncomfortable silence that followed, Sue offered, meaninglessly, "There wasn't really enough time. I mean to see him. It was quick."

Ben moved closer to Elizabeth. "Tall as I am?"

"No. Not that tall. He was . . ."

Another interruption from Elizabeth's mother and both the girls were as aggravated by it as Ben was. "It's obvious, Lieutenant Hamilton," she said, "very obvious that the children can not be any more specific than that. They're upset. They're children and you can see that they're upset." Her eyes were soft and smiling.

An intense quiet filled the room. Ben clenched his jaw and looked at the woman. Control. "All right. If that's all they can give me, then that's all they can give me." He turned back to the youngsters. "But I'll want to see both of you again."

Immediately Avis ushered him to the door, relief flooding her face. "I think that's much better," she whispered. "They're all upset. You understand." She loved winning out over a man.

Elizabeth turned to Sue in disgust. "It's stupid."

At the door, Ben again faced Avis Mitchell, his voice hard with control. "I'll call tomorrow."

"Stupid," Elizabeth whispered.

Ben faced the girls. "There are some pictures that I'll want you both to look through."

Sue hated to see him leave. He was so handsome. "Tomorrow? All right."

Elizabeth went to him. "No. Wait. Not all right."

Her mother gave warning with her voice. "Elizabeth."

"But, Mother. It's so stupid. We haven't told him anything."

"He's said that he'll call tomorrow and that . . ."

Ben interrupted, "Just a minute." He turned to Elizabeth. "Is there something specific that you can tell me?"

"I can show you. It's dumb to just talk when it's so easy to show you."

At the entrance of the building, Elizabeth and Sue stood in the doorway. Elizabeth put her hand on the glass panel. "Right there. His eyes were right there. Right above the V-I-S in Vista." She referred to the name of the building that was emblazoned on the glass, VISTA DEL MAR MANOR. "That's how tall he was. His eyes were right there. They were gray. And he was . . ." She paused.

Very quietly Sue finished the sentence for her. "He was hand-some . . . At least that's what Elizabeth said." Her voice softened to a whisper. "I never really saw him."

Ben took Elizabeth's arm. "What did you say exactly?"

After a moment Elizabeth answered. "I did say something like that, I suppose. About his being handsome. He was."

"What else?"

"I said that if you could choose . . . you know . . . an older brother or something, that . . . well, it would be nice to have him look like that."

In silence they watched her and she turned away, looked down. "He had beautiful eyes." And as she whispered the words, her eyes clouded for she considered herself a plain girl and was embarrassed for others to know how much she loved beauty.

CHAPTER FIVE

As Charles drove along the winding road in the hills above Hollywood, he tried to convince himself that he had not been seen clearly but the deception was futile. The girl had seen him as plainly as he had seen her. As always he imagined the police activity that must have been set in motion. But there was a difference this time. How accurately would the girl describe him? Would she lead them to him? Was that possible? Always before he had thought that it was not. But now . . .

Slowly the car turned and twisted through the hairpin curves,

the movement relaxing him. And if the worst that could happen
happened? There was excitement in that too. A new excitement.
The depression that he had felt began to lift and he was filled with
the beginning of elation. Tomorrow morning he might find an artist's sketch that resembled him on the front page.

Tomorrow morning.

Tomorrow morning his life might change.

He smiled . . . Tomorrow morning.

He did not understand why but the words had a nice sound and
he repeated them several times.

He turned into the drive which was bordered by runaway vines
and tall grass. He knew that the neighbors sympathized with their
financial inability to keep the place up, never understanding or even
suspecting that the three of them—Charles, his mother, and his
sister—liked the feeling of comfortable decay that surrounded them.
The sun was gone and in darkness he walked toward the house, the
elation that he had felt, fading, but not completely. It came and
went, making him feel almost drunk. He smiled as he thought of
the three of them together, warmed as he imagined them looking at
the paper.

Tomorrow morning.

The house was Italianate in feeling but, unlike the classic exam-
ples of that style, there was no lightness in the structure. It was a
heavy yellow building, so sturdily constructed that, excluding the
possibility of fire, earthquake, or the demolition crew, it would
most likely stand for hundreds of years—a monument to the once-
grand architectural mistakes of the Thirties.

The door closed behind him and Charles walked through the entrance hall which was dimly illumined by yellowish low-watt bulbs
in wall brackets. Fragments of light spilled into the living room
which, obviously never used, was uncomfortably furnished in what
had once passed as grandeur; multicolored lamps with fringe shades,
dark furniture of baroque design and on the wall a massive hanging
which featured the frolic of Diana, the Huntress.

From above a television set blared out the artificial excitement of
a give-away show. Over the confusion of muted sounds, a woman's
voice called, "That you?"

Charles stopped at the sound of his mother's voice and tried to
imagine her as she would be the next morning, skimming the paper,

seeing the drawing. He smiled but the smile faded into weariness and, leaning against the wall, he reached out and snapped off the light.

"It's me," he replied, almost to himself and started up the stairs.

The only light in the upper hallway came from an open door at the end of the corridor. It was his mother's room and Charles moved toward it.

Again her voice rose over the sound of the television set. "Charlie?"

He paused for a moment outside the door. "It's me. I'm home." He leaned against the doorframe, looked in, "And how's my girl?"

The warm odors of the room surrounded him as he entered. In the middle of an ugly, high-back bed, his mother was propped against a mound of wrinkled and soiled pillows. Ann smiled and held her hand out across the bedside table that was covered with countless small prescription-filled bottles and empty cigarette packages. A ravaged Whitman's Sampler was half hidden by the covers of the bed. It was a dark room and not even on the most smog-free day could the California sun make its way in for the blinds were always half drawn.

Situated so that it could easily be seen from the bed was a giant color television set, flickering and ranting with the pandemonium of the quiz program, the babbling rise and fall of sounds filling the room. Ann's clouded, aging eyes seemed to flicker like the picture on the screen as she watched, captured by the antics of the Master of Ceremonies. Without looking, she patted the bed, signaling for Charles to sit beside her.

Ignoring Ann's casual command, Charles looked to his sister and winked.

Elise smiled, almost laughed. "What about Baby Sister? Isn't she your girl too?" The words were a chant, an obvious game and she rolled her eyes in imitation of pique.

Charles relaxed into the familiarity of the games that had always been played in the house.

Tomorrow morning.

He wondered if then the games would change. Would suddenly become real. "Both my girls," he said, enjoying the poorly concealed rivalry between his sister and mother. "You too, Billy Boy." And smiling, Charles winked at the thin aging man who was combing Ann's tangled hair.

"Watch out there, Little Honey," Billy drawled and then in pro-
jected imitation of the almost-forgotten Dr. I.Q., intoned energeti-
cally, "Give the man in the balcony ten silver dollars and a Mars
bar." His voice was heavy with the bitterness and humor of camp
that was not a game, not a façade. "Hold still, Beauty." He popped
Ann playfully and continued teasing her dry, brittle hair.

Charles laughed. The reception was so completely expected. That,
combined with the thought that none of them knew the excitement
that he had come from, amused him.

"Here, Baby." Again Ann patted the covers and Charles sank onto
the bed and into the comforting awfulness of the room. He studied
his mother's pampered face, selfish and vain; leaned over and kissed
her. She caressed his hand without taking her eyes from the set.
Considering the possiblity of the next morning's revelation, he
laughed and kissed her again.

This time she did look at him. "How do I rate that?"

And, continuing to laugh, he nestled his knees against her as she
turned back to her program, content.

His enjoyment increased as he wondered if this would be the last
time that they would ever be together in such a casual, unclouded
way.

Together. All of them.

Together in Mama's room . . . And Billy—the eternal visitor—
watching as always and making his bitter, bitchy remarks.

Charles glanced about. It seemed that a lifetime had passed since
he had had more than a vague impression of the room and what it
contained.

It was, even to the smallest detail, his mother's room, a shrine to
her past. The walls were covered with cherished mementos of better
days, photographs from years and adventures so long past that they
seemed to be myth rather than something that had actually happened. (Every day Ann studied them, and always with a sense of
wonder that they were pictures of herself, for they revealed a very
pretty, rather taunting blond girl who appeared more remote to Ann
than the years that separated her from her own youth.)

The majority of the photographs were stills from motion pictures
of a slender and lively Ann, a B picture version of "flaming youth."
The walls of her room were a memorial to her lost career: costume
dramas, bedroom comedies, social message films and Westerns. All
smacked of Republic. Or, at best, RKO.

And there was a wedding portrait. Ann was standing on a terrace, smiling at the camera while her groom, a rather serious and stiff young man, looked at her. The other members of the wedding party were grouped about them. (Several of the faces were vaguely familiar as having once been famous.) The light on the terrace had diffused Ann's hair into a blond halo.

Charles turned and watched his mother, her once-saucy face now ravaged by the pain of arthritis, lined with age. The light from the television flickered, catching the brightness of her eyes. A product of the romantic period of the Silver Screen, still she lived in constant expectation of the great give-away.

Ann leaned toward the set. Someone was about to win something. Her eyes sparkled.

And as she strained forward, Charles relaxed against the pillows, a feeling of contentment touching him. He was home. And he waited for the games to begin, knowing that soon they would; smiling with the knowledge.

Home.

Mama.

Baby Sister. (Although she was in her thirties and carelessly crashing into middle age, she was still thought of as the baby.)

And Billy, too.

He was home.

He watched his sister, wondering what her reaction would be if the police came, if the games ended and she had to look into the secrets that were part of him. Her shoulders stooped as always ("Stand up. Straight, Baby. You look awful stooping over," their mother had always said.), Elise hovered over a card table, "working." Spread before her were large sheets of names and piles of envelopes which she was carefully addressing by hand. (She was paid three dollars a box.) With a flourish, she finished another envelope and called to an imaginary servant, "Mr. Ashley's home!"

Charles laughed, kicked off his shoes and drew his feet back onto the bed. A movie game.

But Ann was not amused. At any other time she would have been, but she was involved in the drama of the give-away show and for her that was serious business. "Shhh," she warned.

The reality of the house was completely overridden by the game-playing fantasy of the movies. Whether speaking of Melanie and Ashley or Alice Faye and Tyrone, it was obvious that they were old and very comfortable friends. "A good day, Ashley?" Elise whispered as she returned to her work.

But for Ann this was definitely not a time for games. Without looking away from the set, she snapped, "Elise. I am watching this," her voice even and sharp. "Ow," Ann winced as Billy tugged at her tangled hair.

"Well, if you'd hold still like I said." He combed and caressed.

Charles and Elise exchanged a look and Billy laughed. It would be a good game.

Charles gently soothed his mother's hand, leaned across and whispered to Elise with exaggerated concern, "Now you've upset her."

"Should I call the doctor?"

Charles almost laughed. It was just the kind of ridiculous opening that he enjoyed. All of them sensed that a movie game was about to begin and it was difficult for Elise to keep a straight face.

Finally Billy started, quietly and seriously. "Call *Tammy and the Doctor*. Starring . . ."

The rules of the game had been established by the four of them years before. Going clockwise around the room, each of them had to name an actor who had been in the picture.

Charles smiled. "Sandra Dee. And . . ."

Elise finished another envelope. "Peter Fonda. And? . . ."

Ann was torn and frustrated. She wanted to watch the show but at the same time, she could not bear to pass up the pleasure of the game. For a moment she could not think of another actor who had been in the picture. "Oh . . ." She very rarely missed one and the thought of failure upset her. "Wait . . . Sandra Dee. Peter Fonda . . ."

Elise leaned back in the chair. "That's right, Mother. Charles said Sandra Dee. I said Peter Fonda. And you say . . ."

Ann closed her eyes. "Now just a minute. It's hard. I mean with the television going and everything."

"Hate to do it," Charles said quietly, "but I'm going to have to call time."

Ann's face wrinkled with panic. Then she relaxed, triumphant. "*Tammy and the Doctor* starring Sandra Dee. Peter Fonda. And . . . Mitzi Hoag!" And with a cackle she took a piece of candy from the box and stuffed it into her mouth. "And just be quiet, all of you. I mean it. 'Cause I wanta watch the rest of this show." She settled back, smugly chewing the honey nougat.

Elise tossed the ball point onto the table and laughed. "Bravo!"

With an abrupt move of her hand, Ann signaled for quiet. "Wait. They're drawing for the trip now."

Billy continued combing and patting. "Hope they send 'em to Albuquerque, New Mexico."

Ann's patience was going. "Billy!"

After a warning glance from Elise, Charles stopped himself from laughing. Neither of them shared their mother's enthusiasm for quiz shows but if they made fun of her she would pout for days. Leaning against the headboard of the bed, Charles picked through the box of candy. Accidentally he rolled onto Ann's hand and when she gasped in pain, he was immediately contrite. "Bad tonight?" He cradled her hand in his as she nodded, biting her lip to keep from crying.

Elise knew that her mother's tears must not start, that if they did, the night would become a confusion of medicine-giving and whispered sympathies. With a half smile, she looked to her mother. "It's no worse than usual and you know it."

A flash of anger jarred Ann and conquered the tears that she was about to shed. Charles took her swollen hands. "Let me warm them." Gently, he rubbed.

Ann nodded toward the TV and in a quiet, unsteady voice, whimpered, "Buenos Aires. Bet that's where they go."

Charles laughed and kissed her hands. "Feel better?"

Ann loved attention. "Uh huh."

Elise wished that Charles would stop, let their mother forget about the pain. "That means good air."

Ann sniffed. "Huh?"

"Buenos Aires. Good air. Good Air, Argentina."

"We could use a breeze or two of that," Billy drawled. He loved the intimacy of combing Ann's hair.

The arthritis now on the verge of being forgotten, Ann took another piece of candy. "Spanish names are prettier than English."

Elise knew that if she could keep the chatter rolling for a while, the pain and pampering would be forgotten and her mother would be all right. "The Angels is pretty."

Ann's attention was wandering back toward her television program. "Ssssh . . . The angels?"

"Where we live. La Ciudad de Los Angeles."

"Hold still, Angel," Billy hissed. The effect was almost as he wanted it.

"Sssh!" Ann demanded and again leaned forward, recaptured by the suspense. The studio audience was becoming more and more excited as the announcer droned on. Ann loved to guess the destination of each winning couple. "Buenos Aires," she whispered.

"Los Angeles," said Elise, hoping that her mother would be right.

With the usual blaring, building fanfare the orchestra gave the announcer his cue and his voice rode over the music with the high, artificial excitement used by all his brotherhood. "And you and your husband are going to fly first to . . ." He paused theatrically while the contestant fidgeted and the audience murmured. "Are you ready?" The housewife from Ohio was. "Are you?" The studio audience was. "Is everybody ready?" The home viewers were. "To . . . Los Angeles!"

"You were right!" Ann said to Elise, stunned that her daughter had guessed correctly.

"Yes, Virginia, there is a Law of Averages," Billy smirked.

Charles laughed and Ann turned to him. "She was!"

"Let's hope it's the beginning of a winning streak," Elise sighed.

Ann was about to continue the exchange but there was another fanfare from the orchestra and again she signaled for quiet. "Sssh . . . Let's hear where they go after that."

Elise didn't care where they went. "Papeete, Hong Kong, and Yokohama, Mama."

"Wonder what Yokohama means?" Ann whispered.

Who cares, Elise thought, and said, "Fish heads and rice."

Charles laughed. "And Yamaha."

To Ann, Charles's laughter was one of the most beautiful things in the world. She joined in. "Oh, Charlie. Yamaha. Where's that?" She nudged Billy. "Charlie speaks Jap."

Charles's laughter increased. "Jap?"

Billy began giggling, "Careful, dear, your hubba hubba's showing."

Within the growing confusion of the television show, the announcer's irritatingly smooth voice once more soared over the noise. "And after a wonderful three days in golden Los Angeles you are going . . . yes, you are . . . you and your husband are going to fly JAL to . . . here you go . . ." On the screen the couple from Ohio waited with fixed, imbecilic smiles on their faces. "Up. Up. Up and over the broad blue Pacific to . . . Yokohama! Japan!" The audience and the contestants went wild.

Rocked by her daughter's heretofore unsuspected prophetic ability, Ann gasped and turned to her. "Elise!"

Elise was equally stunned. "I can't believe it."

Immediately Ann agreed. "I can't either."

Elise despised the show. She looked on the announcer as a freak and the feather-brained contestants who were jumping about screaming and kissing everybody, as pitiful. "No," she said. "I mean who would be dumb enough to send somebody to Yokohama?"

But Ann was not listening. She had grabbed Billy's hand. "She got them right. Both of them."

Elise laughed, glad that the ridiculous program was over. She started putting her work table in order. "And for a prize I get to fix Charles's supper. Right?"

"Yes. And bring me my ice cream." Ann patted her son's hand. "Get Rocky Road, Charlie?"

Every Tuesday with never-changing predictability, Charles "surprised" his mother with a carton of Baskin-Robbins Rocky Road ice cream. Her babyish pampered face amused him, but he concealed his thoughts with a grimace of self-condemnation.

Ann was stunned. "You forgot! . . . But it's Tuesday. You always bring Rocky Road on Tuesday."

"Thank God," Elise mumbled. "An unexpected change."

"A change for the bad." Ann's disappointment turned to anger.

Elise coughed as she lit a cigarette. "What did you expect?"

"I'll get it." Charles looked about for his loafers.

"We can order some," Elise countered quickly.

Leaning against the bed for balance as he forced his feet into the shoes, Charles was glad for the opportunity to leave. "Rocky Road?"

Elise did not want him to go. The simple fact of his being there gave her a feeling of safety. All day she waited for him to return, lived for the weekends when he would be with them. "If we ordered it, we'd get to look at the delivery boy."

But Charles did not smile at the weak joke. Suddenly he was aware of how much he needed solitude. He wanted to relive the events of the afternoon, to be away from the house, the vapid, endless chatter.

Ann pouted like a child. "How could you forget?"

Elise draped her sweater over her legs and pushed the chair away from the table. "And when that sweet ice cream boy came in, I'd be sitting there all covered up with a quilt, or better still an Elizabeth Barrett Browning afghan, smiling a 'come on, baby' smile . . ."

"And I'm not forgiving you either," Ann interjected, her face a lump of petulance.

Always Elise was stunned by her mother's density. Convinced that if it were not for such nagging comments, Charles would stay, she hurried on. "Then when he came close, I'd whip off that afghan . . ." As she brushed the sweater from her knees, the light caught and glistened on the metal of a heavy brace that encased one of her legs. With a healthy Rita Hayworth intake of breath, she turned the leg to the side, displaying the built-up shoe that held her foot tight. She smiled. ". . . I'd reveal my withered leg and go right on smiling like Chiquita Banana." Grinning, she arose and moved away from the table, walking with slow, deliberate steps.

But Charles was not listening. Countless times he had heard variations on that theme and he wanted only to be gone. "Come on, Mama. What kind?"

At the foot of the bed, Elise almost stumbled, regained her balance. "Mama bound my feet in Joan Crawford ankle straps and just ruined the shape of my legs." She laughed, knowing that she had lost, that he would not stay.

"Come on!" Charles's voice was a command.

"Surprise me." Ann refused to face him.

Charles started from the room, his mother's attitude seeming more absurd than aggravating.

"Surprise both of us and come home before midnight," Elise called. She wanted to ask him to stay, but she knew that she could not.

"*Hasta luego,*" Billy crooned as Charles's footsteps dissolved into silence.

Slowly Elise made her way to the window so that she could watch as he left the house. "Wish he hadn't gone back out," she whispered.

Ann was puzzled. "But how could he have forgotten?"

There was silence for a long moment. Then Elise turned to her mother. "Face it, Mama. Charles must be bored to death with us."

The thought had never occurred to Ann and she was startled by it. "What a stupid thing to say," she said.

Elise turned back to the window and watched Charles leave. She loved watching him—his graceful walk, the habit he had of tilting his head a little to the right, the appealing slope of his shoulders. She waited until his car had disappeared down the drive, then she started from the room. "I'll fix a plate for him and leave it in the refrigerator."

Alone with Billy, Ann tried to dismiss her irritation. What had Elise meant when she said that Charles was bored with them? The thought that he did not enjoy being with her was beyond the realm of possibility. She pushed it back where it would not have to be dealt with, took a peppermint cream from the Sampler and relaxed as Billy combed and soothed.

Billy was a comfort. He was loyal. He loved her and that was what she loved about him—that and the fact that his hands were magic. As he caressed and shaped her hair, she drifted into the pleasant warmth of believing once more that beauty was an unlost thing; that it was there still, waiting—just beneath her Billy's finger-tips—to be combed and teased back into place.

Billy hummed one of the old tunes while he worked and he smiled, sensing the power he had to relax her. It was this easy comfort in their relationship that pleased him most. He needed to serve her for she was his only constancy in life. It was the unspoken intimacies of these minor moments that served as proof that he brought deliverance.

Their friendship went back to the early days of her stardom when he had been her hairdresser. Those days had lengthened into long years of closeness, shared secrets, interwoven careers, and caring until finally their need for each other had been sealed by the inde-structible bond of mutual failure. When he touched her hair or took her hand or, in parting, brushed her forehead with his lips, they both were comforted by the knowledge that here was the other person who understood, the only other one who really knew. It was only with Ann that this comfort was possible for Billy. The rest of his life was pretense. It was the façade that others saw but Ann knew him. She was the only one who did.

Billy was not a handsome man, had never been, and that was the source of his greatest bitterness. Failure was nothing compared to that. Always his homeliness had been his pain, for that was the flaw that had kept him from ever being courted. And that was his in-satiable need; to be wooed and made over, toasted and teased in a haze of romance, an endless romp of silliness, of "catch-me-if-you-can." He was a stocky man with pitted skin, haunted hazel eyes, a comic nose and large lips. Only his eyes were appealing, and they were so deeply set that they were seldom noticed. He knew that he was not a pleasant man to look at and was sure that that was the reason that no one had cared, not at any time in his life. His constant anger, his hopelessness arose from the fact that he was homely—homely and ungraceful, abrupt in his bitterness, abrasive in his demands to be loved, to be held, to be soothed like a baby by an endless lullaby from strong, whispering, man lips. For it was a man's love that he had always wanted, and that which he most desired he had never had. Although he constantly dreamed of the man who would hold him, rescue him, whisper dream words, he knew that the chances of its happening were gone—that they had, in truth, never actually existed. Not even when he was young, in the years that should have been golden for a boy from Nebraska just come to the Coast. From the beginning he had believed that his homeliness had rendered his dream impossible. And, believing as he did, he had made it true.

And so his life had become Ann and he held to her. She was the only salvation that he would ever know, for to him salvation was getting through the day. And together they could laugh endless days away; laugh and giggle, coo, taunt, and tease each other as the silent years rushed them into old age. Alone with each other they were still young. Together their terror of time was softened by games, role-playing, pretending; the knowledge they shared of the past making them a part of the same splendid failure.

Billy was her jester. She toyed with his hands as though they were paws, blew smoke in his eyes, and yanked on his ears. She was his goddess and he danced and traipsed to whatever tune she chose. Her beauty was his, her incredible beauty; and when he smiled and whispered, "My Beauty . . ." he was unaware of the depth of truth that was there.

Always he had loved men and it had marked him with a loneliness that had never left him, not even in those endless eternities of forced gaiety and theatrical bitchiness that had become the surface center of his life. In the rare moments of quietness, his face was a vacant thing that caught the unaware passers-by and held them for a moment; for there was a childish puzzlement there that on the surface of the aging woman-man face was at the same time comic and terrible in its innocent prissiness.

He was a man who loved his wounds, for they were the core

of his life; and for hours on end he would sit alone at his breakfast table, reliving defeats as, with soft fingertips, he would feel the smooth, polished, pine arms of the comb-back Windsor chair as though to soothe and caress the humiliation that his life had been.

He did not like the maleness within himself and, despite the fact that his body was that of a ballsy country joker, he wanted to be a woman. Always it had been so. As a child he had wanted men to hold him. And as a man he wanted men to love him as a woman. But he was homely and clumsy and the disgust that he felt for his unattractiveness made him a bitch, and men who preferred men did not want him; so he became an acid-tongued thing who lived only for his own pain and the ghost of Ann's Star Beauty.

He loved her and with her he would relax, the meanness in his face would soften, and the ghost of the country-homely man that he might have been would bring innocence to his eyes.

Ann would smile.

He would touch her hand and whisper, "Beauty . . . My Beauty . . ."

His work finished, Billy studied Ann's face and hair. Yes. It was right. Just right. "Beauty," he whispered and pulled one of the curls rakishly down over her forehead. He laughed. "Right in the middle of her forehead." Quickly he kissed the top of her head. "Gotta go."

Ann fiddled her fingers for the hand mirror which was on the foot of the bed. "Lemme see."

Billy handed the glass to her. "Sensational, right?"

Ann studied herself. Billy was good, there was no denying that. Very good. Perhaps a little old-fashioned, but what was wrong with that?

Waiting for his compliment, Billy paused as he put on his waiter's jacket. "Right?"

"For want of a better word." Ann smiled, knowing his need for praise. And then when he turned to go, she was aware of her need and she reached for him, covering her loneliness with a game. "No. Don't leave me." Her voice lilted with baby tones.

Slowly Billy buttoned the jacket. "Duty calls."

It had been years, but still Ann remembered how to play those farewell scenes. "Everyone deserts me," she whimpered.

Billy took her hand. "Love me, Pet?"

On cue, Ann pouted and turned away. "No."

Billy laughed. He loved her scenes, recognizing them all.

She held tight to his hand. "No, no, no! Won't let go!"

Still laughing, Billy sat on the bed, pleased that he had sensed the scene that she was going to play. It was from the last reel of *Arizona Belle*. The laughter began to fade and they looked at each other, losing themselves in memory. Without speaking, together they remembered the long-ago days of filming. Then, after a long silence, Billy whispered, "Here we are."

Ann tried to smile and as he put his arm around her, she leaned against him. "Wish you'd stay," she whispered. "Hate to be by myself. Hate it."

They remained quiet for a long time. like dreaming children at the end of a country day. Then quickly Billy kissed her cheek and stood up. "Table of five in the back, Billy," he chanted, imitating the proprietor of the restaurant where he worked. "Shake it up!" His coat straightened and neat, he smiled. "Who do you love?"

"Not you!"

Laughing, he leaned closer. "Who do you love?"

"I love us each and every one," Ann chirped.

Billy touched her hand in farewell. "Night, Angel," he whispered. And he was gone.

Ann listened as the footsteps faded. "Night," she called, pulling the covers closer around her for protection from the loneliness that she hated and that she knew would come. She heard the front door close. "Night." She said the word softly to herself.

Alone. She closed her eyes against it. Elise had been right. Charlie should not have gone back out. She sat up and looked to the door. "Elise," she called. It couldn't be taking this long to fix Charlie's supper plate. Ann shivered with the emptiness of the room. On the TV set the endless complications of a *Mission Impossible* episode were unfolding but they did not interest her. With her remote control, she ditted around past all the channels. There was nothing. Nothing! She could not stand being alone. And Elise knew that, too! Where the hell was she, anyway?

Always solitude brought an onslaught of memories. She did not want them. But they came unbidden and she could not control them. That was what was so marvelous about Billy. With him there, those same memories would not be painful at all for he would infuse them with fun. But alone . . . She shuddered. Alone, the memories were haunted things that would finally draw her back to the years before she had left home.

Home. The sound of it was a ghostly sorrow and it haunted her as nothing else ever could.

Home.

The beginning of her failure was there and she could not stand it. Could not think about it. She would think about something else—anything. She fought for thoughts to fill the void.

"Night, Billy. My Billy," she said.

And answered, "Night, Angel," as he had answered.

"City of the Angels," she whispered to the empty room and smiled. The words had a sorrowful sound, lonely. She relaxed against the pillows, her puffy, baby-pretty face grotesque with age and emptiness.

"City of the Angels." A really lovely sound, she thought. And idly she fingered her hair, tracing the curls and waves, thinking of herself as young, admired.

As she started to doze off, she thought, "Not a bad evening . . ."

And judging from what she knew of the evening, she was right. It had not been bad at all.

As their evenings went.

CHAPTER SIX

Elizabeth Mitchell huddled under the covers, her knees drawn up almost to her chest. She stared into the corners of the room, fascinated by the shadowy shapes that she had never noticed before. Despite the fact that her mother had given her a tablet to help her sleep, she had been lying there for over an hour and still was not in the least drowsy.

She heard soft footsteps beyond the door and fear caught at her heart. Then she knew that it was Sue. She could tell by the sound. There was a gentle tap on the door followed by silence. Then Elizabeth watched as the door slowly opened and Sue came hesitantly into the room. Elizabeth made no move to signal that she had seen her.

Sue stood still for a moment, unsure whether or not Elizabeth was sleeping. Then she whispered, "Elizabeth?" There was no reply and she tiptoed closer to the bed. "Liz . . . You asleep?"

Elizabeth did not answer. She simply folded the covers back and gratefully Sue crawled in. "Mama said I could come up," she said, her voice soft in the late-night silence.

"My mind keeps going and going," Elizabeth said. "And the shadows. I never realized the room was so full of them."

"Your mother said it was all right for me to come."

"I'm glad you did." Elizabeth gave Sue one of the pillows.

"I couldn't sleep. It's almost like I'm afraid by myself." She rummaged through a paper bag that she had brought with her.

Elizabeth listened to the crinkling of the paper, moved a little closer. "I can't stop thinking about it either."

"I was lying down there in my room, all by myself. And I thought . . . well, I don't know . . . I thought that at any minute I might just start crying or something. I could still see Jane and I knew that I'd never go to sleep." She fished out a bag of potato chips and ripped them open. "It was so awful. Wasn't it? The way she looked?" With a crunch, she bit down on one of the giant chips.

"Don't get 'em all in the bed." Some of Sue's habits were very hard on Elizabeth.

"Do I ever?"

"Yes."

Sue was stricken by the unfairness of it. "That one time. And those were Sunshine crackers and they do that, they're so crispy." In her agitation, she rolled over onto the bag of potato chips and cringed at the sound of snapping and crunching. "Oh," she groaned. "What a mess. Look. A mess!"

At any other time Elizabeth would have become angry, but the events of the day dominated everything and she remained calm, helping Sue scoop the crumbled bits and pieces back into the bag. "What difference does it make? I don't care . . . so worried I don't care about anything. I thought that my heart would stop . . . That would be the most terrible thing, Sue. To see this person. He's holding you and you can't get away. He's holding you. You know that he's going to kill you and there's nothing you can do."

"Don't talk about it." But Sue knew that they would both continue talking. There was no way to avoid it. They needed to talk about it.

"He has you and you can't do a thing."

"Don't," Sue whispered. "It would be too terrible."

They turned away from each other and there was silence. Then softly Elizabeth began to talk, her voice chilling in its calmness. "I saw a picture once. It was in New York . . . The picture was taken in New York, I mean . . . A boy in New York was in the subway. Somewhere. In the tunnel or something. I don't know because I've never been there . . . Anyway he must have been walking in the tunnel where they have these little places in the walls, the walls of the tunnel in the subway, places just big enough for a person to get in, to protect himself in."

Sue listened to the voice that was so gently leading her on but she did not know where she was being led. The words seemed a mystery to her, unconnected, without meaning; and she did not have to think, she only had to follow. She could see the boy. And the tunnel.

"You're walking in the tunnel . . ."

"But why was he there? I mean walking?" The words were whispers that in the stillness seemed to have special power, capable of carrying beyond the walls and into the street. "Why in the tunnel instead of on the subway train?"

"I don't know why. Nobody does. But he was there . . . Now you're walking in the tunnel. You hear a train. You get in there. In that little place. The train passes by . . . But at the last minute this boy looked out. And that's what the picture was. His head, there where it rolled. Against the wall. I was passing a newsstand, the one on Las Palmas. It was years ago and I saw it and won't ever forget it. Not even when I'm old. When I'm forty years old, I'll still remember. And this afternoon, in Jane's apartment, it was the same thing. But worse. So much worse. This afternoon was real. That's the staggering thing. There didn't seem to be anything real about it. But it was."

Images flooded through Sue's mind, memories becoming more and more real until she could not stand it.

"The way that Jane was lying there. Twisted, so that it almost seemed . . ."

"Let's don't say anything else, either one of us," Sue said. "Just lie here." She moved closer to Elizabeth. "Close our eyes . . . and maybe we'll go to sleep." But the silence was more haunting than the words had been. "It's almost like he's in the room," Sue whispered and closed her eyes against what might be waiting in the shadows.

Elizabeth felt it too and shivered. "Or Jane is here. Or something. It really is like somebody is here . . . somebody else."

"You wonder what it's like to be dead." Sue had never thought of that possibility before and it frightened her. "Don't you wonder that? What happens when you die."

It was a thought that had often come to Elizabeth and she was comfortable with it. "Right now. We die. Both of us. Something, another earthquake or something, a very bad one and we die. Well, the truth is that all this is nothing, what happens here. I mean it's important now but it's nothing really. I mean . . ." She searched for the words but could not find them. "I don't know how to tell you." She loved words and hated not being able to catch the ones that would make it clear, for in her mind there was clarity. "Look. It's this. The two of us." She turned so that she was facing Sue. "Boys don't ever ask us out. We're not pretty and we spend half of our time in mourning for that. It's crazy."

This was a truth that Sue hated so completely that she could not bear to acknowledge it, even to Elizabeth. "I don't want to talk about it."

In disgust Elizabeth looked away. She was trying to explain something, something important, and Sue's ridiculous pretense was stopping her. Suddenly all the pretending, the endless evasions of what she knew was true, seemed to her an exhausting waste of time and, in some way that she did not understand, an insult. It was important that she try to say what she felt. "Why not talk about it? There's nobody to hear us." She wanted Sue to understand. "It's wrong, don't you see?"

Sue refused to think about it. Her unattractiveness, her lack of popularity, were truths that she did not want to examine. If she left them alone, perhaps they were not true after all.

"Insane, Sue. For us to condemn ourselves for not being beautiful, something we have no control over. The most important thing is not how we look. It can't be. That doesn't go on. Not forever. But something does, some part of us goes on and on. Forever, Sue. For more time than seems possible . . ." There was silence. And then Elizabeth continued, her voice a whisper. "We die. The two of us. Right now. And what happens?"

"I don't know what happens."

"But what do you think?" There was no reply. "In a flash the earthquake comes and we're dead. Well, some part of us must continue. Somewhere." She shifted her pillow so that once more she was facing Sue. "Don't you see how crazy it is? I mean for us to spend all of our time moping and whining about the fact that we're not pretty?" Softly, she laughed. "So embarrassed by it. And why? Pretty is left behind. That's what I mean. It's all stupid."

Elizabeth's childish, groping words were the first view that Sue had ever had of eternity and she was awed by it. "You think that after Jane was killed, she was still there?"

"Still somewhere."

"That maybe she could see him, the man who killed her, as he moved away, as he left?"

It was not an easy question and Elizabeth was beginning to lose faith in her revelation. "Maybe," she hedged.

Sue had detected the moment of hesitation. "Well, we'll never know. None of us will ever know what happened to him."

"Yes, we will."

After a moment, Sue reminded Elizabeth of something forgotten. "You liked him."

The words, whispered so softly, echoed through her. Elizabeth turned away and when finally she spoke, her voice was shaking. "That's what I mean. Part of it. About the way people look . . . Don't you see, Sue? It's too easy to care about people, handsome people. And what is that, anyway? I'm glad we saw him. We know what he looks like. We're the only ones. Nobody ever saw him before . . . All those other times . . . And we're the only ones who saw him."

"I bet they never find him."

"They'll find him."

"I didn't really see him."

"I saw him."

"Just for a second."

"For long enough. And I will never forget him. Never. And they'll find him."

There was silence and Sue closed her eyes, hoping for comfort that might bring sleep. "Bet they don't."

"Go to sleep."

About to drift off, Sue mumbled, "I don't think I'll ever sleep again."

In quietness Elizabeth relived the moment of walking to the door of the room, seeing Jane. She closed her eyes. "I thought my heart would stop. Seeing her like that. And that man's eyes. I almost feel . . ." She turned and saw that Sue was asleep. For a moment she felt deserted. Then she was glad for the solitude. She pulled the covers up and whispered, "They will find him. They have to."

CHAPTER SEVEN

Porterton, like most California towns, had outgrown itself in the last twenty years and in a minor way had all the problems of the larger cities. As the police officer drove toward the Atkins home, he frowned in distaste at the way the town had changed. It was a relief to find such an easy outlet for his frustration but the moment was short-lived. Of all his duties this was the one that he most hated—to go to someone's house and tell them something so painful. In his quarter-century of service, he had never become accustomed to it, still found it impossible to plan what he would say.

He believed in prayer and silently he prayed that Tom Atkins would be there. He knew him slightly and that was a help of sorts. But if Tom's wife were alone . . . He had often seen her, a heavy, friendly-seeming woman, but he did not know her. He checked the address that he had jotted down when the call had come from Los Angeles. Why in God's name anyone would allow his child to disappear into that Sodom puzzled him.

He pulled up in front of the house and carefully looked it over, hoping for some sign that would tell him that Tom was there, but he found nothing to reassure him. The front rooms were dark.

As Laura Atkins came around the corner, she saw the car. Police, she thought, and immediately knew that something terrible had happened. She hurried her pace, then slowed almost to a standstill. She needed time to think. If it were something bad, really bad—and she was sure that it was—she needed time. She stopped. She was right. It was a police car. Parked in front of their house. And the man on the porch, ringing the bell, was in uniform. As she cut across the front yard, she recognized him. He was the one that they called Carson. "Good evening," she said and tried to smile.

"Mrs. Atkins." His prayers had gone unanswered. Tom was not at home and it would be only the two of them.

Laura nodded toward the door which was open. "I know I should lock it. I mean with all the new problems and everything . . . But . . . like the man said, old habits are the hardest to break."

"Tom home?"

"No. Wednesday's poker night, you know that." She tried to laugh but was unsuccessful with it and reached for words that might fill the silence. She knew now that it was not Tom. Whatever had happened had happened to Jane and whatever it was, she did not want to hear it. "Just walked down to the mailbox. Our daughter's in Los Angeles and I . . ." No. She did not want to talk about that, was afraid of where it might lead. "Come in." Carson followed her into the house. "I'm not sure when Tom'll be back but if it's important . . ."

"It is important."

There was silence and she knew that she could postpone it no longer. "What is it?" Some awful thing had happened to Jane. She was sure of it.

Carson nodded toward the brightly lit kitchen at the end of the hall. "Let's go in there."

"Of course. I'm just not thinking. I mean . . . well, you know . . ." She made another attempt at laughter and again failed. "Well, you're walking back from the mailbox. You turn the corner. A police car. Right there in front of your house." She stood before the sink, stifling the urge to wash her hands. "Right away you're sure something terrible has happened." She waited for him to speak but he said nothing. "Has something happened?"

He told her. And as his words surrounded her, denying her escape, she felt the air of the room become thick and she could not breathe. She knew that he was talking, but the words had gone beyond meaning and if she asked questions, she was unaware that she had asked them.

Jane was dead. That much she knew and that was all. What else was there? Gone. And there was no longer a reason for anything. No greater defeat was possible. It was complete. Always she had felt the years of her life leading to some mysterious terror and now that she found herself there, she became very calm, her only fight, the fight for air to breathe.

Suddenly the room seemed dusty, as hot and lifeless as the unending road from Kansas that was bound and buried with her childhood just beneath the surface. The image of Carson blurred and in his place she saw herself, her parents, her brothers. The walls of the room faded and they were together again, all of them, young and on the road to "good times, golden times." Memory closed about her and filled her with a longing to turn back.

Turn back.

From the golden times that had never come.

Even then, at the beginning, she had been the one who had wanted to turn back. Back home to her grandfather. The farm. Her brothers had laughed, teased her. And her parents had not looked back.

Calmly she watched the stranger who sat opposite her and tears filled her eyes. "I want to turn back," she said.

The policeman seemed frightened and that puzzled her. She knew that she must make him understand. She grabbed his hands and whispered, "Turn back. Please. Let's turn back."

After Carson had called a neighbor to stay with her, he went to find Tom. He hated this part of his job and, as he drove, he said aloud, "I hate it . . . Lord, I hate it."

The ocean had always been one of Charles's favorite places. It was a mystery to him and he never tired of watching the lazy darkness of the Pacific. Standing on the Santa Monica pier, he let his mind move with the gently rolling swells. It was the power of it that fascinated him.

Unlike many people, he had very few memories from early childhood. Frequently his mother would speak of things that had happened to her in the early years of her life and always he doubted that she truly remembered those long-ago days—was sure that she had heard others tell the stories and later believed that she remembered the incident rather than the telling of it.

One memory from those years he did have. He was unsure of his age at the time, knew only that he was small. His father was still alive and Elise was a baby. The four of them had gone to Malibu for the day to visit an Englishman who had written one of his mother's pictures and while the adults sat under beach umbrellas, Charles had played in the water. He could still remember how cold it was, how the sand seemed to move from beneath his feet as he walked. Then the sand was no longer there. The cold water closed over him and he was lost in it. He had fought and fought but could not find air. Then he was in his father's arms. His father was holding him, carrying him to the beach.

"Don't put me down." Charles could still remember saying the words. And his father had held him for a long time.

More than thirty years had passed, but as Charles looked at the water, the feelings came crowding back, the hidden power of the current, his inability to break free.

Taking a deep breath, he held to the railing of the pier as he had held to his father on that long-ago day. Then he turned and walked back toward the car.

Tomorrow morning. Would it be over then? That possibility held the same fascination for him that the water did. In a way it would be a relief to let go, sink into it. The waves made a pleasant sound and he walked to their rhythm.

His mother's face while she studied the paper, he would enjoy that.

And the things that would follow? He smiled. What might or might not follow did not matter.

It was only seeing her face that mattered.

While Ann dozed before the television set, Elise continued addressing envelopes, but her mind was not on it. She hated it when Charles stayed out so late, worried about him, and as always, imagined the awful things that could happen. Automobiles. They were to her terrifying things and the possibility of an accident haunted her. She had never driven an automobile although her mother constantly urged her to learn, insisted that "if only you would try . . ." Always it had been like that in everything. Ann had never had much patience with her daughter's infirmity. But Charles understood, had for as long as she could remember and she loved him for it. For that and a thousand other reasons. He was her champion, had been all of her life and she wanted him to come home.

"I hurt, Lisey." Ann was awake, her face groggy with bad dreams, pain, and sleeping pills. She lifted her hands and gently caressed first one, then the other. "Mama hurts," she whimpered.

Glad for the opportunity to stop addressing the endless boxes of envelopes, she gave her mother another tablet, held the glass while she drank.

Ann adjusted to wakefulness. "Charlie home yet?"

"Not yet," Elise said. And she walked to the window, looked out.

Tom Atkins dumped the coffee grounds into the sink and watched as they were washed away, relieved that the neighbors and family at last had gone. Why did people make a sort of entertainment of something so awful? He could not understand it. They had stayed for hours, drinking coffee, visiting; the house rustling with noises, chatter. Even laughter.

He turned off the light and for a long time stood in the dark, glad that he was alone. For him, contentment was only possible in solitude. He did not like people, did not trust them, did not want to be with them. Laura was in Jane's room. That was another thing that he could not understand. How could she bear to go in there? That was over and he would never step into that room again.

Everything was over. For too many years his life had been a downhill ride and Jane the only possibility of their ever reaching upward. Now that was gone and if there was any light before him, he could not see it, could not imagine it. He did not feel self-pity, felt instead, with complete dispassion, a deep need to surrender. But to whom? Or what? Except for an occasional beer, he did not like to drink. The usual, even the unusual, profanity did nothing for him. It was wearisome and he was disgusted, sickened. If only he could rid himself of the whole mess that his life had become and watch it, like the coffee grounds, swirl down the drain. Everything had gone wrong. Every goddam thing. The profanity did not help, made his feelings neither more nor less true, clarified nothing.

Marriage. That was the beginning. A cliché but none the less true. Everyone, his parents, his brother, his sisters, all of them had told him that it was a mistake but he had not listened. He had done what he thought he should do. But they were right. It was a mistake. He should never have married her. She had been an unintelligent girl who had grown into a stupid, bovine woman. The sight of her sickened him; her heavy, dense face hovering, gape-mouthed, over the endless pots of stews and soups. And her dark, slumbering eyes, so wounded. He knew that it was wrong of him to condemn her for not being what she could not be, but the feelings were at a depth beyond his control.

His stupidity. He was aware of that too. His initial stupidity that had led to marriage. He had relived it a thousand times, more than a thousand, and could so clearly see the mistake. But that was all in looking back. When he was young, when they both were, and they were married in the Catholic church, friends and family sitting there trying to smile; how could he have known? He had thought that he loved her. But he did not. That awareness came almost immediately, in the first few months. Then, while they were still children, they became parents and it was too late. His friends, classmates, all the people he grew up with, had been at the beginning of the good times while he had already passed to the far side.

Penance. Perhaps the priests were right. If so, he had twenty years of Hail Mary's to his credit. In the darkness he drank the last of his coffee. It was too weak. One of the other women must have made it, his older sister perhaps. Not Laura, that was for sure. He put the cup in the sink. At least she could make a good cup of coffee. He smiled. There was that. For the next thirty years his coffee would be strong. Just like he liked it.

"Tom."

He heard Laura's soft voice as he passed the closed door of Jane's room. But he did not answer.

Slowly he undressed without bothering to turn on the light, letting his clothes remain on the floor where they fell, stepping out of them. What difference did it make?

Jane . . .

Naked, he sat on the side of the bed and, thinking how foolish it was to lie down, he lay down.

Jane . . .

He had been wrong to treat her as he had. He would not think about it. He could not bear to think about it. But stronger and stronger the thoughts came and he did not have the power to hold them back. They floated on darkness around him and he shivered as they touched him.

Jane . . .

Why had it happened? It could not possibly have happened. He needed to say I'm sorry. For years he had meant to say it. And now . . .

Desperately he wanted to call it back, change it, make it different. The familiarity of the thought chilled him with loneliness. He was not a man to change things and he knew it, even the things that could be changed.

When Laura came into the room, she could see from the brightness of the night that Tom was already in bed. He was very still but she knew that he was not asleep, that neither of them would sleep for a long time.

In silence they lay there, lost in thoughts of "if only."

"Tom." Laura waited and although there was no reply, she knew that he had heard. She put her hand lightly on his shoulder.

"Tom." She loved him and the silence was terrible now that the house had become such a lonely place.

"Hold me." She whispered it very softly, not wanting to say aloud what she hated having to say.

For a long time she waited but there was no answer.

CHAPTER EIGHT

The television set flickered in silence, the picture gone. Sitting on the side of the bed, Charles touched his mother's shoulder. "Mama." He watched her, thinking that she would awaken but she did not. And after a moment, he started from the room.

Through the fog of sleep, she saw him. "Charlie?"

He smiled as he turned to her, holding out a Baskin-Robbins bag. "Ice cream."

She blinked, trying to reconcile herself to wakefulness. "Is it Tuesday?" He came back to the bed, laughing softly. "Oh, that's right," she said. "That's right."

He took the quart of ice cream from the bag. "Want some?"

"Where've you been?"

"Driving around . . . The ocean . . . beach towns."

"We waited for you. Waited and waited. Lise went on to sleep."

"Elise never sleeps."

"She sleeps all the time."

"All the time and never."

Ann patted his hand. She loved these times alone with him. Wanted attention. Needed attention. "I never sleep."

He smiled, accustomed to the games that she played. "You always sleep."

"I hurt."

Did she? He was never sure where the games stopped. "Did Elise give you some extra?" He looked at the notepad by the bed where the medication was recorded, saw that she had had an extra tablet.

"No." She saw his smile and realized that her daughter must have given her more than usual. "Did she? . . . I don't know." She relaxed as he gently massaged her hands. "Did you see the fire? . . . Said on the Eleven O'clock News that Malibu's burning . . . Thousand Oaks, too."

He kissed her hands and stood. " 'The fire next time . . .' "

"Hope it doesn't come here."

He held up the ice cream. "I'll put this in the icebox."

Already she was almost asleep again. "Love you, Charlie."

"We'll have some for breakfast."

". . . more than anybody."

"Ice cream and hot waffles."

"More than I ever loved anybody."

Charles watched her for a long time and smiled. Tomorrow morning. He snapped off the television set. "Yamaha."

As he went quietly to the door, Ann tried to follow him with her eyes but she was too tired. "Yamaha, Charlie . . ." He was gone and the door closed softly. "Don't go," she whispered. "Don't," and was asleep again. But it was not a deep sleep. It was that out-of-focus borderland where fragments of dreams come so quickly.

Don't go . . .

With a gasp she awakened. Quickly she looked about the room and was relieved that she was alone.

Don't go. It was her mother's voice that had awakened her and she was filled with anxiety. The dead. They were always with her and she was tired. Too tired to think about them. But she could not command them away.

Don't go. The voice was always there within her, waiting like some miasma to make its way into the room.

The dead. Why did they fascinate her so? Why so powerful, relentless? Was it because she had been holding her mother's hand at the moment of death? Was that the claim? Her haunting was the most private part of her life and no one knew that she believed the dead were with her always.

They were in the room—her mother, her father, and her little brother, Charles Edwin. She could not see them but she knew that they were there. Half sleeping, half waking, she could feel them brush past.

Charles Edwin! Don't go! She could hear her mother's voice calling to the dead, and it was the ghost of that voice that haunted her.

Know what's wrong with you, Annie? . . . Know what? Her father was there too. They would never leave her.

Always the beginning years were waiting just around the corners of her mind and she was in mourning. Not because the dead were dead. But because they lived with her. She could not escape them; and when they came, they brought back the Georgia days of her beginning.

Their life, while her mother lived, was a constant battle to recapture some ghost of dimly remembered gentility. Then, the battle lost, her mother was gone.

It happened midmorning on a Monday. (The day remembered because it was washday.) Ann was there alone with her when, at the moment of dying, a quietness had come into her mother's face and she had looked to the shadowy corner of the room and whispered, "Charles Edwin . . ."

The reality had been so strong that Ann too had turned and looked, but there was nothing there and she had taken her mother's hand, frightened.

"No. Let go. Don't!" Her mother had pulled away, had reached for the shadows, whispered again, "Little Edwin . . . Don't go!"

Ann had watched as she died; and in those last moments her mother's pain had seemed forgotten, replaced by joy at the imagined presence of a son who had drowned years before Ann was born.

Or was it imagined? Ann had never been sure. Were the dead there, somewhere beyond sight, waiting to see the living across?

"Know what's wrong with you, Annie?" Her father smiled and Ann waited, knowing that he would answer his own question. "Know what? . . . You're too damn prissy—that's what's wrong with you." And laughing, he had gone through the hall and onto the porch, leaving her there in the kitchen, her history book open on the table in front of her.

She could hear the creaking of the swing in the still, airless night. Always something about her had angered him but she never knew what it was. The noise of the swing stopped. She heard him as he shuffled to the Morris chair, let himself fall into it.

The Morris chair. She had begged him not to take it onto the porch. Her mother had loved it, had saved to buy it. And as soon as she was dead, he had taken it out there in the weather where quickly it became an old ragged thing, nothing at all like the chair her mother had taken such care of.

She closed the book.

Suddenly she did not care whether Napoleon escaped the dread Russian winter or not. She was not aware of ever having thought it before; but with the sound of her father slugging down into that chair, she realized that Napoleon's getting out of Russia was not half so important as her getting out of Georgia.

The idea was novel. It was breath-taking.

Immediately a regret presented itself. If she left, she would not graduate. She liked school, carefully prepared her lessons, was encouraged by her teachers. She wanted to graduate.

But why? Where would that lead her? All A's and what was that? Still she would go to work in the mill like her father.

Neatly she stacked her books and took them to her room. Her windows opened onto the porch and she could hear her father snoring. In darkness she undressed and got into bed.

For the first time she thought seriously, truthfully about her future, concentrated deeply on it and fought to keep the familiar fantasies at bay—those dreams that were such old friends. In one of them she taught school like Miss Walters, her English teacher. She would be "brilliant," have pretty clothes, all her students would love her. Frightened, she realized the impossibility of it. There was no way for her to go to college. And an even deeper truth was that she did not really want to teach anyway. With that admission, her dreams began to come apart, and she took refuge in another fantasy. She would marry some wonderful man, handsome, bright, successful. But why would a man like that marry her? He wouldn't. Her husband would work in the mill just as she would.

As she continued fighting her way through the fantasies that made her life bearable, she was suddenly angry at all of them—her father, the town, the school. Most of all the school. All those years of study —the work, discipline. And what difference did it make? All of it would finally lead to the same place. Knowing the dates of the Napoleonic Wars would not help her in the weaving room. In fact she could not imagine a situation anywhere in life where that knowledge would help.

On the off chance that she ever did meet some "college" people, what would she do? Stand around and rattle off some idiotic dates?

"1066."

"Oh yeah. And 1861."

"You think that's something, what about 1776?"

She kicked the sheet back, miserable in the hot stickiness of the September night. What could she do? The future was so terrible that she could not bear to think about it. Was she really as prissy as her father had said? She knew that many of her classmates ridiculed her properness but never before had she cared. Suddenly she saw it for what it was. Secretly she had always believed that her bloodless, sterile devotion to study and decorum would be rewarded. But it would not be. Her reward would be an absolutely miserable life.

She heard the neighbor's back door slam. Buddy Brock Fuller was on his way to the toilet. Would she marry someone like that? A man who would shuffle across the yard every night with terrifying predictability? And in his underclothes!

A life without fantasy. It was impossible. A life which daily negated all her dreams. She would not stand for it. Within the hidden part of her nature that she had never before examined, she sensed the necessity for illusion. She could not live without it and since dreams were no longer possible in the town where she lived, she would go where they were possible.

While her father slept, she packed, taking the diamond that her grandmother had left her and the thirty-one dollars that she had saved. She went out the back door and edged her way along the side of the house. Pausing at the end of the porch, she looked at her father, sprawled in the Morris chair as she had seen him so often, his head rolled to one side, his heavy face frowning in uneasy sleep. Then turning quietly, she walked beneath the chinaberry trees to the road. Once, she looked back but she could no longer see her father clearly, for he was lost in the shadows.

In less than an hour she was on the 11:43 to Mobile.

Then West to the Sun.

To Gold.

To a life where dreams were not only possible, but necessary.

As the Twenties roared across America, Ann quietly left the South, headed for the Golden West. To make her way.

And make it she did.

Almost.

But as the years went, the dreams wore thin, would intrude when she did not want them. *Don't go,* she would hear her mother call and, half waking, half sleeping, she would know that her mother was in the room. Her mother and her father and Charles Edwin.

In the stillness of the bright night Ann could feel the ghosts go. And just as her father, so many years before, had then been lost in the shadows of the porch, the pictures on her wall seemed lost, undefined ghost things. She had known then that he was there in the Morris chair, and she knew now that they were there—the photographs that showed what she had done, that proved she had, for a while, made the fantasy real. For her those pictures would always be there, even if the house fell down, if the canyon burned, if all California tumbled into the sea.

In the darkness she could see them.

She closed her eyes. Still she could see them. Just as always she could see her father there in the darkness on the porch. And her mother, reaching toward the shadows in the corner of the room, calling, *Little Edwin* . . .

Dreams. That was all that she had ever wanted out of life and in the end they had either failed her or haunted her.

"I die. I die," she whispered. Often the words came to her when she was alone, but it was not death that she wanted. It was the death of her humiliation. The humiliation of failure. Her haunting was a dual thing. She lived with the ghosts of her dead and with the terrible knowledge of her failure, of dreams that had finally deserted her.

Charles. He was all that she had.

Charles.

He was her victory. And sighing, she slipped into sleep as quietly as her mother had died.

Charles dipped his hands into the tray of solution and massaged the photographic paper. Gradually images began to appear. In the red light of the darkroom, the light and shadow on the paper blended together until a pattern emerged, a figure, caught and twisted in death.

Quickly Charles moved the print from one tray of solution to another. He leaned forward and studied the random pattern of wounds that covered the body. The face. He did not remember stabbing her there. He tried to recapture the moment but he could not. His mind was drifting and as he looked at her features, he found

himself thinking of the younger girl who had faced him in the doorway.

What was her name? And why had she stared at him with such
assurance? Almost as though she knew him, wanted him to know her.
Both of them had stood there waiting. But waiting for what? And
what was there about her that appealed to him? She was too young.
Not really pretty. But there was something.

She was unlike any girl he had ever held and he was puzzled that
she should interest him so.

He took the print from the tray, hung it up. As the liquid drained
across the smooth, glossy surface, the lifeless figure in the picture
seemed almost to move. He smiled. He loved that about it.

In his mind the movements would always be there.

Jane. Her body warm. Trembling against him.

Trembling. Twisting. Moving.

Always.

CHAPTER NINE

"I won't go." Tom Atkins turned away from his wife. Her eyes were
desperate and he knew that he would never be forgiven.

"Tom . . ." With his name, Laura's tears brimmed over and she
lowered her head.

To him her voice was flat and unsweet, had always been so. He
turned from the sight of her heavy, clumsy body, the redness of her
coarse face. He needed to hurt her, make her pay in some small way
for the guilt he felt, for the eternal misery that his marriage had
brought. He ripped a ScotTowel from the roll above the sink and
slammed it into her hand.

"Clean your goddam nose."

She was stunned into silence and he felt a passing reward but it
was not enough. He leaned across the table so that his face was very
close to hers.

Laura wanted to move away but was unable to. Fear kept her
where she was. She was afraid of what he would say, what he would
do. But something in her needed to know. And because that need
was greater than her fear, she did not move.

Tom knew that what he was going to say would hurt her more

deeply than any words had ever hurt her before, and he watched closely, not wanting to miss any part of her small death as the fingers of pain reached through her eyes.

He leaned nearer and whispered, "You're the one that wanted her to go to that goddam town."

His reward was even more complete than he had expected. He had never seen anything to equal the pain that coursed through those dazed eyes. It was overwhelming in its intensity and for a moment she was like some trapped, wounded, dying thing—not human at all.

"I mean it," he said. "I will not go. You're the one sent her down there so you can damn well go get her yourself."

And he left.

As Tom drove, he wanted to just keep going. Head for the highway. And on to Destination Unknown. His eyes filled with tears at the sudden beauty of those words. Destination Unknown.

Oregon. Yucatán. New Zealand. Maine.

But he knew that he would never see them, that the day, in physical action, would be like all other days. Go to work. Go home. Go to sleep. Go nowhere. His shoulders sagged with the truth of it while the thoughts that he did not want to come, came. How badly was his little girl mutilated? How desperate those moments of terror at the end? And the pain.

He should have driven Laura to Los Angeles. Should not have hurt her. She did not deserve that. He should have gone with her. But he could not. He would have had to look at Jane. He could not do that.

He stopped at a traffic light and when it changed he could not see that it had.

The cars behind him were blowing their horns.

It was like a celebration.

Charles stood at the door to the kitchen and watched Elise as she prepared their mother's tray. She dumped the eggs onto the plate and, turning, saw him.

"Good morning, Mr. Chips."

There was nothing unusual in her behavior toward him and he was surprised. Surprised that she did not know. The morning paper was there on the table and she must have seen it. He felt relief and that puzzled him. He had thought that he wanted them to know, had been certain of it. But now he was relieved that there had been no change.

Someday they would know. A pleasure postponed. He smiled. "She have a good night?"

"Same old thing. Went *Flying Down to Rio* with Ginger and Fred." She picked up the tray and started for the door.

"Wait." Quickly Charles went to the refrigerator and spooned a small serving of Rocky Road onto a saucer.

Elise laughed as he put it on the tray.

"Go on. She'll like it. A celebration."

"Of what?"

There was a moment of silence. He smiled. "Another day of ignorance."

After she was gone, Charles sat at the table and studied the headline. ANOTHER SLAYING IN L.A. AREA and there was a picture of the girl. "Jane Atkins, number fourteen." He smiled at that. Fourteen that they knew about.

In the beginning he had picked up the girls in the most casual way—on the street, in bars—and had driven them to the hills or the desert. But he had felt cheated by the way it had to be done, so quickly without time for him to watch them. The police had not connected the two groups of killings.

The earlier ones were safer, of course, but still his luck was holding. Proof was before him on the front page. Beside the picture of Jane was an artist's drawing of "Suspect's Face." Charles was amused. It was nothing like him. Only the eyes. And even they were unrecognizable, for he had not been wearing his glasses when he was seen.

Why had he been so eager to claim the assurance that it was over? He relived the moment of confrontation between himself and the young girl. It was only her eyes that he had seen clearly. The writing on the glass between them had obscured the lower part of her face. Only the eyes. He put his hand to his glasses and firmly adjusted them.

He leaned over the paper, touched his hand to the picture of Jane's face.

Elise stopped in the hallway outside the kitchen, frozen by her brother's attitude of weariness. She rarely saw him like that, vulnerable. Those infrequent glimpses of his unhappiness always frightened her. She never understood the reasons for his dejection, did not try to. But she was afraid. Survival dictated her fear and she trembled, afraid of losing him. What would they do? They would be lost.

With soft steps she moved into the room, careful not to make a sound, fearful that the slightest disturbance would break them apart.

Charles raised his head and with his movement, Elise stopped. He saw her reflection in the glass of the window and spun around to her, spilling his coffee on the newspaper.

His face was so still that for a moment Elise could not speak. Then, when she did, her voice was a whisper. "What is it?"

"You have cat feet." He was a stranger. The words, level and without humor.

Indicating the metal-encased leg, she tried to make a game of it. "And broken bird legs. But what are you so upset about?"

"Spying on me?" It was said with disgust.

The foreignness of it took her breath. "What?"

"It's unusual for you to be so quiet. Couldn't even hear the braces."

Pain swayed through her mind, assaulted her. He never mentioned her leg. Not since they were children. Embarrassed and confused, she turned away. "No fair, Charlie. I'm the only one who can talk about that." Silence followed and she found it unbearable. "I don't understand what you . . ."

"I don't understand either." And he went out of the room, leaving behind only the mystery of words that seemed to drift on the air.

After a moment Elise went to the window and looked out. The day had started with a puzzle that did not fit together. She turned, searching for some familiar activity that would bring her back to the comfort of everyday routine. She saw the coffee that Charles had spilled and, taking a paper towel, went to the table and cleaned it up. The front page of the *Times* was soaked and she spread it on the counter to dry. She glanced at the headline, the girl's picture, and thought, as thousands of others did that morning, *Terrible. Horrible.*

In Homicide, Ben Hamilton and his staff were ready for the rash of telephone calls that they knew would come. Always after the drawing of a suspect appeared in the paper there were countless calls.

Again he studied the sketch and was filled with frustration at the incompleteness of it. The girl, Elizabeth Mitchell, was the perfect witness. It was almost as though she had been schooled in observing detail. She was absolutely positive of what she had seen; the shape of his eyes, the path of his hairline, his height, coloring. But as the drawing proved, she had seen only a fragment and the likelihood of its leading to discovery was very slim.

He tossed the sketch back onto the desk and crossed to a large wall map of the Los Angeles area. Small rectangles of paper were pinned at different points on the map. On each a girl's name was printed and a date, some reaching back for several years. In the Hollywood area one of the policemen pinned another tag. On it was printed, JANE ATKINS, the date and the number 14.

At the window, Ben looked out over the confusion of metropolitan Los Angeles. He was tired, had slept poorly. Someone put a container of coffee on his desk and as he sat and sipped it, the telephones started to ring.

Perhaps one of the callers would lead them to their man.

But Ben doubted it.

Elizabeth and Sue had stopped as usual at the drugstore on the corner of Hollywood and Highland and as they walked the remaining half block to school, they munched Butterfingers in silence.

Everything that could be said, they had said. And said again.

As they approached the steps of Hollywood High, friends surrounded them and the questions began. Throughout the day, and for several days to come, they would tell the story over and over. For the moment they were celebrities and it was not an unpleasant experience.

Tom Atkins did not go to work. People were here. He did not want that. He drove past the building. They were waiting there, beyond the walls—people, friends, fellow workers. He did not want them. He turned a corner and so quickly, all were gone—people, building, job—everything. It was a neat trick—turning corners. In his youth, he had thought himself good at it. But youth, for him, was gone. The trick no longer worked. (Had it ever worked? He was not sure.) But he knew that now no corner, no turning was sharp enough—complete enough—to take him away from the truth that the night before had brought.

He wondered if he should call in, let the boss know. But decided against it. He did not want to talk to anyone. "I'm so terribly sorry . . ." "If there's anything we can do . . ." "Such an awful thing. And if there's anything you need. Anything in the world . . ." People. There was nothing that he wanted from them. The story had been in the morning paper, on the TV and radio newscasts. Everyone knew and if he went to work, there would be the endless questions.

Slowly he drove through the gently rolling ranchland that

surrounded the town. It relaxed him. Years before he had wanted to move to the country, but he had been alone in that desire and so they had stayed in Porterton.

Porterton. It seemed impossible that he had spent his whole life in that town. He had not intended to. Had, in fact, planned a much more adventurous life. Hawaii, that had been his secret plan. After his service in Korea he had stopped there, and the beauty of those islands had awakened feelings that he had never experienced before. Of course he had done nothing about it, but the feeling had always remained there, dormant.

In some secret, discontented part of himself, he blamed his inability to act on his wife, his child. But even as he blamed them, a part of him knew that they were not at fault. The fault was his. That was his frustration, his fury, the disjointed incompleteness of his life that others could not understand, could not put right. The self-knowledge that the weakness was within him—that was the burden for which he wanted others to pay.

For some mysterious reason that he could not understand, never even attempted to examine, it had always been impossible for him to venture out; to say to the world, "My name is Tom Atkins. This is what I'm going to do . . ." and do it. In thought it seemed such a simple thing, but moving it from thought to action had been impossible.

He looked over the gray-brown hills. Fire weather. Everything, the earth itself, seemed parched and dry, ready to burst into flame. The papers were filled with accounts of fires in the south of the state. The hills around Los Angeles, from the ocean to the San Fernando Valley, were burning.

For the first time since Carson had brought him the news, he almost smiled.

"Let 'em burn. Let the whole damn place burn."

Laura Atkins stood by the window so that she could see the taxi as it turned onto the street. She knew that any one of a dozen neighbors would be glad for the opportunity to drive her to the bus station. "If there's anything . . ." "Please. Just let me know . . ." "If I can help. Please . . ." The offers had been sincere, their friends, shocked and saddened, wanted to help but Laura could not ask anyone for this particular favor. She never wanted any of them to know that she had had to go to Los Angeles alone. They would not understand it, would think it unforgivable of Tom. No one knew him as she did. Not even Jane had. Laura loved him. Would always love him. And even when he disappointed her as desperately as he had that morning, she wanted to protect him by hiding his childish actions from others who would not understand.

The taxi was there, driving slowly, looking for the number.

Laura hurried from the house and across the lawn, hoping that she would not be seen.

"Greyhound Station."

She did not look toward her neighbors' houses as the cab headed for town. If they saw her, she did not want to know it. Clutching her overnight case, she sank back into the seat. Los Angeles. She closed her eyes and listened to the whirr of the tires on the pavement. The dream of going to that city had been continuous for so many months. It was not far, did not cost much, but always she had postponed it, convinced that she would be able to persuade Tom finally to accompany her.

Tom. He had refused to come with her, leaving her to face alone official terrors that she could not even imagine. Why? He loved her. She knew that he did. That she must never question. And if the ghost of doubt came to her, she must push it quickly away, not look at it, not think about it.

The taxi pulled up at the station and she dug into her purse for the correct change. The driver would be cross when she did not tip him and she steeled herself for it, was careful not to look him in the eye.

"Oh, Mama. Everybody tips these days." She could hear Jane saying it. Jane had always been embarrassed by her attitude, had had little patience with it. But the new generation, they did not know. It was impossible for them to imagine what exalted value the quarters and dimes that they so casually tossed onto counters had once had. But Laura could remember. And if taxi drivers and waitresses wanted to frown, give her curt looks, let them. She remembered the devastating depression that had happened once and was aware that it could happen again.

She waited in line before the ticket window. Bus stations had always depressed her and she preferred trains. They were so much more . . . She searched for the word, gave it up. Anyway, they were better and she thought it a shame that they were disappearing. She could remember what excitement, an odd excitement heightened by pinpoints of fear, she had felt as a child when, in the distance, she had heard the trains. Sound there on the plains of Kansas had carried so far across the endless openness and the cries of the trains had always touched her with a lonely fear.

She was at the window. "Los Angeles."

"Round trip?"

"Please."

Twenty-five minutes to wait. An eternity. In the coffee shop, she sat at the counter and sipped a cup of badly brewed coffee. How did they ever get it to taste like that? And it would cost her fifteen cents. She did not even want it but the action of stirring it, lifting it to her lips, sipping it and putting the cup back onto the saucer filled her mind, kept her from thinking of what awaited her, just as her memory of trains and childhood had done.

But the thoughts came anyway. She could not keep them back.

Los Angeles.

In less than twenty-five minutes the bus would leave.

"Refill?"

"Please." The waitress was a pretty girl. Jane's age.

Jane.

Laura nodded to the clock on the wall. "Is that time right?"

"Don't worry. They announce all departures over the loud speaker." The girl laughed. "'Course you might not be able to understand what they're saying."

When the announcement came, Laura could hardly force herself to stand.

"The Express for Los Angeles now boarding . . ." As she moved toward the line of listless people waiting beside the bus, she was overcome with weariness.

She wanted to stop, to rest.

But she could not.

It was her bus.

CHAPTER TEN

They sat before the television set, Ann and Billy and Elise.

There was absolute quiet in the room except for the Thirties dialogue that came from the midmorning movie on Channel 13. It was one of Ann's early films and her devotion to it was complete. Silently she watched the soft, youthful image of herself moving gracefully through the scenes, speaking the dated words. As an actress her choices were obvious, unsubtle. But she had a quality that was touching in some undefined way, a ghost of vulnerability that had nothing to do with acting.

Intent, Ann leaned forward with the reverence of one seeing a long-awaited wish image come to life. With economy of movement, she smiled as the girl on the screen smiled, turned as she turned.

Elise divided her attention between the picture and her mother, slightly saddened by the realization of the importance Ann attached to the dated film.

"Look . . . look . . ." They had all seen the picture countless times, but still Ann was deeply moved by the final scenes. Whispering, she pawed the air for Billy's hand. "Billy. Billy. Remember that shot?"

"Wasn't I there?" He spoke softly, not looking away from the screen.

The camera of more than thirty years before moved smoothly in for a closeup. The girl on film smiled, tears filling her eyes, as a young man stepped into the frame and caressed her, kissed her. The romantic music built as in all love stories of the Thirties.

"One take. One, Billy. One take. Remember?" Ann's voice was a sigh of love that expected no answer. She watched, trembling, as the picture began to fade. *The End.*

Abruptly the overorchestrated theme was sliced off by a commercial jingle which accompanied an animated advertisement. Ann and Billy looked to each other and there was a moment of quiet, of memory.

A soft laugh began to build and Ann squeezed his hand. "Now was that good? . . . Huh?"

Billy gave her a pat. "Few more like that and it would've been, 'Marion Davies, look out!' "

With the mention of Marion, the fantasy area of her memories began to fade. The picture that they had just seen was not really good. Always, she had known that. Everyone had. It was cheap, a B picture from Fade In to Fade Out. The script was rotten and the director, a fool.

Marion Davies. She had been a Star.

A real Star.

Marion Davies and Norma Shearer. The Talmadge girls. Gloria Swanson. Lillian Gish and her sister Dorothy.

All of them, Stars.

Ann watched Billy as he stood before the mirror putting on his waiter's jacket. He was going to leave. "I'm old, Billy," she sighed.

From the sigh, Billy recognized the game before she spoke the words. It was the endless replay of *Prove to Me That You Love Me.* Through the mirror his eyes met hers and he played the scene as Time had dictated that it must be played. "Old!?" he trilled.

Ann's voice was low, her eyes, pleading. "It's gone, Billy . . ."

Smiling, he went to her. "You? . . . Old?"

Ann laughed, delighted. "That's my Billy."

He bent and kissed her on the top of the head. "Bye, bye, Pet."

"Wait!" Desperately, she reached for his hand, nodded to the TV. The Late Morning Feature was starting, a picture from the same period as Ann's. "Evelyn's in this one. Don't you want to see?"

Together they watched the credits. As the director's card flashed on and off, Billy sat on the bed. "It's one of Edward's. I'd forgotten that Evelyn did a picture for him."

"I don't think Edward ever really liked me." The memory awakened was not a pleasant one for Ann.

"He never liked anybody, but he could direct."

In quietness they watched the opening scene of the film. It was immediately obvious that it was a better picture than Ann's had been and she turned away, lit a cigarette. "Remember that time I called Edward? 'Call him, call him,' you said. And I did."

"I remember." Billy's voice was as haunted as hers, for that was the call that had been final proof of Ann's failure. And her failure had been his.

"Edward," she said and no other words were necessary; for the name triggered in both of them the same memory which led them along a chain of memories, all linked by deceit, by promises broken, by the disloyalty of friends. "I'd love for you to play it. But . . ." "If it were up to me, Ann, you know what the answer would be. But . . ." "I fought for you to the end. But . . ."

Only Edward had told her the truth. After she had asked him about the part, there had been a long pause. For a moment she had thought that they had been disconnected. Then the words had come, the terrible lilting syllables in that light fey voice that she could never forget. "Sorry, darling. Nothing in this picture. In fact the truth is . . . I don't know why I should bother with truth but you've caught me at a rare moment. Nothing in this picture and nothing in any picture I ever do. Face it, Ann. It's passed you by."

Immediately she had hung up and Billy, hovering nearby, awaiting the verdict, had listened as she repeated the words.

"Edward," she said again, her voice deadened by the pain of failure. She tried to dismiss it with a laugh. "Well, I had it for a while anyway."

"In spades, My Beauty," Billy smiled, touching her face in farewell.

She caught his hand. "And Edward did get his, didn't he?"

"That's right, Little Sunshine. Died alone. And that's something that'll never happen to you. Not while Billy Boy's still here. And Lise. And Charlie." He turned the smile to Elise. "Right?"

"As 'Raindrops Falling on My Head,'" Elise answered and bobbed her head in a comic vein. She did not like for her mother to linger over past failures. That led to sleepless nights, "sinking spells."

As Billy headed for the door, Ann's voice stopped him. "Why do you always leave?"

"That damn restaurant. Twenty years ago somebody said to me, 'Split shift.' And I thought, now there's an interesting word."

"Call in. Say you're sick. Lise'll fix lunch. Won't you, Lise?"

Elise stood up. "An Alice Faye salad and some Don Ameche tea."

"Can't do it. I was always lousy at lying. To other people."

"Killjoy," Ann pouted.

"I can tell you this, Sugar Pie," he said. "That damn job is gonna be the next thing to go. Next year, sixty-five. And Little Billy Softshoe is breaking through the Social Security barrier." At the door, he winked. "Medicare, here we come!" And he was gone.

Elise straightened the envelopes that she had been addressing. "Want a salad or an omelet?"

"Wish Charlie had been here."

"Wish he had," Elise said, then added, "Salad all right?"

"Nothing like the movies, Baby," Ann laughed. "'Specially when it ends with a closeup of you. Fountain of Youth, that's what it is!"

"I can fix a mushroom omelet."

"Salad's fine." She nodded to the television set. "That was me, Lise. And Young! . . . How 'bout that!?" She laughed. "Shame I didn't save my money, huh?"

"Something like that," Elise said as she disappeared into the hall.

"Damn right it is," Ann whispered to herself and tried to smile. But she didn't quite make it.

Money. There was never quite enough. But they owned the house, thank God, and with Charles's salary and the pittance Elise got for the envelopes, they somehow managed to manage. And as long as they did that . . . Money had never been the driving force in Ann's life. Always it had been a secondary thing, a cousin that tagged along with the real Success. Success. She mourned the passing of it.

Sometimes when she was alone, it would come over her and she would clench her pudgy, swollen hands and make little mewing sounds of pain—not the pain of arthritis, but the torment of memory —for interwoven among the layers of illusion that her life flight had been, was recognition of failure. Failure. To be brutalized, forced to reality by that word. She despised it. "Why? . . . Why?" she would whisper. But always she stopped herself from seeing the answers. Her excuse was the all-inclusive "them," the evasive "they."

"They" had never given her the right pictures, had always shuffled her about like some cheap thing. Her thoughts stopped, for she had great fear of that word. Cheap. She hated the sound of it. Perhaps it was that one shrill word more than any other that had been the reason for her flight. Yet, like some private haunting, it had always gone with her and she did not understand why. She had done something with her life, accomplished something. Still the haunting was there.

But she had been a star. Nothing would ever change that. She tried to take refuge in it. And if those long-ago executives had laughed at her pretensions, had nudged one another and compared notes, had snickered and whispered like children scribbling dirty words on a wall, what difference did it make? She had starred in twenty-eight pictures. And she had lived to see most of those executives dead.

When she saw their notices in the Obituary, her nervous, uneasy eyes would snap with coldness and pleasure. The death of all who had contributed to her humiliation pleased her. But always the moment was ruined for immediately memory would fold about her, take her back to those quiet offices, to the dark forgotten apartments and she would see the men as they had been, would hear again their lies. Lies. Their promises had not been kept. Always the pictures that should have been hers were given to others. All those years and only two good pictures. And those two given to her only because they could not get the actresses that they wanted.

They had lied. And when she read of the death of one of them, she was relieved. Not because she was a woman who hated, but because it meant that there was one less who could remember those private moments that had made her ashamed.

"Lise," she called. "Hurry up!" She was starving. She wished that the salad would be shrimp, knew that it would be egg.

CHAPTER ELEVEN

In his office, Charles continued stamping the books, his mind attuned to the news releases that came from a small transistor radio. The morning announcements had contained no further information and he was sure that they would never find him from the fragmentary drawing. No one, not even those closest to him could recognize his eyes without the glasses he always wore.

Slowly he submerged himself into memory, relived the moments of waiting. Jane . . . He saw her again as she was when she first came into the room, enjoyed her lack of awareness.

Then he had her. He was holding her. He trembled with the clarity of remembrance and it was over. For a moment he closed his eyes, searching for the image of her as she had been, afterward. In some ways that was the most fascinating part for he was then removed from it, was no longer a partner in what had happened and he could see so clearly the twist of her body, the stillness of her eyes and the places where the knife had entered. Every time it was different, for he struck without thought of where the wounds would be.

The face, always there were some wounds there. And the abdomen. Jane. He loved the simplicity of her name. With her, the slashes there on the lower part of her torso had been so deep that the wall of muscles had been completely sliced through and the inner parts of her, released from their confinement, had spilled onto the bed.

Charles opened his wallet and studied one of the pictures that he had developed the night before. He pressed the picture to his chest remembering how, when he had finally undressed, he had fingered the coagulation that had covered him there before lowering himself into the bath. How, as the dried fluid dissolved into the water and slowly swirled on the surface of it, he had gently swayed his body so that the oily patches had caressed him.

With sure precision, the coroner sliced into the mutilated hundred and fourteen pounds that had been Jane Atkins. He nodded and his assistant started the water that would wash the blood into the drains that bordered the shiny metal examination table. Deftly he peeled back the layers of skin. The depth of each wound, the width at point of entry, the area affected; all were carefully recorded. With professional grace, the torn skin that had covered the abdomen was slit and laid back and as the water washed the blood and globules of fat away, the network of ripped muscles could be seen, studied.

It was a clinical and thorough examination, conducted in the most dispassionate manner.

VISTA DEL MAR MANOR. Laura Atkins stood before the rather shabby apartment building trying to recapture her high school Spanish. View of the sea? Yes, that was it. But why? The sea was twenty miles away.

She scanned the mailboxes. *MILDRED HIRSCH—APT.* 209. And there near it was Jane's name. She turned quickly from it and hurried into the lobby.

Mildred had been waiting all morning but when the tap on the door came, it was so soft that she almost missed it. "Who is it?" she asked, leaning close to the door.

"Laura Atkins."

Mildred was surprised to see that she was alone. She looked farther down the hall.

Laura was unprepared for the clumsiness of the moment. Of course the woman would expect them both. "Tom couldn't come . . . He . . . He just couldn't stand it."

They sat in the kitchen drinking coffee. ("Sanka really, hope you don't mind. It's gotten to where coffee makes me nervous, I don't know why. Used to drink . . . oh, eight cups a day, no exaggeration." This from Mildred while the two women tried to work slowly toward some area of easy rapport.)

"Of course I didn't know really exactly what the noises were. I mean there was nothing about them really that seemed to warrant the concern I felt. That's what it was, I guess. Just a feeling. Intuition, if you like . . ." She refilled their cups. "Anyway, I went to Mr. Chambliss after I couldn't get Jane to answer . . . and . . . well, you know the rest. When we came back the door was open. It was chilling, the door open like that and everything quiet. And then . . . then we went inside . . ."

Mildred took the key that Mr. Chambliss had given her and together the two women went to Jane's apartment. At the door to the bedroom, the older woman turned to Laura. "You're sure you want to go in?"

"I'm sure."

Although she had never been there before, the apartment was totally familiar to Laura. It was exactly as Jane had described it in her letters. Quickly she turned from the sheet-covered bed and lingered over the pictures that surrounded the mirror, studying each as though she were seeing it for the first time.

The confusion that she had felt began to lift and she was left with only sorrow. This room. It was in this room. In this room that Jane was killed. Like a litany she repeated the phrases in her mind. Each short arrangement of words, a response to the one that went before. And the rhythm of sounds was like "My fault. My fault. My most grievous fault . . ."

Mildred turned away. She could not bear to watch the loneliness that lined the younger woman's face.

Charles waited while one of the high school pages slipped the afternoon paper onto a stick and put it in the rack. As the boy moved away, Charles took the paper and studied it. Three pictures were featured on the front page: a shot of Jane Atkins, a picture of the apartment building which, under the circumstances, was sinister in its sun-splashed whiteness, and the artist's sketch of Charles. Beneath the drawing was the caption. *Teen-age Witness Supplied Details for This Composite Drawing of the Suspect.*

The girl. Charles was puzzled by the confusion of feelings that the thoughts awakened. He returned the paper to the rack and went into the lobby.

"Let me have the City Directory, Frances."

Without speaking, the librarian behind the circulation desk handed him the book. She did not like Charles. He was handsome and that she found appealing, but at her age that was an appeal that was fast losing its power and when she saw him she could think only of his coldness. She remembered when years before one of the old librarians had been opposed to his being given a permanent position. She watched Charles as he went to one of the tables and began studying the book. Idly she wondered if perhaps he were homosexual. There was definitely something strange about him, and these days so many homosexuals were handsome and masculine in appearance. The world had become too confusing. With a sigh of disgust, she returned gratefully to the Grace Livingston Hill novel that she was rereading.

Charles leafed through the pages of the Directory where residents were listed by address. There it was. Beachwood. 1600 block. He smiled. Jane Atkins was the first resident listed. He ran his finger along the column of residents of the building. Only two children were listed. Laughton, Sue. And Mitchell, Elizabeth.

Which was his? He smiled. His. Why not? Either was possible but to him Elizabeth had a nicer sound. Again he studied the brief paragraph concerning her. "Mitchell, Avis. Occupation: dental technician. Daughter, Elizabeth . . ."

He jotted down the names of both girls and their telephone numbers.

"Yes." Laura immediately looked away. "That's Jane."

The formality completed, Laura joined Mildred who was waiting for her in the corridor, and they were led from the morgue by an attendant. The day was ending; and as they walked into the soft twilight, Laura stopped. Mildred turned to her without speaking.

The colors of the sky were intensified by the smoke from the distant burning hills, and the ceaseless hum of traffic stretched like a tight wire through the air. "Think how afraid she must have been," Laura whispered.

Mildred did not reply.

"How desperate." The sound of straining trucks and cars seemed to grow. "One of her eyes was covered and when I asked them why, they didn't want to answer. Then finally . . . 'One of the wounds was there' . . . That's what he said."

"We're down this way," Mildred took her hand.

"Her eye. Just think, Mildred. Through her eye. And into her brain."

"Come on." Mildred led her to the parking lot.

As the car flowed smoothly into the treacherous flood-stage traffic of the freeway homeward bound, Laura closed her eyes to the noise that surrounded her.

"I'm glad Tom didn't come," she whispered.

Charles had been waiting for a long time. Finally he saw the two girls as they walked along the sidewalk toward the building where they lived. He had been on the point of giving up. It was after six and he had been waiting for over three hours. He watched the girl who had seen him in the doorway. She was worth the wait.

"Elizabeth," Sue called. "Don't go so fast." And she hurried to catch up.

Elizabeth. Charles smiled, almost laughed. It was ridiculous how easy things were sometimes. Almost as though the whole world waited to do his bidding. He watched as the girls disappeared into the building.

Elizabeth. A nice name.

Elizabeth and Sue were studying in the Mitchell living room, the record player blaring forth one of the loud, haunting tunes of The Moody Blues. The ringing of the telephone was lost in the music. Finally Sue heard it.

"Telephone," she shrieked above the din.

Elizabeth looked up, had not understood.

"Phone!"

Elizabeth hurried across the room and grabbed the receiver. "Hello." Only silence greeted her and she cupped her hand to block out the sound of The Moody Blues. "Hello . . ."

"Elizabeth . . ." The voice on the other end of the line was low, seemed almost a whisper.

"Yes?" Elizabeth signaled for Sue to turn down the volume of the music but Sue was leaning over her schoolwork and did not see.

Again the voice came. "Elizabeth . . ."

"Who is this?" She listened and when there was no answer, she became uneasy. Then she heard the sound of breathing and was frightened. "Who is it?"

"Elizabeth . . ." The whisper now seemed sinister and she felt that the man, whoever he was, was smiling. "You know who it is. Don't you? . . . Don't you know, Eliz . . ."

Quickly Elizabeth put the receiver back in its cradle, then slowly backed away. Desperately she turned to her friend. But Sue was tapping her pencil to the beat of the music and, her eyes on her book, she did not notice that anything was wrong.

It was he. Elizabeth could not get her breath.

It was that man. It had to be. But how had he gotten her number? And her name. He knew her name.

As the upbeat rhythm swirled about her, Elizabeth trembled with the fear that had come into the room.

CHAPTER TWELVE

Finally the kitchen was in order, or at least as close to that state as it would ever be. Elise took one last drag on her cigarette, stamped it out in the sparkling ashtray that she had just washed, and pulled the garbage can from beneath the sink.

The door slammed behind her as she maneuvered her way down the cement steps and emptied the trash into a larger can. At last she was through. At last. "Thank God," she whispered and immediately smiled at her own foolishness. For several months she had been in the habit of talking to herself but had not reached the point where she was comfortable with what she looked upon as a sure sign of middle age. She knew that others considered it odd. Smiling, she lit another cigarette. The last thing in the world that she needed was another quality of oddness. "What the hell," she said. She was going into middle age, and so what.

She sighed with aggravation. The can was too full and she was unable to force the lid on. She would have to pack the contents deeper with her hands. She hated that. Fortunately the morning paper had fallen so that it was resting on top of the garbage and a silent thought of gratitude drifted through her mind. At least she would not have to put her hands in the coffee grounds and egg-shells.

Something about the paper caught her attention. She coughed, tried to turn her head so that she could evade the smoke that swirled up from the cigarette that was clamped between her lips. In frustration she flipped the butt to the ground and stamped on it.

The morning paper. The article about the murder had been torn out. The coffee stains were still there on the part of the front page that remained. Charles had spilled his coffee, had been so cross when she had come into the room. He must have torn the article out after he came home, while she was serving her mother's dinner.

But why? She had never known him to express any interest in the more macabre happenings reported almost every day on the front page.

It was a puzzle.

Only a minor puzzle. But Elise was vaguely disturbed by it.

The evening was cool and she began to tremble. Hastily she forced the lid onto the can and hurried into the house.

Elise paused in the hallway outside her mother's bedroom, the sounds of a television variety show enveloping her. From that distance she watched as though she were seeing a scene from a play. Charles was lounging on the bed beside Ann who was completely absorbed in the splashy production number. He was not looking at the screen. His gaze seemed to reach for some point beyond the room, beyond the life of the house that was their world. In silence Elise studied him and was chilled by the sense of loneliness that came to her. Was he as unhappy as she feared? Tired of home and women? Some day would he leave? Not call, not write. Just leave?

Feeling her presence, Charles turned and after a moment, smiled. "Come watch, Lisey."

"Glen Campbell," Ann called. Glen Campbell was one of her favorites. "And Dom DeLuise." She loved him too. "It's a Special."

Charles winked at his sister and laughed.

He had a very nice laugh.

Laura was alone in the living room of her daughter's apartment. The afternoon had exhausted her to a point beyond weariness. If Mildred had not been there to help . . . Shivering, she left the thought unfinished. The room was cool and she was unfamiliar with the heating apparatus. It did not matter. She would not have to be there very long.

It was not good for her to sit alone as she was doing and she knew it. It was an invitation to the most terrible ghost images; and Laura knew that the longer she stayed, the more deeply they would be entrenched. She must do what she had come to do.

At the door to the bedroom she paused, but only for a moment. Then she went in. The only light came from the room behind her. She adjusted to the half light, then went to the closet. Quickly she rummaged through the dresses that were hanging there. They were almost all familiar to her. Together she and Jane had made the majority of them. The hours they had spent looking through the books of patterns . . . *Seventeen* . . . *McCall's* . . . The care that went into the selections of material.

She found the dress that she was looking for and carried it to the light. The color was so soft, a pale green. Like Jane's eyes. Her eyes . . . No. She would not think of that.

Before the mirror, she held the dress to her, studied it. Then slowly lowered it, looked at her reflection, the heaviness of her body, the puffy mask that her face had become. For the first time she was aware of how she would look as an old woman; the lines around her mouth, the weight of years that bent her shoulders to a slant.

She turned away, gave her attention once more to the garment. Holding it to the light from the living room, she gently swayed it back and forth so that the folds of soft material flowed and cascaded over and around each other, gracefully.

Her daughter would never grow old, never become heavy, never feel the weariness of age. That light, soft dress was the one that Jane would wear for all the years to come.

Book-laden, Elizabeth and Sue trudged up the hill on Cahuenga that led from Hollywood Boulevard to Franklin.

"Elizabeth! I do not worry about that!" Controlling her urge to stamp her foot, Sue stopped.

Elizabeth continued walking, did not look back. "You do."

"I don't!" Sue's voice was rising.

Elizabeth turned, more exasperated than angry. "Oh, we both do, and it's stupid and that's the point."

"Elizabeth, that does not worry me." Sue caught up with her friend.

"Why lie about it?" Elizabeth said softly and nodded to the deserted street. "It's just us, nobody else. Why not tell the truth?"

They turned onto Franklin, the hill behind them, and the going was easier. Elizabeth wanted to explain, but hesitated. Certainly she did not want to upset Sue. Still it was ridiculous. Almost as though Sue believed that if things were not spoken, they were not true; that unpleasant things could be discussed only if they were totally removed from her. It was frustrating; and Elizabeth took the silence as long as she could, then started again, trying to outline what she had meant although she did not see how she could make it any plainer.

"Boys don't ever ask us out," she said, her voice matter-of-fact. "We're not pretty and that's why they don't and we do worry about that. Both of us. Worry all the time."

Charles's car was parked in the hills above Franklin; and as he watched the girls in the distance, he was a little angry with himself. Following her seemed pointless for he did not truly find her appealing. But there was something about her that had caught him and he could only act as that need dictated. He reached into the glove compartment and pulled out the camera.

As he focused on the distant figures, he thought, It's like a gun sight. And, his face intent, he began to take pictures.

Elizabeth stopped and turned to Sue. "Listen. Why don't we go to the Drive-in any more? We tell each other we don't like it. But why?" She waited for an answer but of course there was none and so she continued. "Because now everybody there has dates and we don't and we're embarrassed . . . Well, that's crazy."

"I don't know why you always have to bring all this stuff up."

They stopped for the light, paying no attention to the cars that whipped past.

"Because it's something that concerns me," said Elizabeth. "Concerns us both."

The light changed and they started across the street.

"It does not concern me," Sue replied, her face tight with controlled anger. "I don't think about it, Elizabeth, so I don't worry about it. But when you talk about it, I have to think about it and then it just worries me to death, makes me sick." Trembling, she paused to get her breath. "Now I'm really worried," she rasped. "I am!"

"Well, I didn't mean to worry you," Elizabeth mumbled, contrite.

"You did!" said the heavy girl, her face building red. "You meant to and you did and now I'm worried frantic!"

For a moment they walked on in silence, Elizabeth now sorry that she had insisted on going over the whole thing again. She knew that Sue hated the kind of self-analysis that she so enjoyed. "Well, Sue," she said quietly, "it's something I can't help thinking about, can I?"

"If you want to think about it, think about it!" Sue barked the words, determined that there be no misunderstanding. "But don't make me think about it. All right?" She felt some relief but still her frustration was there. "And anyway, I do not worry about that!"

Elizabeth studied her for a moment and then whispered, "You do."

"I do not!" Sue was furious.

Again there was silence while the girls looked at each other. Finally Elizabeth turned and walked on. "Well, I do," she murmured.

Charles lowered the camera and from the hillside street, watched as the girls disappeared into the underpass that ran beneath the freeway. Only the confusion of traffic remained and for a while he studied it, fascinated by the graceful maneuverings of the cars.

CHAPTER THIRTEEN

Without warning the car changed lanes and in the five-thirty traffic it was impossible for Charles to follow. The cars beside him closed the gap and he knew he would lose her.

His excitement building, he waited and watched. There was an opening . . . Almost . . . There might be enough room. He tightened his grip on the wheel and tried to nose his way into the next lane, but the car behind him and to his right would not ease up and let him in. Bastard, Charles thought. The stranger increased his speed, closing the beginning of that opening in the flow of traffic that Charles had tried to use.

He had lost her. If she took the next off-ramp it would be over. He would never find her again.

He had first spotted her at Wilshire and Sepulveda just as she was turning onto the San Diego Freeway. It was a treacherous hour to try to follow someone. Usually he enjoyed that about it, but this time it had become too difficult and the pleasure was gone, replaced by frustration and anger.

"Don't take this off-ramp. Don't take it. Don't." Tense, he watched her car, a Vega. "No, baby. Keep straight. Don't get off. Straight. Straight." They were past it and he took a deep breath. She had not turned. Now he had no difficulty easing in behind her. She was a good driver and he smiled in admiration. "All right, baby. I've got you now."

As Margaret Connor maneuvered her car through the ever-changing currents of flood-stage traffic, she pouted and sighed. She was not happy. Her life had become a messy, confusing thing, not at all what she had wanted it to be. Carefully, she had planned everything; but those immature standards, the little-girl dreams she had so painstakingly nurtured, the strict demands with which she had burdened herself had taken too many wrong turns and she was caught in the discomfort of self-acknowledged ruin.

There was no cure for it, of that she was certain. She had betrayed herself and no forgiveness was possible. Repeatedly she told herself that she was a fool; a stupid, silly cow, mooning and mooing her way from one guilt-ridden week to the next. But there was nothing constructive about her superficial inner dialogues. She could only answer herself in total agreement. "Yes, you are stupid. Stupid and silly and a great fool. And so what?"

It was all Brian's fault. No, not all. But in a way it was. If she had never met him, then none of it would have happened, would it?

Of course not.

So, judging in light of that questionable logic, it was definitely his fault.

Brian. The corners of her pouting, childish lips turned downward at the thought of the name. It seemed impossible to her that he was a lawyer. How could he be? And a successful one at that. It made no sense. He was so silly. But she was silly too, sillier than he was. (Of this she was quick to remind herself.) Silly and stupid to get herself into such a mess. Hopeless. She sighed.

Her mind was narrow, repetitive, and vapid to a point verging on the ridiculous; but if this had been pointed out to her, she would not have believed it, for she considered herself a borderline intellectual.

She continued her self-castigation. If she had not devoted such energy to the meticulous planning of her life then it might have been all right to find that suddenly everything was such a shambles. Well, not all right exactly. But at least understandable. To an extent.

But she had planned. Very carefully.

Planned.

And what good had it done her? Brian was a buzzard. A dirty, no-good buzzard. And he had ruined all her plans.

Ruined!

She gritted her sparkling little teeth and swerved through the traffic. Silly. Silly! She sniffed and started to cry.

When she had first met Brian, he had seemed so very serious, almost insultingly so. It was at one of her cousin's "Saturday Afternoons" that her parents were always so eager for her to attend. ("Rich people, successful. No telling who you'll meet!" At least they were right about that.) Margaret had been in the den at the pool table, a game she detested but it was better than the sun that always left her blotchy and red. (And sticky, she hated that.)

Brian had stood and smiled while she made a complete fool of herself. She had tried to ignore him, but all afternoon he had followed her around making inane statements like, "I can't really talk to anybody but lawyers. Nobody else has the kind of mind that can follow quickly enough." Finally she had turned to him and said, "Is that right? Well, I'm a legal secretary and know for a proven fact that lawyers are the biggest ass holes in America." She had been certain that that would turn him off, but she was wrong. He had laughed and begged for more, had thought that she was very funny.

And during the months that had elapsed since, he had continued to think so. Whatever she said, he laughed. Whatever she did, he giggled. When she was silent, he smirked. It was driving her to a state of near collapse.

The puzzling thing to her was that, feeling the way she did—and she had felt it from the first moment—she had still allowed herself to become involved in a serious affair with him. At least as serious as any affair with Brian could be. He was everything that she did not want in a husband. What woman in her right mind would want a . . . well . . . a silly man for a husband?

Perhaps that was the explanation. Perhaps she was not in her right mind. But even as she thought it, she rejected it. The explanation was obvious. And it offended her. Deeply! She was in love with Brian, silliness and all.

She groaned in aggravation. In love or not, she was going to break it off.

She nodded her apple-dumpling head in agreement with her more "serious" self.

Yes. She was definitely going to end it.

Charles followed as she changed to the Golden State Freeway, pleased that his quest was leading into new territory.

She took an off-ramp and he fell a little behind so that she would not suspect that she was being followed.

The area was quiet and residential.

Perfect.

As Margaret approached the block in which she lived, another worry took priority. Parking. That was the only thing that she did not like about her apartment. The building was old, erected before the new regulations that demanded that parking space be provided for the tenants. She saw a place not far from her building and with a sigh of relief, parked, lit a cigarette, and exhaled wearily. She had faced the ordeal of the freeway once more and had lived. Los Angeles was becoming impossible. Perhaps the solution to all of her problems was a move. Phoenix. Or maybe Tucson. Perhaps even some small place like Wichita. There was something nice about the sound of it. Wichita. Country. Kansas. Salt of the Earth.

On the sidewalk she stopped. Brian was waiting. There at the entrance to the building. Sitting on the steps like some silly teen-ager. A three-hundred-dollar suit. She had gone with him, had helped select the material for it and now he was sitting on those dirty steps as if he had on jeans or cords. She groaned as he dropped ashes on the beautifully tailored jacket, casually thumped them away. Then he saw her and his homely face rearranged itself into a rather sheepish grin.

From across the street where he was parked, Charles watched as the girl approached the building. It was obvious that she knew the man sitting there and that she did not want to speak to him. Then the man was standing and they were arguing. Charles tried to catch the words but he was too far away. The exchange was brief, ending when the girl abruptly turned and hurried into the building. For several moments the man stood there, undecided, then got into his car and left.

Again noting where the girl's car was parked, Charles slowly drove past the building.

It was late and the street was deserted. Charles tried the door of the car but it was locked. Once more he glanced about and, reassured that he was unobserved, he snapped on the flashlight and shined it through the window so that he could see the registration card that was strapped to the steering wheel.

Margaret.

The last name was not as easy to read. It started with a C. C-o-n . . . that was as much as he could see. But it was enough. Conway, Conrad, Converse?

In the foyer of the building, he checked the mailboxes. Connor. That was it. *MARGARET CONNOR—APT. 318.*

And she lived alone.

He smiled, imagined her curled up asleep there two floors above where he was standing.

Asleep. Undisturbed. Unaware.

Margaret. Elizabeth.

Slowly he drove home, thinking of the two girls.

Comparing.

Planning.

CHAPTER FOURTEEN

The neighborhood theatres in the San Fernando Valley were their favorites. They were quieter somehow, the audiences more attentive and to Ann that was mandatory. The movie houses in Hollywood had become impossible havens for the most boisterous behavior and the prices in Beverly Hills were outrageous. They were left with only two choices: Santa Monica or the Valley, and Ann preferred the Valley. They all did. It was so much more convenient. The Valley seemed far away but it wasn't really. All they had to do was drop over the hills, wind around a bit and there they were.

Every day Ann carefully studied the movie pages in the *Times,* a very complicated process for there were hundreds of theatres and the listings were needlessly confusing. With a magic marker, she boldly checked each picture that they had not seen. Then together they would discuss the desirability of seeing this one or that one. At least once a week, they went to the Movies.

They especially liked Previews and this had been a lucky night. Ann had found a Major Studio Preview playing in Encino with a double-feature that none of them had seen. The marquee billed it as *ALI MCGRAW FESTIVAL . . . GOODBYE COLUMBUS . . . LOVE STORY . . . ALI MCGRAW FESTIVAL . . . ALI . . . ALI . . . ALI.* All that and the Preview as well for a dollar twenty-five each. It was a bargain.

They had gone in a little after six and they came out six hours later just past midnight, pleased with the evening.

The dozen or so other patrons who had possessed the stamina to sit through all three pictures hurried toward their cars. It had rained while they were in the theatre and the streets were still wet, the air cool and damp. A teen-age usher in an ill-fitting uniform was on a ladder changing the marquee. Ann, depleted by the outing, set a slow pace and together the three of them ambled toward the parking lot. Behind them there was a clatter and, when they turned, they saw that the usher had dropped the plastic letters that had so recently spelled out *ALI MCGRAW.* As if on cue, they all burst into laughter.

"There she goes, folks!" Charles called. "Ali McGraw!"

"Ali was really marvelous," Elise mooned, in imitation of a teen-age fan.

Ann was unsure whether it was a game or not and she did not wait to find out. "Irene Dunne was marvelous," she said, immediately defensive, just as Charles and Elise had known that she would be.

Charles turned to the usher and clasped his hands in pleading, "Ali. Ali. Don't die, Ali!"

The usher laughed and with another clatter, *LOVE STORY* came down.

"Myrna Loy was marvelous." Ann was not ready to let it go.

Charles winked. "The Oldies but Goodies."

"Ryan O'Neal wasn't so bad himself." Elise picked up an imaginary telephone. "Hello, Ryan? Come on over, baby. We got some Rocky Road."

Ann was on the road of memories and was not to be detoured. "Remember *Sentimental Journey?* John Payne and Maureen?"

"Then after," Elise whispered to the phantom Ryan, "you can polish my braces."

"*No Sad Songs for Me*," Ann continued. "Introducing Viveca. That was marvelous."

It was a pastime that they all enjoyed and Elise gladly forgot the telephone conversation. "*The Clock* with Judy and Robert Walker."

Charles joined in. "*Sunday Dinner for a Soldier.*"

"Anne Baxter."

"John Hodiak."

Now they were totally caught up in remembering. It was a serious involvement for them, much more emotionally rewarding than the pictures that they had just seen. But still, while they recalled the films of the past that had held such excitement for them, they were aware of the foolishness of it. At least partially so.

"Right . . . Oh, and *Waterloo Bridge*," Elise said. "Our Vivien."

For a silent moment they were lost in memories of Vivien Leigh. Then when they spoke, their thoughts came almost on top of one another, each instantly triggering the next.

"*Streetcar.*"

"Scarlett."

"*Ship of Fools.*"

They walked on in silence. And again their thoughts, when they were verbalized, fell so close to one another that they seemed one sentence, one uninterrupted tribute.

"All American pictures."

"And her best pictures."

"By far the best."

There was quietness and then the same pattern was repeated.

"The English never treated her right."

"They never loved her like we did."

"They didn't even want her to play Scarlett."

During a moment of silent rage, their thoughts lingered on Vivien, the legendary prophetess who, in her own country . . . They were angered and saddened by the injustice of it.

Finally Ann sighed, "I hope the English have a depression."

Charles laughed at the depth of his mother's feeling. The two women joined in, aware of the foolishness of it. But it was a foolishness that they all enjoyed and Ann could not desert her thoughts. Laughter or not, she needed to remind her children that she was serious. "Well, I do."

The moment was pleasure and Elise did not want to let it go. "*Waterloo Bridge* . . ."

In silence they paused at the entrance to the parking lot. The air was nice; clean from the rain, cooler than usual. Ann knew that tomorrow she would pay for going out in the dampness but she did not care. "I'm sorry de Gaulle died," she said. "He never would've let 'em in the Common Market, whatever the hell that is . . . *Waterloo Bridge*. Train station scene. Brilliant. Perfect." In silence she remembered the romantic way in which the scene had been filmed. She could recall them so clearly. Vivien. And Robert Taylor. "Now Robert Taylor was handsome."

Elise laughed in appreciation of her mother's loyalty. "You can swing that in Ragtime," she said and again reached for the imaginary telephone. "Hello, . . . Heaven?"

"Elise!" Ann was truly shocked.

"Sorry."

Ann chose to pass over it. "Handsome and nice. Robert and Barbara both."

Into her "telephone" Elise began singing snatches of the turn-of-the-century hit, "Hello, Central, Give Me Heaven. Is My Daddy There?"

Ann reminded herself that the game was over but she hated to leave it. "That's the way it oughta be," she whispered.

Grabbing her words as a cue, Charles started singing the Coca-Cola theme.

Elise joined in. "Coke is . . ."

Ann had wanted it to continue but it was finished and she had to admit it. With a shrug, she let it go.

Elise saw how she felt and whispered, "Vivien was my favorite."

Ann stopped. "Vivien and Clark. Jeanette. Gary Cooper. Even Marilyn . . . It's unbelieveable."

Elise put her arm around her mother, gave her a hug. "Love my mama."

Ann was pleased. She looked to Charles for the same declaration, waited.

With deliberation, Charles studied her, as though trying to decide. "Well . . . Sometimes."

Laughing, Ann saw it as another game and, in mock anger, she hit at him. "I'll get you."

Joining her in laughter, Charles dodged away and together they walked to the car.

The three of them.

Ann, smiling. These were the best times.

Elise, still singing "Hello, Central, Give Me Heaven . . ."

And Charles, planning.

Margaret Connor believed in breakfast. While others in her generation might settle for a dry cereal, or grab an instant this or that, Margaret held fast to the old-fashioned belief that "breakfast is the most important meal of the day."

While she finished off her two eggs (over medium), two pieces of buttered whole wheat toast, sliced tomatoes, grapefruit juice, three cups of coffee and generous globs of strawberry jam, she fed bits of bread to her myna bird whose cage was on the nearby counter. A gift from Brian, she had at first hated the ill-tempered creature. Then slowly, just as Brian had said that she would, she had gotten hooked on him. (The bird *and* Brian.) Often she found herself talking to the funny-looking feathery thing and that was comfort in a way, to be able to say whatever came into her mind. For a while she had worried that what she was actually doing was talking to herself, but after a few weeks of relaxing monologues, she had convinced herself that that was not the case at all.

"Well now, what the hell would I do in Wichita?" She addressed the myna bird in rather defensive tones, as though it had been his idea that she disappear into the mysterious and healthy Midwest.

There was an ear-splitting squawk as the feathered creature demanded more toast. And a little jam. He loved sweets.

"All right, McGoo." The nearsighted manner in which he stared at everything seemed to denote some difficulty in seeing and Brian had named him for the myopic cartoon character. Margaret watched as the bird gobbled up the toast. "Wichita sounds just awful. Awful. And frankly Tucson and Phoenix don't sound much better. Anyway why should I have to leave just because of him? Leave. All by myself. Go to some dreary place I don't even know anything about?" She was angry. It seemed almost as though Brian had suggested—no, demanded—that she leave Los Angeles.

"Well, I just won't go," she said, loading the dishes into the sink.

As Margaret backed the car around and started for the freeway, she was unaware that she was being watched. Followed.

Charles would be late for work but that was all right. Because of his mother's illness, he had an understanding with the director of the library that he could make up any time that he missed by staying late. He had no difficulty in following the compact car, for he knew the route that Margaret would take. The Golden State to the San Diego and off at Wilshire.

Easy.

In Westwood he watched as Margaret walked across the parking lot and disappeared into an office building.

Fine.

She would be just fine.

"Mother! I simply do not have time . . ." Margaret clutched the telephone in frustration and rat-tat-tatted a pencil on her head. Her mother always called at the worst possible moment. "Now I know that . . ."

"But, dear, I felt I just had to call," Alice Connor interrupted. "Believe me, I tried not to. I know you're busy. But I just could not help it." She was sure that her daughter was making a mistake— a very bad mistake—in so casually dismissing Brian's proposal. "Of course I realize you don't like to talk to me about it."

"I don't like to talk to anybody about it, Mother. But it's not just that. It's that I don't have time to talk about it. Not right now." Margaret was under pressure to finish the brief that she was working on and she knew that this kind of extremely disturbing interruption would throw her behind.

"I know that you're busy and I won't keep you but a minute," said Alice. Always there had been minor friction between them and that friction threatened to break into open hostility over the issue of Brian. "It's just that I've been thinking about it all morning." Her voice was artificial and grating. "Here all by myself trying to get the spots out of the Aubusson in the dining room. Your father spilled the fricassee. He's playing golf with Sam this morning. I thought that he would hate retirement, but he seems to thrive on it. I was afraid that he'd be around the house all the time. Under foot and all. You know. But he's never here. I don't see as much of him as I did when he was working."

Margaret was tempted to just slam the receiver down. She did not have time! Why couldn't her mother understand that? "I'm right in the middle of this brief and I'm trying . . ."

"Oh, I know. I know you can't talk. And I won't keep you. I

promise. I just called to find out if there was any new news. You know. You and Brian. I mean have you come to any real decision or anything?"

"No." Margaret continued typing while her mother rambled.

"Nothing at all?"

"Nothing."

Mrs. Connor was disgusted by her daughter's casual dismissal of such an excellent opportunity. Of course, eventually, Margaret would find out what a foolish mistake she had made. But that would be cold comfort, for then it would be too late. She had an overwhelming urge to spank her daughter, send her to bed without dinner, lock her in her room. Why was she so stubborn? Refusing to realize that this was an opportunity. An opportunity! Golden. Truly golden! And perhaps the last one. Surely the last one this good. Margaret was already practically an old maid. Twenty-four. All the girls she had grown up with were married. All except Hazel Rutland and Audrey whatever-her-name-was. And they were revolutionaries or something. (That's what came from sending a child to Berkeley. The Rutlands had always been Liberals and it just served them right!) ". . . Just wanted to be sure you didn't make a mistake or anything, darling." She could hear the hum and clatter of the IBM typewriter. Margaret was still working. Wasn't even listening to what she was saying. "Margaret! For God's sake. I want you to listen to me. Just stop all that stupid typing and listen!"

"I have to finish this thing before lunch, Mother. And for once you're right. It is stupid. I'm so bored with it I could scream. Sometimes I just . . . Oh, dammit. Damn. I made a mistake. Now just wait a minute. I made a mistake."

"Margaret, this is a toll call."

"Just hold on." Margaret made a quick correction and completed the transcription. "Now. I'm through. What were you saying?"

"I was saying, Margaret, that this is a toll call and it's costing me a lot of money, that's what I was saying."

Margaret handed the typed sheets to one of her fellow workers. "Proof them for me, will you?"

A bit disgruntled, the girl took them.

"Now." Margaret sighed, relaxed. "I'm through with that, thank goodness. It's just that you call at the worst times. I do work, you know."

"Yes, I know. And that's what I called about. That and Brian. He wants to marry you and you're a fool, an absolute, total fool not to accept him. Marry him. Right away! You think you're tired of that job now. In your twenties. Well, just wait 'til you're sixty and still slugging away. Change of life. Middle-age nerves. Getting old. And there you are! Still pounding away at your stupid typewriter! Still Miss Connor. Living alone. And typing ninety to nothing trying to keep up with the rent and car payments and scrape together enough for two weeks in San Francisco or Carmel once a year. How's that for a future?"

"Mother, you're just being ridiculous."

"I am not being anything of the kind. I'm telling you how it's going to be. Your generation may be expert at telling it like it is; I won't argue that. But believe me, we're the ones who can tell you how it's going to be. You're going to get old, Margaret, like the rest of us. And you're going to be sitting by yourself in some awful place, absolutely alone, without any money except the pitiful amount you'll be able to make yourself and you've already found out how quickly that goes. Goes! Whoosh, it's gone! Just two weeks ago, two weeks, you had to borrow twenty-five dollars for a new fan belt and whatever that other thing was that was shot, so now you know how quickly a paycheck just evaporates, vanishes, just Kazam, my dear, nothing left. And where does that leave you? It leaves you somewhere in your sixties, that's where, and still Miss Connor. Living on Social Security and praying to God that you don't get sick before you're old enough to qualify for Medicare, that's exactly where it leaves you, my baby."

"The most exaggerated thing I've ever heard in all my life."

"Did you or did you not have to borrow twenty-five dollars from your father last week?"

"Week before. And yes, but . . ."

"But nothing. Last week, week before; what difference does it make? The point is, you had to borrow it. And why? Because you didn't have it, that's why! You've been working at that job for over two years now and you haven't been able to save a penny. Well, let Mother clue you in; if you can't save anything in two years, you can't save anything in forty. Believe me, I may be an old fool but there is nothing, absolutely nothing that I can't tell you about financial desperation. Desperation! Just how do you think your father happened to have that twenty-five dollars? The twenty-five he lent you. Because he saved it? Not on your life. I'm the one who saved it.

That's how he had it. And it wasn't easy. It's been a struggle. We haven't burdened you with that, Margaret. We've always tried to shield you from money problems and I guess we were wrong to do it. We didn't want you to worry, to be burdened with all that. I suppose that . . ."

"I don't know what you mean, you tried to shield me. For as long as I can remember there was constant panic about finance. I can't recall a time at home when one of you wasn't moaning about this bill or that or arguing about how . . .'"

"Well, now you have a little taste of that yourself, don't you? I mean the twenty-five-dollar repair bill on that insanely expensive car that you never should've bought in the first place."

"It was not expensive. It's one of the least expensive models."

"Sure. Only twenty-three hundred dollars. What's twenty-three hundred? You could have had Loreen's Malibu for seven-fifty. A '67. And in good condition. Perfect condition. She would've sold it to you. You could've saved almost two thousand dollars. And you . . ."

"Fifteen hundred."

"What?"

"It would've been a saving of fifteen hundred."

"Fifteen-fifty, if you want to get snippy. About finance, I'm an expert . . . But no. You just had to have that Vega. Well. Now you've got it. And you've got payments for the next God-knows-how-many years and I just called to tell you that you better go on and grab Brian while you still can so there'll be somebody around to pay those payments because believe me by the time you've paid the last fifty-three-dollar installment that Vega or whatever it is'll be a piece of junk that you'll be lucky if they'll take as a trade-in on a new one and you'll have to start the whole thing all over again. That's the future, my dear. And, believe me, I know." Exhausted, Alice paused and lit a cigarette. At last she felt that she was making some headway. "Brian is nice," she said sweetly. "Nice as he can be. Your father liked him as much as I did. He's handsome, too. At least handsome enough in his own, funny kind of way. And he is rich! Far be it from me to suggest that you marry for money. But if money happens to come along with the rest of the package, who's to complain? Now I know that you're busy and I don't want to keep you. I have an appointment with Irene. My hair. Eight dollars. See. I have to think about that. Eight dollars here. Ten there. Well, if you marry Brian, those days will be ended for you. Ended, Margaret. Ended. Forever. What's eight dollars to Brian? Nothing. You told me yourself that he wears three-hundred-dollar suits. Of course on him they don't look it, but posture can be corrected. I knew, just knew that if you went to those parties at Anita and Emory's you'd meet somebody eligible. Worthwhile. Not just a passing nobody but a substantial somebody. With money! And I was right. Anita says he's just rolling in it. Covered with it. Santa Barbara money at that. And you know money up there is really money so I don't want you to be silly any more. I want you to tell him yes. Just say, yes, Brian, I will marry you. I love you and I will marry you. Just say that, Margaret. And don't argue with me. I can't stand it any longer. Just say it. Do it. And stop being so damn silly before you drive me absolutely crazy. Now I simply have to go. I've wasted enough time on this and I have to get to Irene's and get my hair done. She has a fit if you're late. You just think about what I've said. Just think about it. I certainly don't want to rush you into anything, darling. Mother loves you too much for that. But let's face it, at twenty-four, and that's where you are whether you choose to admit it or not, you have to jump where you see a hoop. Bye bye. Just think about it, darling. Think about it. Bye."

Margaret put the receiver back in its cradle and thought about it. It almost drove her crazy, but she thought about it. Brian. For months she had been unable to think about anything else.

Charles was parked near the entrance of the building. He recognized the car as she turned into the street, smiled, for like so many women she was excessively careful when driving slow. On the freeway she was an extremely bold driver, but on the absolutely quiet street where she lived, she was hesitant. At last, the car safely anchored in a parking place, she walked up the steps. The door closed softly behind her.

Margaret.

Charles drove slowly through the almost deserted streets to the freeway. Margaret.

The decision was made. But for the first time the excitement was not there. His heart did not quicken. No fantasies came to him and he was puzzled. There was no tension, no enjoyment.

The image of Margaret began to fade and in the mystery that his mind had become, thoughts of Elizabeth came to him. Unbeckoned, they filled him with softness. She was too young, not pretty . . . Then what was it? He did not know. Knew only that thinking of her gave him pleasure.

The telephone call. That catch in her voice when she realized who he might be.

That was pleasure.

As always Charles heard the television set when he stepped into the entrance hall. He smiled. His life at home was an absolutely expected thing. And the certainty that he would be greeted by those familiar sounds was the most unchanging of all. There was always that hum.

For a moment he listened, trying to guess which show it was. An action series. Most likely a Western. There was a burst of gunfire, hoofbeats, and his guess was confirmed. Probably a rerun of *Big Valley* or *Branded*. It was about that time.

"That you?" His mother's voice carried above the din of the program.

Smiling at the predictability of it all, he bounded up the steps. "It's me," he called, suddenly in a very good humor.

Ann was relieved that he was home. Always, when either of her children was away, she felt a vague uneasiness. She liked having them with her. There, in the room, where she could see them. She relaxed onto the pillows, waiting for him to come in. But he didn't. He passed quickly by the door on the way to his room. "Aren't you even going to say hello?" she called.

Elise looked up from her endless involvement with the envelopes. Charles was playing the kind of game that their mother most detested.

"Hello," he called from a distance, his voice almost festive.

Ann didn't like it. After a moment of pouting, she mumbled to Elise, "Hate it when he does that."

Quietly, Charles had retraced his steps to the doorway. He popped his head into the room. "What's that? What's that?"

"I said . . . Oh, you know what I said. And you know you know it!" Ann was not amused. "Hate it. I do. I don't like to be teased."

Laughing, he came into the room.

"I mean it, Charlie. I'd rather be dead."

For a moment he was quiet. Then he took a silver letter opener from the table, slowly lowered himself onto the bed, and, smiling, whispered, "Then I'll just have to kill you, won't I?" And, steady, his eyes held hers.

"Charlie!" Ann laughed uncomfortably. It was one of his games. She did not understand them, did not like them for she never knew how they would turn out. Sometimes they dissolved into nothing. But at other times they led to the most unbearable moments with Charles losing his temper and saying terrible things. Unforgivable things. She did not want that. She hated unpleasantness, saw no need for it.

Gently, Charles held the blade to her throat. "Like this?" He snapped it down to her breast. "Or this?"

Ann waited, not moving as he flipped the blade a few inches lower, angled it up under her rib cage.

"Or maybe," he smiled and leaned toward her, their faces almost touching. "Maybe this is best of all." He increased the pressure slightly, carefully watching to see if fear would come into her eyes.

Ann's discomfort gave way to confusion. She was not afraid of physical wounds. It was the other. He had the most terrifying ability to hurt her with the things he said. She blocked the possibility from her mind. She must not let it go that far. With the quickness of a bird, she darted forward and gave him a peck on the cheek. She laughed as a stunned expression crossed his face and she could not suppress the joy she felt at her moment of triumph. It was so seldom that she surprised him.

"I got ya! I got ya!" she called. "Mama got Charlie!" And she gurgled with pleasure.

With excessively slow movements, Charles placed the letter opener back on the table. Then he smiled, nodded, acknowledging her win. As he started to stand, he rolled onto her hand. Hearing her gasp of pain, he turned back and, still smiling, looked at her for a long time.

Elise went to the bed. "Are you hurt, Mama?"

Ann nodded and cradled her hands before her. Then, aware that she was the center of attention, she laughed as tears filled her eyes. "Arthritis is a terrible thing," she said, her chin quivering.

Elise sat on the bed. "Horrible."

Ann looked toward Charles with forgiveness, smiling weakly. "The most terrible thing in the world."

Charles sat on the other side of her, kissed her ear, and in soothing tones, whispered, "The most terrible? I don't think that's true." He looked across to his sister. "Do you, Elise?"

Ann was annoyed. More so than she had been by anything that had gone before. "It is," she whined. "And if you ever had it, either one of you, then you'd know." She was trembling with self-pity.

Elise knew that unless the moment was brought quickly to a close, the evening would become an endless complication of medicine-giving and heating pads. "I'm glad I don't have it," she said.

Ann whimpered. "Absolutely awful."

Covering her thoughts with a conversational tone, Elise glanced to her brother. "Hope you never get it, Charlie."

Ann was almost crying with the full enjoyment of the moment. "The worst thing."

Casually Elise turned to her mother. "I'm glad you don't have it."

"The most . . ." Then Ann realized what Elise had said. She was stunned. "I do have it!"

"No, you don't." Methodically, Elise rubbed her mother's swollen hands.

Pretending to come to his mother's aid, Charles whispered a harsh condemnation. "Elise . . ."

Ann was so touched by his support, that once more she was near tears.

Elise seemed unconcerned. "She doesn't. And you both know it." She leaned closer to her mother and whispered, "Do you know what you have?"

Ann fought to hold the tears back. "Don't joke, I'll cry."

"Don't cry, I'll joke." Elise leaned closer. "What you have . . ."

Ann turned to Charles. "She's insane."

Elise dismissed it with a shrug. "So what? What you have is a simple . . ."

Again Ann interrupted. "Stop it now!"

Charles had difficulty in forcing himself to remain serious. "Yeah. Lise. Stop."

Elise gave him a sour look and continued, ". . . A simple case of demon possession. Among other things too numerous to mention."

Ann closed her eyes in disgust. "Born insane."

Elise stood, knowing that she had won. The tones of self-pity had disappeared from her mother's voice, replaced by healthy anger. "Wrong," she said with a smile. "Born with braces on my heart and a crippled mind, but maniacally sane."

Ann turned away. "I won't even listen."

With irritating control, Elise once more started addressing envelopes. She smiled with condescension. "Of course you won't. Your demon won't let you . . . We're all demon possessed."

Her daughter's stubbornness was maddening. "You'll end in an institution."

Elise laughed. "Where the hell are we now? Or did I sleep right through Prince Charming's kiss?"

"I don't think you'd sleep through that, do you?" Charles asked, his voice a conversational throwaway.

"No. I'm a light sleeper. And it's a shame, I'd like never to get up again." She smiled at Ann. "Not even to give you your Darvon, Mommie." She finished an envelope and started another. "All of us are demon possessed."

Ann started to laugh. "It's so ridiculous!"

"Of course it is," Elise whispered, relaxing. "Everything is."

"Where did you get this?"

"Look around. A demon is a demon is a demon."

Suddenly it was a game. And Ann loved games. She laughed. "What's your demon?"

"Regret." Elise's answer was immediate. "Yours?"

After a brief pause, Ann snapped her head toward Charles. "Love." She smiled. "Charlie?"

Charles thought for a moment, then stood. "Three o'clock in the afternoon," he said softly and without looking at them he went to the door.

"Charlie! Tell us now!" Ann did not want him to leave. In irritation, she called to Elise. "He won't play."

Charles laughed. "Who's playing?" he asked, his mood suddenly light. And he left the room.

For a long time they waited but he did not come back.

They could hear him moving around.

They knew that he was in the darkroom.

CHAPTER FIFTEEN

Elizabeth Mitchell hurried out of the school building and down the steps, the thick foliage of the trees shielding her from the sun. From across the street, Charles watched as she sat on the grass, talking to some of her classmates. He tried to isolate the quality that made her seem special to him, but could not. She was important in a way that he could only sense, not understand.

Someone called her and as she turned, her forehead wrinkled in expectation, Charles took the last picture on the roll. What was the appeal? She was too thin, had birdlike eyes that snapped with intelligence, challenged.

She was a mystery and he could not dismiss her. She would take time. More than the others.

Slowly he drove past them. Elizabeth was talking as she always did while Sue, lumbering along silently, made only an occasional nod of affirmation.

Charlie felt a rising anger. She was nothing really, not even attractive. Why was he wasting so much time? Through the rearview mirror, he watched as the girls turned up Argyle under the freeway. She was gone and he realized how much he loved watching her. If she was nothing, why was he trembling?

Again he saw her eyes as they had been when she had first faced him. Was that what it was? The fact that she had so calmly looked at him without turning away, without shyness, without artifice? A look that asked nothing, expected nothing; eyes that gave nothing.

Finally he would see fear come into those eyes. Fear and the knowledge of dying. And perhaps, too, desire.

That would make it perfect.

"Well? . . . Look, do you want to or don't you?" Kevin Bedsole was hacked. It seemed beyond the realm of possibility that a girl like Elizabeth Mitchell would be hesitant about going out with him.

At the break between shows, the lobby of the cheap Hollywood movie house was crowded and noisy as the incoming and outgoing tides of people slapped against one another. Elizabeth had been unprepared for the invitation. Why would Kevin Bedsole ask her out?

Sue edged closer, whispering, "Come on. Let's go!" With an overly theatrical smile, the pudgy girl turned to Kevin and raking her hand through her oily hair, she laughed. "Sounds great to me, Kev."

"Elizabeth?" Kevin was absolutely stunned. Who the hell did she think she was anyway?

Still Elizabeth deliberated. "I don't know. I told my mother that . . ."

Kevin interrupted. "It's only nine o'clock, for God's sake." Where at first he had been rather cavalier in his attitude, not caring whether she accepted or not, he now was challenged. She would accept. She had to! He moved a little closer, dropping his voice to a more intimate resonance. "Come on."

"Call your mother up," Sue hissed impatiently. She definitely wanted to go, had no intention of letting such an opportunity slip past her. Not even in her most outrageous fantasy could she have imagined, when she and Elizabeth went into the theatre, that they would leave with Kevin Bedsole. The fantastic Kevin! At school his presence was the only thing that made her chemistry class bearable. Of course Elizabeth would get him. So life went. But Mel was with him. A nice foursome. Silent Mel. Really cute too. Sue gave Mel a sidelong glance and smirked in what she considered to be an attractive manner, silently thanking whoever the divine power was who had led her into such an incomparable circumstance. She leaned a little closer to Mel, grateful that she had worn her new suede serape which, she was confident, made her look thinner.

"Yeah, that's right. Call her. I mean, it's not like it's midnight or something. Or like we're taking off for Mexico or someplace like that. It's just a drive-in on Sunset." Kevin was sure that he had her and was again disgruntled. Imagine. A girl like that. Hesitating for even one second.

"What kind of car you got, Kevin?" Sue was doing her utmost to compensate for Elizabeth's incomprehensible reticence.

"Mustang." Kevin spit the word out with a casual, ballsy arrogance.

"Great!" Sue, of course, had known what kind of car it was. She had watched often enough as, tires squealing, he took off from the school parking lot.

Kevin waited while Elizabeth dug through her purse for a dime to call her mother. "Need telephone money?" Was that what it was? Was she stalling so that he would be stuck for the lousy call?

"No. No, that's all right. It's here somewhere." As Elizabeth rummaged about for the coin, she looked Kevin over coolly. Even more surprising than his asking her out, was the fact that she had not immediately agreed to go. She was mystified by her reaction. Kevin was extremely handsome, that was immediately obvious. And popular. Until recently he had gone steady with Marilee Johns. They were both famous for their beauty, their good times. "Did you hear about Marilee and Kevin?" . . . "They say that last night, Kevin and Marilee . . ." Everybody talked about them, wanted to be what they were. So why was she not pleased? Perhaps because when he asked, it was so obvious that he had expected her to fall all over herself in gratitude. And why should she? Certainly she was not as pretty as Marilee of the golden skin and brilliant smile. But for the first time, Elizabeth realized that she did consider herself a person of importance. Special. It was his condescension. But she did want to go with him. He was handsome. Incredible. His face. His lips. She was glad that he had asked her.

Kevin waited while she searched for the coin, fascinated by her lack of pretense. She had made no attempt to lead him on. He was surprised to find that that was a distinct relief. Marilee had been so dazzling that it had exhausted him. And just let him offer Marilee a dime for the telephone. It would make his head spin to see how quickly she would grab it up. Too bad Elizabeth wasn't better-looking. Not that beauty was all-important . . . And she was all right, in her way . . . But . . . It would be almost embarrassing. After Marilee had broken it off and everything, he would feel . . . well . . . funny, starting up with somebody like Elizabeth who was . . . well, not in the same league as Marilee, really.

"Back in a minute." Elizabeth made her way through the crowd, skirting her way around the jumble of patrons who were clustered about the popcorn stand.

"We won't be real late or anything," Kevin called. It might be a relief, he thought as he watched her disappear into the crowd. Somebody quiet for a change, somebody who wasn't always laughing, moving fast, demanding more and more of whatever. And anyway, what difference did it make what people thought? He was sick of it, trying to pass the pace setters. Marilee had finally turned so frantic and freaky that he had turned sour on the whole thing, let her walk out. Elizabeth would be a change. A few quiet afternoons in the park with her might be just fine. Perhaps more than a few. And perhaps more than fine. Bet she's never even been kissed, he thought, smiling. . . . Not really kissed. Well, he'd fix that. A kiss and maybe more.

The vibrations of the din of voices that surrounded them made Sue uncomfortable for it gave her a terrible awareness of the silence that covered the three of them. Her mind scrambled desperately to catch a thought worthy of utterance. If only one of them would say something. But they did not. They stood there mute, gazing at nothing. She could feel them slipping away. They would think her unattractive and stupid, would not see the interesting person that she knew herself to be. She felt the tension building. It was up to her but the thought of speaking filled her with a fear of clumsiness. The car. Both of them loved cars. "Don't you think a Mustang's great, Mel?"

"Huh?" Mel was sullen and unenthusiastic about the whole thing. What the hell was with Kevin, anyway? And just look what he was stuck with. A beast. A sloppy, fat, unbelievable . . . Disgust stopped him from a further search for descriptive words . . . A beast!

"Mustang!" said Sue, laughing what she hoped was a provocative laugh.

"Yeah. Just great." Mel turned to Kevin, making no attempt to lower his voice. "Now look, I told you I don't have much money."

"I know. I know." Kevin understood Mel's anger and did not blame him. And where the hell was Elizabeth? How long could one lousy phone call take?

Sue stood between them, a smile frozen on her lips. She did not want to smile but she was afraid to stop. She did not know what would happen if she stopped smiling, for it seemed almost that it was that, the smile, that held her firm, kept her safe. It was obvious that Mel did not want to go with her, that he had to go because Kevin had asked Elizabeth. Against her will, she started laughing. "I love a Mustang. Just love it," she said to cover the laughter which quickly faded, leaving only the smile. *What would happen if I stopped smiling?* she wondered. *Just stopped. Right this minute. And never smiled again?* But she did not stop.

"Love it," she said. And laughed.

"Just for a Coke, Mother. A drive-in somewhere." Elizabeth had already explained it once and was getting edgy. Why was her mother suddenly so nervous? Elizabeth cupped her hand over the earpiece to block out the noise that encircled the telephone booth.

Avis Mitchell was not at all pleased. She did not, in any way, consider herself a prude, but she would like to meet the boys before agreeing to turn her daughter over to them for an evening. She wondered if possibly she had been secretly relieved that her daughter had never been one of those very popular teen-agers, always going. "Late to bloom" was not exactly an undesirable thing considering the new sophistication of youngsters. "These boys. What are they like?"

"Nice."

Nice. Avis felt like pitching the receiver into the air, going on a vacation, becoming the oldest drop-out in town. Nice. Now there was a great word. It meant nothing. "Now listen, Elizabeth . . ."

Elizabeth listened as her mother began to caution her against the most incredible series of possibilities. Finally, exasperated, she interrupted, "Mother! That's ridiculous!" And without giving her a chance to start again, she hurried on. "It is. And embarrassing. It's not going to be anything like that at all. We'll be right there at the drive-in with a thousand people. Just drinking a Coke, that's all. And I called to tell you that you don't need to come for us. Kevin and Mel will bring us home . . ."

Kevin and Mel. They sounded like arrogant cocks of the walk to Avis and she did not like it. She knew that she must seem terribly stuffy to her daughter. But what, after all, did Elizabeth really know about the trouble that a man could give?

Avis knew all right. A day never passed that she did not remind herself of the cost. Her memory was at perpetual flood stage with images of Dan, Elizabeth's father. The cost. She never looked at her daughter without remembering how casually she had stepped into that mistake which had literally ruled the rest of her life. The impossible cost. And waste. Married at seventeen, divorced at nineteen, fresh out of Saturday nights.

Well, Elizabeth could think what she liked. Avis knew. It was too easy to make those mistakes. "Elizabeth, I don't like this. I don't know them. And when I say I want you home early, I mean early. Ten-thirty. I've told you time after time that I want to meet the people you go out with. Now when those boys bring you home, I want you to bring them in and introduce them to me. Is that understood?"

"Yes." Elizabeth had heard it all so many times before that it was now only a minor irritation. "You call Sue's mother and I'll see you later. Bye." But before she could hang up, her mother started again. "They're waiting, Mother," Elizabeth exclaimed. "They're waiting and I have to leave. Goodbye!" Hanging up, she sighed with weariness, "Honestly!"

As she started to turn, someone stepped into the telephone booth behind her. It flashed through her mind that it must be Kevin, playing a joke but immediately she knew that it wasn't, for hands reached out and touched her. It was not a game.

And she knew who it was.

Even before he spoke, she knew.

And as he pulled her against him, pressed close; she knew that she was going to die for she could feel the knife.

"Don't make a sound."

The voice whispering close to her ear was the voice that she had heard on the telephone. He was holding her, closing about her; all so quickly. There was no time to think.

"Here." He took the receiver from the hook and held it close to her ear. "Take it."

Trembling, she did as she was told.

"See? You're still talking to Mama." And he laughed.

Then he leaned closer, whispering. His words were fragments of thoughts that surrounded her and she closed her eyes as the images he spoke covered her with terror. She tried to turn.

"No. Be still." He loved the feel of her against him. There was something special. He had been right. There was. "There"—he nodded toward the glass wall of the booth that they were facing— "in the glass. That's what I look like."

But Elizabeth could see only the dim outline of his reflection.

"Lean against me." He was whispering and the words were soft; love words. "I love to feel you against me." He kissed her neck, smiling as she trembled. "Smooth," he whispered as he ran his hand across her lips. "Nothing else in the world feels like that." His voice was lost in whispers. "Love that . . . I do . . . I'd love to . . ."

He was speaking so quietly that she could not hear him. Or was it that she did not want to hear?

". . . and with my hands . . ."

No! She did not want to hear. She would not listen. All around the booth, there were people but none of them were watching. They were standing only inches away but they did not see her, had no awareness of what was happening to her. Two men were just on the other side of the glass, leaning against it. She wanted to call out but fear kept her from it. Still he was whispering, holding her too close. She could feel his body against her, could feel him move, could feel the sharp edge of the knife. No. No . . . Without realizing that she was doing so, she spoke the word. ". . . No . . ."

He stroked her hair, coaxing her to silence. He did not want it to end, wanted it to go on forever, wanted to hold her for a longer time than he had held anyone before. "Look," he whispered, his lips warm against her neck. And as he spoke, he kissed her, his kiss as soft as his voice. "Look at us." He smiled, nodding to the reflection.

But when she looked, still she could not see his face clearly, only the shadows that were there where his eyes should have been. They held her as firmly as his hands and she felt herself being drawn closer. Her breath caught as his hands moved over her.

"You like that?" he whispered. "Tell me that you do . . . Tell me . . . I love it."

She had never before had such an awareness of any man and she felt herself dissolving into him. "No . . ." She tried to pull away but he held her.

"Elizabeth," he whispered. "Tell me."

"Please." He was hurting her. "Please." She could not think. He was kissing her and she could feel the length of his body as he pressed against her. "You're disgusting," she said, forcing her voice to calmness. Immediately he looked up and she studied the blur that was his reflection. Was he smiling? It seemed, almost, that he was.

"Did you know I've been following you? Watching you?" He played with her earrings, lightly brushed his fingertips over her lips and when she shivered, he laughed. "I want you to know one thing," he said. "I want you to know that finally I'm going to kill you. Not now. But finally I will and there's nothing you can do about it. Of course, right now you could scream but if you did that, you'd die now." He laughed softly. "There's nothing you can do . . . I watch you all the time." He took some pictures from the pocket of his jacket and held them in front of her, encircling her in his arms as he showed them to her. "See? . . . I was there . . . there . . . there."

As Elizabeth studied the pictures, she trembled with the knowledge that he had so often been that close and she had been unaware of it.

"It's the two of us. That's all," he whispered. "I could've killed you a dozen times. In fact, right here." He nodded to the crowds beyond the glass walls. "All those people and we might as well be alone. Right here. I could do anything I wanted. I could do anything."

As he tightened his hands around her throat, Elizabeth gasped, certain that he was going to kill her.

He smiled. "I could kill you as easily as kiss you." He kissed her and when he felt her tears on his hands, his smile lengthened into the ghost of a laugh. "I love that," he whispered.

For a long moment he looked at her reflection. "I love it." Then with an abrupt movement, he was gone as quickly as he had appeared.

Elizabeth was trembling so badly that she could hardly stand. She leaned against the glass walls, unaware that she was crying.

Elizabeth's bedroom was a confusion of tension and worry. Verging on shock, she was the center and desperation ebbed about her. Her mother hovered on one side of the bed, the doctor on the other.

"It'll be all right," said Avis. "Be fine, Baby."

Elizabeth tried to draw away as Dr. Tullis searched through his bag for the hypodermic. "It's so stupid. I don't need a shot."

"Just lie still a minute, darling." Avis wished that she could have a shot too. She had been foolish enough after Elizabeth had first returned home to call her former husband and now he was there, standing about ineffectually, actually wringing his hands. Why had she called him? His presence was enough to make her want to scream.

"I'll call Alma as soon as the telephone's free," he said. "And you can . . ."

As Avis watched Dan, his voice just seemed to fade away. Calling him, asking him to come had been the final stupidity. Since he had arrived, he had done nothing but talk about Alma, that simpering girl he had married shortly after the divorce. As if she could do anything! At least he had not brought her with him. That would have been the one last thing that would unquestionably have driven her over the edge. Avis looked at him, her cool fury building. It was maddening that he had not in any way lost his physical appeal. In fact, if anything, he was more attractive than ever. It was not fair. His eyes were as clear. His waist, as trim. His hair, as thick. And if there was a little gray there, that too was appealing. While Dan cracked his knuckles and looked worried, his body automatically fell into the physical attitude of a dirt-lot pitcher on the mound, awaiting the American-boy moment of truth. Avis turned away from him. He was as handsome as ever. It really was not fair.

"Won't hurt a bit," Dr. Tullis said as Avis stroked her daughter's forehead.

"But it's stupid, I tell you." Elizabeth was groggy from tablets her mother had given her before the doctor arrived. "I'm all right!" She started to laugh. Why couldn't they understand that she wanted to be by herself? It seemed to her that anyone should be able to understand that. Even a fool. Even the worst fool.

In the living room, Ben Hamilton was on the telephone talking to one of his subordinates in Homicide. What had happened did not seem part of the pattern and that concerned him. The girl was too young. She in no way fitted the description that they had grown to expect. And why had he not killed her? Certainly he could have chosen an opportunity that would have afforded more privacy. Why not after school, before the mother returned from work? Something must have happened that had caused a change in their man's thinking. And that change, Ben prayed, would be what would lead them to him.

"That's right," he said into the receiver. "Two men, all shifts. Tonight I want Folmar and Rosa. And in the morning, I think probably Avedon . . . Yeah, Avedon and Lesser. Logan and I'll take it tomorrow afternoon." For a moment he listened. "Look, Logan's the one I want to work with, I don't care how new he is." He hung the phone up, his mind still boiling, trying to sift the new facts.

The girl's mother had not been as co-operative as he would have liked. Of course it was understandable that she would be overwrought. But still . . . They had to have more information. If they hadn't given the girl so much medication before he got there . . . The girl. There was always the possibility that she was lying, had made the whole thing up. He had had several cases like that. True, there had been nothing in Elizabeth's previous behavior to make him suspect that she would fall into that category.

But who could tell? On one case in West Hollywood he had devoted two months to careful investigation before discovering that the crime had never happened at all.

But this girl. Elizabeth. He did not think that she was one of those. Still she was the only one who had seen the man. A phone booth. In a crowded theatre lobby. It was unbelievable and that was one thing that made him believe her. He was sure that if a girl like that decided to fabricate a threat, she would choose a more immediately acceptable situation.

As Ben went back into the bedroom, the doctor, his face a study in Tender Loving Care, was ready with the hypodermic. Ben turned away. The shot meant that it would be the next morning before he could question her again.

"Dr. Tullis is just trying to help," Avis said and put her arms around her daughter.

Elizabeth started to laugh, tears streaming down her face. Everything was foolish. They were treating her like a baby when the only thing that she wanted, the one thing that she needed, was solitude so that she could try to understand what had happened. Not the fact that she had been threatened or held, but that, for a moment, she had wanted to surrender, had almost wanted to be held. She could not understand it and certainly she could not talk to anyone about it. Never. But these minutes, the ones that were going by so quickly, they were the ones that held the answers. Still she could feel his hands, his lips, and she knew that with time the feeling would fade. There would be other hands, other thighs pressed against her and she might never know what had made her tremble as she had. What beyond fear? For she knew that there was something. Immediately after it had happened, she had felt the truth of whatever her feelings were beginning to dissipate. It was Kevin's hands that had helped her to the car, his shoulder that she had leaned against, his fingers that had soothed her hand. And, calmed by his steadiness, she had felt herself dissolving into him. It was not the same but it did blur to an extent what had happened.

Elizabeth looked up as her father leaned over her, his face distorted by concern.

"We love you, Sugar," he said.

His hands caressed her and she shivered.

"All of us love you."

His hands. He had such nice hands. They were . . . She closed her eyes. Always she had been captured by the beauty of men but it was not until this that she had realized what the slow magnificence of them could mean. Hands. Her mind a confusion from the medicine, she fought for clarity. Hands. Too exhausted to stop herself, she grabbed her father's hand and kissed it. Hands. Never before had she realized how beautiful they were. She looked at her father and her smile faded as he pulled away.

Dan Mitchell was startled by his daughter's need. He knew that the others watching saw it as only a child's call for comfort, but he recognized it as something deeper and had withdrawn his hand. They had seen it as a child's kiss. But he had felt it and knew that it was more. Always he had neglected Elizabeth and now he was stricken with guilt because he had. "You can come stay with us in Encino for a while," he said. "I'll call Alma . . ."

"That won't do any good, Dan." Avis's voice was cool with contempt.

Dr. Tullis hated emotionalism of any sort, and the highly charged confusion in the room was very distasteful to him. He knew that he would hit them for seventy dollars. He would like to make it a hundred; but he was afraid that if he did, they would not agree to further consultations. If he handled it right, he was sure he could get the girl for a session a week at fifty a clip. The father looked like he'd be good for it. Maybe more. His shoes were custom. Probably eighty dollars. His shirt, Meledandri. The best. He was sure that with proper planning, it would all go well. The girl was not to his taste but few of his patients were. She seemed a whiner, and he hated whiners. He had purposely postponed giving the shot hoping that she would furnish a clue that he could use. But she had shown nothing. She seemed a vapid, weak thing, and he was sure that in therapy she would bore the hell out of him with the usual stories of masturbation and parental misunderstanding; but that was par for the course. During medical school he had realized how intensely he disliked the profession and had fortunately veered toward psychiatry. Inwardly he smiled. All it took was a little con.

Fortunately he had that.

"Now, Elizabeth, if you'll just relax . . ." His voice was one of his best qualities. All of his patients said so.

Elizabeth wanted to smash him in the face. "Relax? . . . Oh sure, relax. What is there to be excited about?"

Dr. Tullis jabbed the needle in, receiving a minor pleasure from the grimace of pain that crossed the girl's face. It was good to let them know at the beginning who was in charge.

Ben leaned against the window frame near Sue. "Sure you didn't see anything?"

Already she had explained it to him twice but she did not mind going through it a third time. In fact, she enjoyed it. "Like I said, I was talking to Kevin and Mel. We were . . ."

"All right." Checking his notes, Ben went to the side of Elizabeth's bed. He could see her relaxing and his anger built as she began to drift. Dammit. They should have let him question her more thoroughly. She had wanted to talk. He had felt it.

Mothers. He would never understand them.

He watched as Avis stroked Elizabeth's brow. "Mothers," he whispered and when she looked up, he again checked his notes but he could not force them to contain anything except what was there, a very usual recounting of assault and threat.

In the quiet that had settled about them, they listened as Dan, in the other room, talked in hushed tones to his Alma.

"Alma? . . . Dan." There was now a little-boy quality in his voice, a tendency, almost, to mew. "Afraid so . . . Very bad . . . Now listen, I think the best thing for her to do is to come stay with us for a while . . . Well, Betty can move in with the twins, can't she?"

Avis enjoyed the soft, whispered conversation. It was so like the Dan that she had known and had grown to despise. That "I'm a little boy lost, so love me" thing that had always been just beneath the façade of strength. She smiled, knowing what would happen next, knowing that the bluster would begin.

"Alma! I am not going to argue about it," Dan rasped. "Elizabeth is my daughter and I am telling you to have those arrangements made by the time I get there."

Avis wanted to laugh. He was so predictable. As always, his energy, when it was aroused, was misdirected. Anyone but a near catatonic would know that Elizabeth was unable to go anywhere. And even if she were able, Avis certainly would not let her go there.

"I do not know for how long!" Dan barked the words as though they were orders from a boot camp sergeant. "A week. A month. A year. I don't know. Just do it!"

Bang. The receiver was slammed down and they listened as he stomped into the kitchen to calm himself.

Avis turned her face away so that her smile would not be noticed. It was amazing that Dan had been so successful. But then how much sense did it really take to sell real estate in California? Dan had the perfect temperament for it; all bluster and no brains.

Elizabeth wavered in and out of control, fighting to keep from slipping away. "He held me," she said. "Close. Against him . . . And he said . . . all those things. And . . . And . . . The pictures. He showed them to me. I didn't know. Following me and I didn't know . . . Watching me. Waiting for me . . . He is going to kill me."

Dan came back into the room. "Just talked to Alma, Baby, and she . . ."

"Don't baby her, for God's sake," Avis snapped. "You don't even know her." She was grateful that she was no longer married to him, angry at herself for still considering him attractive.

"Go back to Encino, Daddy," Elizabeth whispered. "Go back. All of you. Go on." If only they would leave. She could think if they did. But with so many people in the room, it was impossible. And there were so many things that she needed to think about. So many things. She needed to think about . . . About . . .

But she was falling. Falling and she could not focus, could not think. Desperately, she tried to hold on but she could not. The bed, the floor, everything was dissolving beneath her and she was falling.

She was falling.

They watched as her face relaxed and she slept.

Sleep, Baby, Avis thought. Sleep.

She kissed me, Dan thought. Really wanted to kiss me. Not like a child. And she's my own child. He leaned against the dresser and buried his face in his hands. *Alma. Oh, Alma.*

Why is it I never saw him? Sue thought. Elizabeth saw him two times. And talked to him once on the telephone, too. And I never even saw him once. It's just not fair.

A year. Maybe two, Dr. Tullis thought. Should be able to stretch it at least that long. Maybe more. And when private sessions wear thin, I can channel her into a group. Have to convince them to send her to one of the colleges here so she won't be changing to one of those jokers up in San Francisco or anything. Ten thou, she should bring that at least. Maybe more.

The theatre, Ben thought. Check out the phone booth. Some fingerprints maybe. Won't be any. But there might.

Quietly he left the room. Why didn't the guy kill her? That's what I can't figure. He could've. Easy . . . And the girl. There's something she's not telling.

Softly, he closed the door.

Hands. In her sleep, Elizabeth could feel them caress her.

Hands. She loved them.

And she loved the warmth of the man's ghost body as it covered her, pressed against her. She moved within the dream, wanting closeness.

Hands—strong, warm.

They were holding her.

CHAPTER SIXTEEN

Charles stood before the mirror, studying himself as he emptied his pockets onto the dresser top—wallet, keys, change. He took a drag from his cigarette and rested it in the ashtray, his hand trembling slightly. Slowly he unbuttoned his shirt. Soft music from the radio encircled him and in fantasy, the girl was with him, watching as he unbuckled his belt, waiting for him to turn and move toward her.

His jacket was lying across the foot of the bed. From one of the pockets, he took the pictures that he had shown her. Elizabeth's face looked back at him, serious and questioning. He ran his hand over the image, smiling, and lay across the bed, pressing his face against the pictures. She was the only one of them he had ever wanted and, eyes closed, he dreamed that she was there and he was holding her, leading her to the same usual eagerness that all the world had. And it was pleasure. But a paler pleasure than his need dictated.

He knew that now she would be watched. But that was all right. The way he wanted it really. Let them plan and watch as thoroughly as they liked. He would find a time when she was alone. And then . . .

Sitting on the side of the bed, he trembled as he leaned into the circle of light from the lamp. Again he studied the face. The promise of beauty was there, untouched by the ghost of fear. Where the face in the picture asked nothing, he knew that that same face in future pictures would be interwoven with expectation, fear, the need for deliverance.

He glanced at the second picture, knowing that it would be the same. And the third . . . But there were only two pictures.

There had been three.

He had taken three with him. Hadn't he?

Yes. He was sure. "There and there and there." That's what he had said as he had shown them to her.

Three.

And now there were only two.

Quickly he checked his coat pocket. Only two. And the third? Had he dropped it in the theatre?

And what if he had? It was printed on rough paper so there would be no fingerprints. If it were there and if it were found, there would be nothing to bring it back to him.

It was the stupidity of it that bothered him. Unbelievable that he might have dropped it there. Still, even if they did find it, he was sure that he was safe.

Perhaps it was good that he had dropped it. A reminder to take care.

He put the pictures away and turned off the light. It had been a good night, better than he had expected.

"Good night," he whispered to the ghost of the girl who was waiting to come to him through the shadows of his mind.

He turned out the light.

"Wait a minute. It's here somewhere." Vincent Somers was the manager of the theatre and he was riled. Just like the cops to call him in the middle of the night, demand that he come down and let them in. The lobby was pitch black and he was trying to find the switch. "Damn!" He tripped over one of the cigarette receptacles. "Wait." He felt along the wall and found the switch.

As the lobby flooded with light, he turned to the two policemen, not caring if they saw how disgusted he was, hoping that they would. "I don't know what the hell's so urgent that you have to . . ."

Nodding to the telephone booth, Ben cut him off. "This the only pay phone?"

"That's right," Vincent mumbled, rubbing his shin where he had skinned it in the dark. "Middle of the night and I have to . . ."

"Shut up," Ben intoned casually as he went toward the booth.

"What!" Vincent was stunned.

Ben turned back to him. "I said shut up. It's the middle of the night for all of us and . . ."

"You can't talk to me like that," Vincent gasped.

"I just did." Ben's voice was calm, almost conversational, and for a moment the two men stared at each other silently. Finally, Ben started once more for the telephone booth.

The theatre manager had mistakenly read Ben's turning away as backing down and he followed the detective, his voice rising in fury. "I'm going to report you and if you think . . ."

"Do!" Ben whirled around to face him. "You do that!"

Ben's assistant, Bud Logan, shook his head at the stupidity of the manager. How could anyone be blind enough to challenge Hamilton?

Still Vincent did not see the writing on the wall. "I will! You think that you can . . ."

Words ripped from Ben's throat with staccato speed. "You report me! Do it. Right now. And I promise that by tomorrow afternoon when all the hustlers and fags come streaming in off the Boulevard for their midday 'do,' two of our best-looking and youngest Vice studs'll be stationed up there in your men's room and you'll lose half your afternoon trade for the next six weeks. So, like I said, shut up!"

Logan smiled, suppressed the urge to laugh. Old Hamilton was really something. It was a privilege to watch him operate.

Aware of the thoughts that were going through the mind of the young policeman, Ben decided to unload a little more of his hostility. "And Logan, you can quit grinning like a fool and give me that flashlight, unless you want a transfer to Vice so you can be one of them stationed up there in that toilet."

"Yes, sir!" Snappily, Logan presented him with the flashlight, his face serious, dedicated; his posture, militant.

While Ben shined the light in the area of the booth, Vincent, disgusted by the situation and frustrated by his defeat, watched the detective, a petulant expression settling on his florid face. After a moment of silence, he could stand it no longer. As he opened his mouth to speak, the young policeman at his side took his arm in a viselike grip and mouthed silently, "Shut up!"

The manager of the theatre continued to fume, but he did so silently.

The beam of light played across the popcorn-strewn floor of the telephone booth. Seeing something, Ben knelt and brushed the popcorn and candy wrappers aside. It was a picture lying face down on the floor. With a handkerchief, he picked it up, being careful in case there were fingerprints. Noting the type photographic paper that it was, he was sure that there would be none. He turned the picture over.

It was the girl. Mixed with the excitement of discovery was relief that she had not been lying. He liked her. She was honest, serious, innocent—all qualities that he admired; and he would have hated for her to be caught up in lies. As the light played across her face, he was moved. With surprise, he realized that his hand was trembling slightly. He felt an urge to reach out and touch the face.

What was it about her? There was something. She was his to protect. Perhaps that was it.

Or was it? He did not know. But he would protect her. Of that he was certain. And finally she would lead him to the killer and the moment he had awaited so long.

Avis was stunned. Seeing the picture had made the full horror of what was happening more real than before. She sank down onto the sofa and buried her face in her hands.

"It's all right." Ben knelt beside her. "Nothing will happen to her. We'll be close all the time until he's caught. And he will be." He put the picture in his coat pocket. "I wanted you to see this. We've checked it for prints and there are none. But this is the first actual clue we've had. And finally this and Elizabeth will lead us to him. Or him to us."

He stood, uncertain how best to introduce what he felt must be discussed. Then, after a moment, he continued. "There is one thing. We'll need your help. From the beginning you've fought me in a way and I don't understand the reason. You've never really allowed me the freedom to question Elizabeth as I would like. I want to know why."

Avis turned away. "I don't know what you mean."

"Of course you do. And I want to know the reason. Whatever it is, we have to discuss it, get past it."

Still not looking at him, she rose and moved to the window. "I don't like you." In the quietness that followed, she relaxed. "I know that that must seem a weak excuse. But it's the nearest I can come to the truth." She laughed, a soft bitterness in her voice, as she turned to face him. "I'm not saying this to insult you. I hope you'll believe that, for it's true. I'm rather old-fashioned in that really. I believe in manners, the civilized approach. To me it makes everything more bearable somehow. But you did ask and I realize that it could be important. In the future, I mean, since obviously we'll be seeing a lot of you. We'll need to trust each other. And there's the problem. Trust. The truth is that I don't trust you. Let's face it— all of us make immediate judgments, right or wrong. That was my judgment of you. I may be wrong but I don't believe that I am. You asked for honesty from me. Well, here it is. You're exactly the kind of man that I despise." She took a cigarette from the box on the table, lit it, her hands absolutely steady.

For a moment Ben was speechless. "But why?" he finally managed to ask.

"Elizabeth's father was here earlier. You met him. I'm sure you won't see it, but to me you are very alike. At least in one respect. Both of you present the image of one thing and are another. That's why I don't like you." She smiled, enjoying the puzzled expression that covered his face. "You even look alike, in a general kind of way. That same handsome, athletic exterior, the same covered eyes. Covered. That's the word. You're very guarded, and beneath the façade is something that I truly do not like."

Ben was astounded. She was accusing him of dishonesty. No one, not even those who most disagreed with him, had ever before done that. "I don't know what you mean," he said; and when she continued looking at him, that smile on her lips, he repeated it. "I'm serious. I don't."

"And I'm not sure that I can explain. It's something that I feel."

"Try." He wanted to know. "I saw no similarity between your husband and . . ."

"Ex," she interjected.

"All right, ex-husband. If the two of us have anything in common, I don't know what it is. Oh, a general physical thing, maybe. From the look of him, he probably likes handball. And I do. He's in pretty good shape. And of course I have to be. But that's nothing. Not if you are talking about what we are really like."

"That's eaxactly what I'm talking about. About what's beneath the . . ." She was lost for words. ". . . the . . . magnificence of that." She nodded to him, the smile gone.

"What is?"

"There you do differ. But it's the fact that you're covered, guarded people, both of you, who appear to be one thing, but are, in fact, something very different. That's what I don't like. And if I'm hostile to you, it is for that reason. Perhaps you don't even know what's under that façade yourself. I don't think that Dan does." She went toward the door. "Regardless of all the things that I've said, I am grateful to you for coming and I . . ."

"No," Ben said. "I have no intention of leaving it like this. You must know from my reaction that this is not a conversation that I'm accustomed to. Perhaps I am guarded. It's necessary to my profession. And if I seem to you to . . ."

"Are you divorced?"

The interruption shook him and for a moment he was too stunned to reply. When finally he did, his voice held a challenge. "That's right."

Again she laughed and was immediately contrite for she could see that he was stung and that was not what she wanted. "I'm sorry," she said. "Truly. I care nothing about scoring points in this. In fact I wish I hadn't gone into it at all. Remember, you insisted. And if you really want me to tell you what I think is beneath that façade, I will."

"Tell me."

"With one provision." She smiled, but it was so obviously an inner smile that Ben did not resent it. "I'll tell you what I think of you if you promise not to tell me what you think of me."

Now it was Ben's turn to smile. He nodded his acceptance of the rules.

"I couldn't stand it. Not tonight. I really don't think I could." She took a deep breath. "All right. You. It's control that's the most obvious thing about you. I believe that if right now bombs went off in this room, you would remain as cool as you are. There's something inhuman about it. And I think that that control covers a totally self-absorbed being. And a cruel one. I think that you are genuinely cruel and that if you were crossed, you would be as relentless as the killer you're waiting to catch. In fact, I guess I think you are a killer. If any eyes were ever colder than yours, I've not seen them. That's what I don't like about you. The sure knowledge I feel that if you were not trained to serve the Law . . . conditioned for it . . . totally . . . that at this very minute, you would kill me . . . I think it would be easy for you. As easy as . . . well . . . If you allowed yourself a life without control, I think it would, for you, be a natural act."

Unaware that he was doing so he had, while she was talking, assumed a militant stance. In the silence that followed her words, he nodded to her. He had allowed her to say what she needed to say and had dismissed it as soon as he had heard it. She was right, of course, but it was a truth that he already knew and the fact that now she knew it as well, was meaningless. In fact, it had been rewarding hearing another say the things that he had, for a long time, already known. "I'd like to check the windows in Elizabeth's room," he said and smiled.

Avis watched as he disappeared into the hall. There was something chilling about him, and she felt uneasy with him in the apartment. Why had she bothered telling him what she felt? He and Dan together would have made one hell of a man. Some of his strength combined with Dan's softness. What a man that would make. She wondered if anywhere in the world, there was such a being. And if so, what lucky woman had him. And did she know that she was blessed? Probably not. Probably made his life hell. She laughed and reached for another cigarette.

She heard the door to Elizabeth's room gently close. Elizabeth. She had never had an easy time of it. For that Avis was truly sorry. And suddenly guilt-ridden. She lit the cigarette. When this was over . . . But would Elizabeth be the same then? She blew out the match.

Of course she would be the same.

She had to be.

Ben watched the sleeping girl. Why had he lied, saying that he needed to check the windows? He knew that they were locked, had made certain before he left. It was the girl that he had wanted to see. But why?

He was watching over her, the ever-faithful upholder of the Law. He smiled, relaxed, sat on the bed beside her. He loved watching her. She did not appear terribly vulnerable, even lost in sleep. She was a child, her face pure, unspoiled. He touched her hand and she stirred, but he knew that she would not awaken for he had seen how much medication she had been given.

In sleep, Elizabeth closed her fingers about his hand and Ben was surprised by it, touched. He studied her face, ran the back of his fingers down her cheek, across her lips. He closed his eyes. There was nothing in the world that could equal the beauty of women. A terrible loneliness passed over him like a cold wind and he shivered, walked to the window and looked out. He knew that Folmar and Rosa were out there somewhere, watching. He leaned his forehead against the cool glass. Why had he spent so many years alone? It was senseless. The girl there. He could have children her age. Older. But there was no one. The rest of his life, like most of the years that went before, would be spent alone. And that was wrong. It was a waste. Except for his work, his entire life had become waste.

Divorce. How had the Mitchell woman known that? Was it branded in his forehead, a scarlet D. He smiled, laughed softly and the ghost sound in the darkened room comforted him. Branded. In a way, he supposed it was like that.

Divorce. He had not wanted it. No matter what she did, he had never wanted to be without her. It was Vivian. He would have gone on, regardless. But not Vivian.

Loving was a terrible curse. The most hated part of his life. And although he did not want to think of her, a day never passed that she did not come to mind.

His wife. They had been divorced for eighteen years but still he thought of her as his wife. Vivian. No other name would ever haunt him as that one did.

For the first few years after she left him, he had kept track of her, had known always where she was, whom she saw, what she did. Finally she had gone to his superiors about it, had threatened legal action, begged him to leave her alone. She had refused to understand that he still loved her. Then she had remarried; married a man who was exactly like she was—wealthy, soft, undisciplined. And he had never seen her again.

Why had it gone wrong? Why? He could not understand.

From the beginning of their marriage he had done everything he could to please her; but because he never understood her, he had failed. For her, he had, in a major way, compromised his life but all his concessions had led finally to defeat. Nothing could have changed it, for Vivian was willful, spoiled, insatiable and she wanted life on a grand scale.

After he had returned from Korea, Ben had wanted to remain in the Marine Corps, make it his life. He had found complete satisfaction in the order and challenge of the military; but Vivian had hated it, was uncomfortable with the people, despised the rootless transience of it. Finally he was forced to choose. But there was no choice really. Vivian came before everything else.

He had left the service, had become a policeman in her beloved Los Angeles, but still she was not content. In fact, it was worse, for then she was embarrassed. Always when they were with her friends or family, especially her family, she would give that funny little apologetic, theatrical laugh of exasperation when referring to his work, like a parent suffering through some temporary absurdity from a child. It was hopeless. He had chosen her. And because the choice was his, that choice had to be right. He loved her and refused to see that she was incapable of ever returning that love, that she was a creature devoted solely to self, a woman who would never be content, for whom there would never be enough, who would always want more and more. Of everything.

The one possibility that he had never considered was Vivian's unfaithfulness; and when he had found out about it, the initial fury had almost immediately given way to puzzlement.

He had, by accident, one day run into the wife of one of his former friends, a major who had served with him in Korea. The surprise of seeing someone he had never expected to see again had quickly worn off and on impulse he had asked her to have lunch with him. He had known her only slightly, had never particularly liked her, but he was eager for news of friends that he had not seen in a long time; so together they had gone to one of the sidewalk cafes on the Strip and had enjoyed a pleasant, slow lunch exchanging remembrances of Marine Corps life that seemed almost an existence that belonged in some former incarnation.

Ben had relaxed into the easiness of it, but there had been some vague shadow that puzzled him. Perhaps if he had not gone into police work, he would not have sensed it. To him that was one of the most fascinating things about his work. It had developed in him a professional awareness of the thought patterns of others, unspoken thoughts as well as those openly discussed. It was this ability that had made him a success and; although he was unaware that it was an extremely rare quality, he did recognize it as a plus factor and used it to advantage.

The waiter had brought the coffee; and as they sat for a moment in silence, watching the traffic, the woman absent-mindedly stirring the steaming liquid, Ben had become convinced that there was something that she wanted to say and his professional curiosity had gotten the better of him.

"What is it, Leona?" he had said.

She had looked up with such surprise, such obvious guilt, that he had immediately been sorry that he had spoken. It was his turn for a moment of discomfort. For a long time she had looked at him and her face, as it had been at that moment would always be with him, the smile of that woman he had never known well, had never really liked, would become one of the firmest memories of his life.

"You really don't know," she had said, her voice so quiet that it had blended into the sound of traffic and he had been unsure whether it was a simple statement or a question.

Then his vanity had come to the fore; and for a still, very uncomfortable moment, he had been sure that she was about to confess some hidden passion. Several times that had happened, always with rising panic, for he cared only for Vivian; and when women looked at him, when men told their endless locker room stories of fantasy conquest, he felt isolated from it for he wanted no other woman. From the beginning he had been sure that it would be Vivian and only Vivian for the rest of his life.

Leona had laughed. "Sorry." And had turned from him. Still he could remember the fragments of light as they seemed to catch and tangle in her hair. "I don't mean to laugh," she had said. "It's confusion really. Or something."

The provocative nature of women was endlessly interesting to him; and although he had not wanted another woman, he had always loved watching them, trying to understand, to capture for a moment the logic of their eternal illogic. "Tell me what it is."

"I thought you knew." She had sipped her coffee, added a cube of ice from her water to cool it. "That's why I was so surprised when you said, let's have lunch. Stunned really. I mean after what I was sure you must have known."

"Are you going to tell me, or aren't you? I've always been lousy at guessing games, always hated them."

"Vivian."

"Yeah?" Immediately he had been on guard. That name that was the core of his life, used in such a threatening fashion. Frozen, he had waited for whatever would follow.

"Vivian and Jack, of course." Her voice had been quiet and only the palest ghost of malice had shadowed her eyes. "After Korea. When we were all stationed there at Parris Island. We weathered it, of course. But it wasn't easy. I think . . . I don't know, one thing maybe that made it almost bearable was the knowledge that Jack wasn't the only one, neither the first nor the last. And so I held on. There was nothing else to do. I wanted what I had. A trait that's strong with us helpless little Southern ladies. We hold on. Forever. And before it's over, all scores are settled. And in the most charming manner." She smiled. "Across a table, for instance. Stirring coffee. And smiling."

Ben would never forget that smile. Nor the sweetness of that Southern voice as the soft, cloying accent clothed the lethal words with the fragrant suggestion of rainy afternoons and distant lush country.

After she had gone, the waiter, sensing some possibility of violence, had taken care not to indicate in any way that the table was needed. For the rest of the afternoon, Ben had sat there.

That night when he had confronted Vivian with it, she had, after a silent moment, answered honestly, giving the names of his friends that she had slept with, describing in graphic detail the performance of each—what they had required of her, what their comments had been, how they compared. To each other. And to Ben.

While she talked, his anger had quietened; and he could hardly hear the words, for his mind was filled with images from the past, memories that had seemed to have no connection with Vivian.

Korea.

The girls there.

The ones who had become whores.

At night they would come to the fence, there at the back of the camp. The men would stand on one side of the fence and the whores would kneel on the other.

At the time he had thought nothing of it.

It was an activity of war. Nothing more.

In war there are whores. Always it's been that. It's nothing. And if Korean women knelt there . . .

What was the difference?

Finally Ben had become aware of silence. He had looked at Vivian, who was sitting quietly on the sofa. How long had they sat there? He never knew. She had shifted uncomfortably as he smiled.

There was no difference. His wife was no better than they . . .

Was worse in fact. Much worse. At least the Korean women had needed the money. They and theirs would have gone hungry without it.

Silently he had studied Vivian's face, had touched her hair with his fingers. And as he sat there, the memory of those girls had come back so strongly that he could almost see them.

They were kneeling before him, their faces serious, their hands reaching out . . .

Vivian. Ben had never been able to understand it.

In the months that had followed, he had told himself repeatedly that she did not love him.

But he could not believe it.

How was it possible for someone who was so completely loved not to love in return?

And he had chosen her.

She was the one he had chosen.

He had fought but he could not hold her and finally she had divorced him.

Everyday he wondered about her—where she was, whom she was with . . . He would always wonder.

And whenever he thought of her, ghosts came with the memory. And in his mind he would see for a moment, a Korean girl—very young, almost a child—kneeling in the soft foreign night air . . . beyond the fence.

At the window Ben spotted Folmar in a car across the street. He lit a cigarette, signaling hello with the flame.

At the door, he turned back and looked at Elizabeth.

"Sleep well," he whispered and went out.

CHAPTER SEVENTEEN

"You are not going." Avis Mitchell stood in the doorway of Elizabeth's bedroom, watching her daughter dress. "And I mean it."

Without looking up, Elizabeth continued buttoning her blouse. "Mother, we've been through all that."

"You're supposed to see Dr. Tullis again today."

"I don't intend to see Dr. Tullis again ever."

"That attitude won't do."

"Won't do, will do, I don't care."

"He could help you."

"I don't need his help. I hate him. Those clammy hands. Makes me sick."

"You have a three-o'clock appointment and you're going to keep it."

"No."

Avis was uncomfortable, disconcerted by the new composure that seemed to have settled over her daughter. "But this other thing . . . There's no point in it, darling."

"If you think about it long enough, there's no point in anything

. . . I mean what's the point in getting out of bed? . . . There's nothing out there but another day. But we do get out of bed. And we continue doing things that others think are pointless. We do them because they're not pointless to us. Now I've told you that this is something that I have to do and I'm going to do it."

Avis wanted to reach out and slap her. She was almost beyond the point of endurance. "Why?" she demanded, her voice harsh, no longer attempting to conceal her frustration.

There was a moment of quiet. Then Elizabeth turned from the mirror and faced her. "I don't know," she said, the puzzlement she felt, clouding her face. "Jane and I are tied to each other."

"No!"

"But we are, Mother. And it's ridiculous to pretend that it's not true. We're part of the same thing in a way. And I am going to Porterton for Jane's funeral."

"It's dangerous."

"Everything is dangerous." She went to her mother, touched her arm. "I can't stay in the apartment forever, can I? And anyway, that policeman will be following us. I'll be safe." She went into the living room. "I'm going to call Mildred Hirsch. She's driving up to Porterton and I'm going with her."

Avis did not understand anything. It was all happening too quickly. Her child was no longer the little girl that she had been and it was frustrating. She wanted to cry, to take the events of the week and banish them, dissolve them into fantasy things that had never happened. If there was any point in going to that funeral, Avis could not see it. She wanted to keep Elizabeth in the house until that man was found, caught, killed. And if people thought that she was foolish, let them. She had called the dental clinic where she worked and they had given her a leave of absence. They understood. Everyone understood. Why couldn't Elizabeth? Of course that detective, Hamilton, would be pleased. She knew that. He would be delighted for Elizabeth to wander about the streets endlessly, giving him ample opportunity to catch the man. But Avis was afraid and did not want either of them to leave the apartment.

And Dr. Tullis was coming at three, what about that?

She listened while Elizabeth talked to the Hirsch woman, her voice assured as though nothing had happened. They were insane, placing themselves in such terrible danger.

Elizabeth hung up and turned to her mother. "I'm going," she said, the words soft, containing no hint of argument.

"We're going." Slowly Avis went to the closet and got her raincoat. They would be traveling north into the hills and you never knew what the weather would be there. "We're both fools and we're both going."

Laura Atkins sat in Jane's room, the shades drawn. "Baby," she whispered into the quietness, for that is how she had always thought of her daughter. "Sweet Baby."

Already she was dressed for the funeral. It would be an hour before they would leave and she did not know how she could stand it. An hour. It was eternity. The word caught in her mind and she whispered it over and over to herself. ". . . Eternity . . . Eternity . . ."

She remembered her grandfather in the years before they had left Kansas, an old man who sat on the porch, gazing out over the flat land, talking to himself. It was a habit that always had made her uncomfortable, to hear people mumbling their silent thoughts aloud. Now she was doing that same thing, finding comfort in it.

"Eternity," she whispered and sighed just as her grandfather had sighed as he sat on the porch, rocking back and forth. Suddenly a deep longing for that porch of years before swept over her and she wanted once more to hear the screen door slam, to run barefoot down the sagging wooden steps and into the dusty yard that stretched to barren fields of endless gray.

"Eternity . . ."

Silently, she wept, the tears staining her pale, unpretty face. Jane's death had been terrible. Their loss, indescribable . . .

But that had not been the worst.

The most desperately painful part of it was a certainty that Laura carried within herself. It was the terrifying, sure knowledge that her daughter was Lost.

Lost.

For all Eternity.

Lost to God. For she had not believed.

Jane had not known Salvation and, because of that, Laura's mourning was not solely for the fact that her child was dead, but for the even more terrible truth that Jane was Lost. Forever separated from the Love of God.

Eternity.

They would never meet again, for Laura knew that Jane had not truly been a Christian. For the last two years Laura had been concerned about it but she had said nothing, done nothing. Always she had meant to. But there had been so many things, important things, endless things that had so foolishly taken her time. And then she had been so sure . . . So absolutely sure that with maturity . . . That then Jane would see . . . That everything would be all right.

Then . . . With such terrible suddenness . . . It was too late.

Eternity.

And Jane Lost.

Laura's tears offered no comfort. They filled her with hopelessness.

There was a tap on the door. "Come on," Tom called softly. "Won't do any good, sitting in there all by yourself. Come on."

But she did not answer.

Soon it would be time. Soon the priest would say the words. Then it would be over. Forever. With only the sound of those Catholic words that Laura had never been at ease with, never understood. She had been raised a Methodist, had joined the Catholic church because of Tom. But she had never found comfort there. She missed the old friends, the preachers who had talked so urgently about Salvation, longed for the country songs. How she had loved them, still would hum them as she moved about the kitchen. "Rock of Ages," "Amazing Grace," "On Jordan's Stormy Banks I Stand."

She was filled with sorrow for all that was lost. Jane. The church and the songs. Her grandfather. All of it.

Again Tom rapped on the door. "Laura . . . Come on now."

She heard him walk away. And then, after the footsteps had faded, she rose and went to the door. As she opened it, she caught her breath with longing. She wanted the door to be the screen door that led to the porch of childhood. She longed for her grandfather to be waiting there, for he had been the only one who had understood her heart. He had stayed there in the muted, remembered Kansas when all the rest had left for California. In memory she could see him still, standing there on the porch as the old car pulled away.

Crying, she had looked through the back window of the Ford and had seen him move down the steps, the dust from the car swirling about him. He had shielded his face and called her name.

"Laura!" he had called.

Was he calling her back or bidding farewell? She had never

known. Quickly she had turned away, covered her tear-stung eyes. And so he had remained through all the years, a thin old man, frozen there on the edge of the fallow fields forever, dust the only movement, and that billowing about him as he called her name, Laura.

She had never gone back. Before she was grown, he was dead and there was no reason to go back. But in her mind, he was still there, forever close. And now that Jane was . . . gone . . . Lost . . . Laura felt closer than ever before to the old man. Over and over she relived their parting, never grew tired of it.

She stepped into the hall, almost expecting to see him there. But, of course, there was no one. Still she knew that somewhere he was waiting; that when she died, he would be there. And that then, lighter than air, holding to each other, they would skim across the road that led to the porch. They would pass over the house, quiet and deserted.

And then they would go on, memory dissolving into eternity.

Eternity . . . And Jane, Lost.

She went into the kitchen and Tom handed her a cup of coffee.

"Hope it's not too strong," Tom said. But there was no reply. He was worried about her. Was she losing her mind? God! What would he do? Since she had come back from Los Angeles, he had often heard her whispering. Finally he had decided that it was her grandfather she was talking to. If she broke completely, what would he do? He had never imagined that she could be like this. She seldom even looked at him, had made no attempt to clean the house or prepare the meals. Was it because he had turned away from her that night Carson had told them about Jane? Because he had not gone with her to Los Angeles? Well, he had been wrong about that. He had told her so. What more did she want? What more could he do? He had told her that he was wrong! It was a difficult thing to do and he had done it. But she had only smiled, a smile that he had not understood. She had said nothing.

He watched as she stirred the coffee and wondered what she was thinking. It almost seemed that she was about to smile and it bothered him. He was unsure of her. Always she had been so easy to read. Aggravatingly so. But that openness was gone, replaced by something that he did not understand.

He watched as she sipped the coffee.

"Coffee all right?" he asked.

But she did not speak. There was nothing that she wanted to say to him.

"Tried to make it like you like it," he said.

But she did not look at him.

"I don't know what's the matter with me." Elizabeth's voice shook as she felt sorrow close about her. "I can't stop myself." She started crying.

"It's all right." Silently condemning herself for agreeing to come to the funeral, Avis put her arm around her daughter. It will be over soon, she thought as she watched the priest. But would it? How long were Catholic funerals? She had never attended one before. She had been surprised that it was in a funeral home rather than the cathedral. And the priest. It was all foreign and confusing. Pagan, somehow. She did not understand it and longed for it to be over. At least the police were there. They had followed close behind all the way from Los Angeles and that was a comfort of sorts.

"I can't help it. I can't." Elizabeth's crying increased.

Avis cringed as she sensed the people around them stealing quick glances. Her voice hushed and tense, she whispered, "We should not've come. I told you. I told you." Without realizing that she was doing so, she tightened her grip on Elizabeth's arm as though to force her into discipline.

Elizabeth knew that her mother was right. She must control herself. She must. But she could not. Sue and Mildred Hirsch were sitting behind them. It had been too crowded for them to sit together. She felt a hand on her shoulder and knew that it was Sue. She reached back, took the hand and was comforted. Slowly she regained control and, taking a deep breath, she looked back to her friend, grateful for this proof of what friendship could mean.

Ben Hamilton stood in the back of the chapel, watching. He had not wanted the girl to come into a crowd as large as he had known that this one would be, but she had been determined; and so he and Logan had followed. He glanced about, knowing that he had been right. There were too many people. And six exits. Still he had a clear view from where he was standing and felt confident that if anything happened, he and Logan, who was across from him on the other side of the chapel, would be able to move quickly enough.

For a moment he studied the dead girl's parents who were sitting in the front. What kind of man would send his wife alone to a strange city to claim the body of their child? But why not? He was no longer shocked by any human behavior. Disgusted perhaps but not shocked, for he had seen it all and there was nothing left that could shock.

The thoughts made him weary and he wanted to sit down. Lately he had begun to feel the erosion of age and although he knew that it would be years before others noticed it, he was not as quick as he once had been, no longer had that high, limitless energy which belonged exclusively to the young. His attention was drawn to Logan. Total alertness belonged to that age. Ben clenched his jaw in rhythm with the priest's words. He was a long way still from slippers and a fireside but the quickness of the early years was going and he alone was aware of it.

Elizabeth was turning to the girl who was seated behind her. Ben felt a quickening. She was his to protect and for that he loved her.

Feeling her calmness returning, Elizabeth nodded to Sue. Then as she started to turn back to the front, she saw something. Someone.

And she was caught, held as firmly as though hands were holding her.

He was there. The man who was with her always.

He was standing in the back, partially hidden and she could see only his eyes. Those same eyes. He was there.

Elizabeth gasped with the certainty of it, trembled as those pale, death eyes held her, would not let her go.

Ben watched Elizabeth as she turned back to the front. What was it? He and Logan exchanged a quick look. They had both seen it. Something had happened. But what?

"You must control yourself!" Avis whispered.

Elizabeth buried her face in her hands, began to sob, the uncontrollable sounds echoing in the chapel.

Faces were turning, people whispering, everyone looking. "Elizabeth!" Avis shook her. "Stop it!"

But it was as though Elizabeth had not heard and with a terrible, low moan, she lifted her head, trembling.

"Everyone is looking, Elizabeth . . . That girl's parents . . . Everyone. You must control yourself!"

She began to sob violently, struggling for breath. The priest paused and in the hush the only sound was the sound of Elizabeth's struggle for control.

Ben hurried down the aisle, unconcerned by the faces that were turned toward him, the whispers that rustled through the chapel. He was certain that the girl would not have broken unless there had been an extreme reason.

"It's him," Elizabeth whispered to her mother.

But the words were so choked by tears that Avis could not understand them. "What?"

"He's there." Elizabeth's voice was rising. She did not care that people were turning, whispering.

Then Ben was at her side and she grabbed his hand. "He's there," she repeated.

"Where?" Ben stood, drawing her up with him.

Elizabeth's voice built as she held to the detective. "There . . . In the back . . . Standing." She turned but when she looked, he was gone. The confusion in the chapel tumbled about her and as she sank back onto the pew, Ben rushed down the aisle, signaling for Logan to join him.

In his car, Charles was trying to get out of the parking lot but he was blocked by a funeral procession from one of the smaller chapels in the complex. He edged his way into the line of slowly moving cars. Silently he urged them on and as he looked to his rear-view mirror he saw two men run from the building. His immediate tendency was to swerve around the cars, make his way as quickly as possible to the street and freedom but he knew that that would be a mistake. He remained an unnoticeable part of the slow, silent rope of cars and, headlights glowing in the afternoon sun, made his way into the street. Two motorcycle policemen, young and snappy in their freshly pressed shirts, led the funerary procession, stopping cars so that the mourners could glide past without pause.

As Ben and Logan hesitated on the steps, movement in the far parking lot drew Ben's eye. Someone was going toward a car, getting in.

"You stay with the girl," Ben called to Logan as he ran for his car.

Logan watched as Ben's car bumped over the curb onto the lawn and headed for the street. Then he turned and went slowly back into the chapel, disgusted that life was passing him by.

As the string of cars continued its slow pace through the town, Charles began to relax. He had seen the plainclothesman maneuvering his car in another direction. If the procession continued as it was going, he knew that he would pass an on-ramp for the interstate. "Lucky," he whispered to himself and smiled. Always, he had been lucky.

Ben sped through the traffic, skidding and sliding. The car was still in sight and he knew that he would overtake it.

Two patrolmen in a squad car watched in dismay as Ben's car crashed past, running a red light and almost careening into a Wonder Bread truck. They exploded into action and, sirens screaming, they pulled up beside Ben's car, signaling for him to stop.

"I'm a policeman," Ben shouted over the noise, but he could not be heard and they continued to keep pace. "I'm a cop, you silly sons of bitches," he shrieked and flashed his badge.

Charles saw the overpass and knew that he was free. Smoothly, he curved onto the freeway and was immediately lost in the chaos of traffic.

Ben swerved into the path of the car that he had seen leaving the funeral home. He slammed on his breaks and, drawing his gun, leaped from the car. As he spun around, he froze. The driver, who at a distance he had assumed to be the wanted man, was, to his disgust, a sixty-year-old matron in a severely tailored pants suit.

Shaking uncontrollably, the woman tried to get out of her car but she was too upset and, crying, she collapsed over the steering wheel.

Ben returned his gun to its holster as the local squad car skidded to a stop, siren still shrieking.

"What is it?" the woman cried as once more she attempted to get out of her car. Finally she made it and, shaking, she leaned against her fender. "What have I done? Oh, what have I done?" She reached toward hysteria as cars all around skidded to a stop and people poured out of shops, offices, and the service station on the corner.

"It's all right," Ben said.

"What?" the woman shrieked, trying to top the wail of the siren.

"Turn that damn thing off," Ben called.

"Huh?" said one of the policemen.

"What's she wanted for?" asked the other.

A clerk from a nearby store, drawn by the noise, hurried toward the aging woman. "Emma," he called. "Emma!" And he waved his hands.

She collapsed into his arms, sobbing violently.

"What in the world is it?" he hollered.

"I don't know! I don't know!" she replied and wrung her hands and cried like some crazy thing.

"Off! . . . Turn it off!" Ben shrieked, nodding to the screaming siren.

"Oh . . ." The younger of the patrolmen snapped off the sound.

Suddenly the street was deathly quiet except for the desperate wails of the older woman.

"What did I do?" she sobbed. "What in the world did I do!"

Elizabeth listened to the hum of the tires on the pavement. Moving. Speed. Feeling the slight vibrations of the car. It was comforting and she wanted never to stop. She looked at Ben's hands as he clenched the steering wheel and she started trembling, shuddered with distaste at the thoughts that came.

Hands. His hands were so beautiful. Would the ghost memories be there forever? She wanted him to reach out to her. Closing her eyes, she turned away and for a long time they drove in silence. She shuddered without being aware that she had done so and then she felt his hand over hers. Quickly she looked at him. Did he know what her thoughts had been? She could not tell. But his eyes were nice, something that she had never noticed before. As he looked back to the road, he closed his hand tightly over hers and she leaned against him, grateful and a little in awe that he had sensed her need.

Hands. She started crying. She loved them.

Slowly Ben moved his hand back to the steering wheel, not wanting to lose the warmth of the girl who was beside him. She was his to protect and he had failed. The man had been right there and he had lost him. He glanced into the mirror to the girl's mother who was in the back seat, knew that she was disgusted and he did not blame her.

The girl was leaning against his shoulder and he was touched by her trust. Touched by her innocence. But puzzled too. For he felt that there was something that she had not told him.

Hands, Elizabeth thought, and her eyes closed as the memory of being touched came back to her and she pressed her head against the back of the seat. Hands . . . They were touching her, holding her. She could not escape for they were holding her, ghost hands.

CHAPTER EIGHTEEN

There would be time.

Charles glanced at his watch as he curved onto the Golden State Freeway. It was only a little after five. She would just be leaving the office. Definitely there would be time for him to get to her apartment before she did.

Margaret.

He checked the glove compartment, leaned back as his thoughts moved free. The funeral had been what he had expected. Elizabeth among the mourners. The police there, too—just as he had known they would be.

And he had gotten away.

He had been seen . . . But not close, and so it did not matter.

Not that it would have mattered anyway . . . for now it was happening.

He could feel himself going.

It was happening . . . and now nothing mattered for he was being claimed. Building fast, it came from awesome stillness; a solemn, airless puzzlement within him. Then confusion and a storm of feeling surrounding him, making him aware. Aware of himself—the slow enjoyment of moving—his hands and arms, his lips . . . his hair falling across his forehead as he turned his head.

It was happening.

Almost a feeling of growing . . . And everything beyond the magnificence of his immediate, immaculate self seemed frail and useless.

Self.

It was happening. And he loved it.

Margaret.

His hands were powerful now . . . graceful, God hands. And he was capable of everything. He reached out to what was beyond, trailed his fingertips across the windshield. I'm growing, he thought. I feel it . . . I am a giant . . . and I am closed away from all small things that are the world. His mind—like waves breaking—surged, broke, and receded with the rhythm of the moving traffic.

"Margaret . . ." He whispered her name and saw the two of them as they would soon be . . .

". . . I am there . . . She comes in. And I see her . . . She takes off her clothes And I watch her . . . She moves toward the place where I am. And I'm waiting . . ."

He trembled with the storm that was breaking. The glory of it filled him. The confusion of it stunned him. The power of it held him. A smile edged his lips.

The day would be a good day. A day when he lived. It would not all be loss.

Margaret Connor's day was over.

At last.

Another day and another week gone forever and two days of blessed nothingness awaited her. Nothing but listening to music, being alone, eating fudge brownies and Will Wright's Vanilla Bean ice cream. Two days of wonderful nothing . . . if only she could keep from worrying . . .

Brian. She would simply have to manage to somehow keep him out of her mind for the weekend so that she could regain her sanity. Brian. Her heels repeatedly clicked his name as she walked across the parking lot toward her twenty-three-hundred-dollar car. Brian. No. She would not think of him. She absolutely would not. Brian . . .

"Have a nice weekend, Margaret."

Margaret turned. It was Nan Dantzler, one of the girls from Tankersley, Tiller, Voltz, and Frazer. "You too." Margaret hurried on.

"You and Brian going away?"

"Brian's gone . . . For good, I hope." Margaret did not look back.

"But that's awful!" Nan's voice contained no hint that she considered it other than delightful.

"Maybe it is," Margaret called. "But I don't think so." She paused by her car. "I don't think I think so."

"But it is!" Nan trudged toward her, a heavy-hipped girl in her late thirties with a pale yellowish face and sleepy eyes. "What happened?" she asked, her voice smooth and thick with artificial sympathy.

"Look, Nan, I'm too tired to go into it." Margaret slid behind the wheel. Twenty-three hundred, she thought. She would never be pleased with the Vega again and it frustrated her. Nothing was turning out right. Nothing. She was miserable. Suddenly desperate, wanting to scream, she turned back to Nan. "Brian is silly, that's what happened . . . I know that that sounds . . . well, silly itself . . . but that's what he is. And . . ." She struggled to find the words, was exhausted by the effort. ". . . and it makes me nervous." She put the car in drive and zipped past Nan. "Give you the whole gruesome rundown Monday."

"Wait!" Nan could not believe that anyone could be inhuman enough to leave at such a time.

With a wave, Margaret drove on.

Nan stood alone in the parking lot. "That's awful." She watched as Margaret disappeared into the traffic of Westwood Boulevard.

She would have to wait through the whole weekend, all the way to Monday to get the rest of the story.

"It is," she mumbled. "Awful."

Elise pulled the vacuum cleaner into Charles's room, grateful that she was almost finished. The house was too big, taking care of it, endless and exhausting. She plugged the cleaner into the wall, then for a moment leaned against the dresser. Why did he always have the shades drawn? The place was depressing enough without that.

Several years before, Elise had tried to persuade her mother to sell the house and look for a smaller place, one that would be easier to keep up but the suggestion had not been well received. She had tried to convince Charles but he had also been opposed to it. Of course it was easy for them. They didn't make the beds, carry the trays.

She sat on the edge of the bed, telling herself as she lit a cigarette that she must not stay too long. There was still her room to clean. The hall downstairs. Endless. And the damn drier had finally broken too, so that she had to hang the things on the line. She smiled, knowing that her complaints would sound to others like the cliché whinings of a discontented housewife. But it was true. The house was too big, much too difficult. With every year it became more so. But they had both been against the move, had refused to even discuss it seriously. So here they were.

Gently Elise massaged the calves of her legs. Always she was careful not to complain of any discomfort, but she was aware that she was not as strong as she had been and it frightened her. Sometimes for no apparent reason, spasms would surge through her legs, she would feel herself weakening, losing control.

It had been over two years since she had seen the doctor. What was the point in it? Always he told her the same things. "Don't exert yourself. Get plenty of rest. Conserve your energy." That last examination had cost over sixty dollars and she had not been back. There was no help in it, and the expense was beyond reason. Realizing that her mother would never agree to look for a smaller house, she had tried to convince her to move downstairs, had pointed out that the library could be turned into a very warm and cheerful bedroom but Ann had refused to consider it. Her room was her room, had always been her room. She loved it as it was, wanted nothing changed. Ever. And so Elise had surrendered.

She had known at the time that it was a mistake; and once when the pain in her legs was very bad, she had tried to talk to Charles about it but she could not, for her infirmity was a source of humiliation to her, had always been. She could remember herself as a child, running toward Charles, her legs free, unencumbered by metal encasement. When she thought of childhood, that was the scene that came to mind. Was it a fragment of memory or a wish image? She had never been sure.

After a last deep drag, she stubbed the cigarette out. She must finish the damn room. Charles would be home soon and she had done nothing about dinner. And Mother's five-thirty medicine, God forbid that she forget that. Carefully she stood. There was no escaping it—her legs were becoming weaker. She snapped the switch and the whirr of the outmoded machine filled the room. "Jonas, baby," she whispered to the unseen Dr. Salk, "where the hell were you when I needed you?"

The metal base of the cleaner hit against the Victorian dresser, chipping off a sliver of mahogany veneer. Wondering why she bothered to save the little pieces that periodically flecked off, she knelt and picked it up. How much would a new vacuum cleaner cost? How many green stamps? She kept meaning to check.

As she started to rise, she realized that something was wrong. The baseboard, there in front of the dresser, was protruding. Surely she had not hit it with enough force to dislodge that strip of wood. She flipped the machine off and pushed against the board but it did not fit.

For a moment she was puzzled, then she saw a tiny edge of material coming from between the two uneven pieces of wood.

She tugged at it and with a jolt the baseboard came forward, revealing a hidden drawer that she had not known was there. The material that had kept the drawer from closing securely was a woman's stocking. Elise studied the contents of the drawer which were neatly arranged, almost like displays. Newspaper clippings. Stockings, some of them stained. Headlines. Accounts of murder.

Trembling, she sat back, turned from the impossible suspicion that would not leave her.

"Lise."

From a distance she heard her mother calling but she did not answer.

"Elise." This time more insistent.

"Coming," she said. But she had answered too softly for her mother to hear.

"I need you!"

Slowly Elise closed the drawer—softly so that nothing would be disturbed, as though her gentle handling of it would negate the fact that it was there, that she had seen.

"Time for my five-thirty, Lise."

"I'm coming."

After a moment she stood and left the room.

It was almost six and Charles knew that he would not have long to wait. He relaxed into the silence of the strange apartment, at ease with the beginnings of excitement. Everything had gone smoothly. No one had noticed him outside or in the hallway. And the lock had been no trouble at all.

The rooms were quiet. He loved that. Loved knowing that it was into this quietness that she would come. Through the doorway, he could see the late-afternoon sun spilling across the kitchen table. The quality of light fascinated him and he studied the particles of dust that floated lazily in the stillness. He went into the room and as he reached his hand toward the light, a terrifying scream shattered the quiet and, gasping, he spun around to face his discoverer.

The shriek was repeated and Charles shook with uncontrollable laughter as he looked at the outraged myna bird who continued to flutter and squawk, indignant at the invasion of privacy. Charles reached toward the cage and whistled softly through his teeth but McGoo would not be soothed. He continued to flap about the cage, pausing only to peck at the offered fingers.

Quickly Charles withdrew his hand and fixed the bird with an amused eye. "Don't like me, do you?"

Reaffirming his hostility, the myna bird fluttered and shrieked, flapped his wings against the bars.

"Smart bird," Charles said and smiled.

The day was going and the house seemed cold. Elise put a sweater around her shoulders and turned on the light beside her mother's bed. She filled her mind with thoughts of the familiar room, looked at the table which was a cluttered jumble of empty and half-filled cigarette packages, match books, old *TV Guides*, combs, candy wrappers. Years before Elise had given up trying to keep it orderly. Ann did not want it disturbed. Something might be lost, something that she valued. The dinner tray was there, resting on the clutter, waiting to be taken back down the stairs. The food had been lightly picked over as it always was. Throughout the day Ann gorged herself on candy and gingersnaps and then, at mealtime, sighed pitifully that she had no appetite. Elise watched as her mother took the last of the after-dinner tablets and grabbed for the glass of water.

"He's late." Ann was in a frail mood. The veal had been tough and the tea, too weak. She hesitated. There was only one medication left, two tablespoons of cranberry juice with eight drops of tincture of opium. Elise handed her the small plastic container. Closing her eyes tightly, Ann drank it, then reaching for the water, grimaced and gurgled, clenched her fist in distaste. It was over and Ann fell back on the pillows, exhausted. She despised the taste of it.

Elise tried to arrange the dishes and medicine cups on the tray so that she would only have to make one trip.

"Hate it when he's late," Ann said as she fiddled with the fringe of the spread. All day she looked forward to Charles's return, never completely relaxed until she knew that he was in the house.

On the pad, Elise entered the time and dosage of each medicine that her mother had taken, glad that it was over. The medicine was taken. Dinner, finished. Everything done. Everything except the tray. It had to be taken to the kitchen. Downstairs. Then upstairs again. And when Charles came, downstairs to fix something for him.

Charles.

She tried not to think of him but it was impossible.

Charles. What did the drawer mean? It was not possible that . . . No. She would not allow herself to think that. She picked up the tray and started toward the door.

"Just hate it when he doesn't come home," Ann said. Almost dark and where was he? She saw the napkin on the spread. "Wait. Wait, Lisey." She held it up.

Balancing the tray carefully, Elise went back and took the napkin. As she started to turn, Ann snapped on the television with the remote control. Always Elise had found her mother fascinating and for a moment she studied the older woman, seeing her for the pampered, selfish, smothering creature that she was; vain and demanding, but through it all, loving. Protective. Especially of Charles. Charles . . . And if the impossible, the suspicion that Elise feared, were true . . . What would that truth do to her mother?

As the picture on the screen began to roll and flip, Ann's face immediately became a mask of urgency. "Lise . . . It's funny, all messed up."

Elise put the tray on the bed and adjusted the set. Then, on impulse, she leaned over and kissed her mother.

"What is it?" Ann was startled. It was so unlike Elise. Then she was touched by the beginning of fear. Why was Elise looking at her like that?

"Nothing."

"No. Tell me." Her voice was a plea. She hated the unexplained.

Elise smiled and whispered, "Who's going to take care of me when I'm old?"

Ann relaxed, laughed. Was that all? "You've got Charlie," she said, her voice a mixture of bitterness and humor. "You and Charlie . . . After I'm dead." It was what she feared, the time when she would have to leave him.

"What's going to happen to us, sweet Mama?"

Ann was caught by the loneliness in her daughter's voice. What was it? For a moment she was silent and then she laughed again. "You're funny, Lise. You know that?"

Elise shrugged and smiled.

Ann nibbled at a chocolate-covered almond. There was really no understanding her daughter. She was an odd thing, always had been. "What's going to happen? . . . Good things, bad things, who knows? . . . No. Good things. Definitely good! . . . This is a good day." She held her hands toward Elise. "Look at that. Hardly swollen at all."

She twisted her wrists back and forth, demonstrating her rare freedom from pain. "It is definitely a good day."

From Margaret Connor's window Charles watched as the day ended. He did not like the moments of fading between day and night and was always glad when they were gone. His clothes were on the bed, folded neatly, and as always he was careful to stand back from the window just far enough so that he could see but not be seen. His field of vision was limited and he could see only a thin sliver of the street. But that was enough, better than some of the others. From some of the windows, he had not been able to see anything.

Margaret was a sloppy girl and he smiled as once more he glanced over the room which was a jumble of discarded skirts, overflowing ashtrays, stacks of magazines, and half-eaten candy bars. In fact her slovenliness had for a moment presented him with a problem. The closet was so packed with clothes and boxes—also a 1958 set of the Encyclopaedia Britannica—that he had had to look for another hiding place. Finally he had settled on the shower stall although it was certainly not ideal. His field of vision would be more limited than he liked but no other choice was possible.

Then he saw it, the blue of the car as it flashed by and quickly he scooped up his clothes. Soon she would be with him. In the bathroom, he opened the hamper that was in the corner and put his clothes there, covering them with towels.

Then quickly he stepped into the quietness of the shower, drew the plastic curtain.

Margaret Connor sighed with relief as she got out of her car. He wasn't there. "Thank goodness," she mumbled to herself. For once Brian was not sitting on the steps. Everyday when she came home he was there. Perhaps he had waited for a while, then given up and left, gone away for the weekend. On the way home she had stopped at Shakey's and had a combination pizza and two Cokes and then had driven around aimlessly, hoping that he would give up and leave. Or had he not even bothered to come? Hurriedly she ran up the steps, fearing that his car might turn into the street before she could disappear into the building.

He had tried to get her to go away for the weekend. To Big Bear. Skiing. She hated skiing. The sun so bright on the snow. It made her face all red and blotchy. It was awful. A thousand times she had explained to him why she hated it but he had always laughed, said that he liked her like that. It was infuriating. How could anybody like for anybody to look all messy and red and puffy-faced?

The sound of the elevator surrounded her and she found it comforting. Like the lost chord or something. She loved sounds. There was something warm about them and they kept her from being lonely. That was one of the things that she hated—absolutely hated —about the mountains in wintertime. Brian liked to be away from people and he would drive miles and miles over the most terrible curving roads to get to the end of nowhere so that they could be alone on some isolated hillside, velvet and death-white with all that awful snow and it would be so quiet there that she could hardly stand it. Always it made her want to cry, for it was like they were the only two people in the world left alive and death was coming for them. If she had to go to the country, she wanted it to be the kind of country where there were animals and insects, yapping and whirring; endless sounds that were unfamiliar yet pleasing. But the hills in the snow, that was terrible—the sky so clear, and the snow too bright, and settled over it all, that devastating eternity of silence. It truly was like being dead. She shivered as the *hmmmmmmm* of the elevator changed to *whrrrrrrrrrr* and, with a *grnnnnnnnn,* the door slid open.

In the corridor the sounds were different, cushioned and muffled, blunted like footfalls on the carpet. They were all around her, thousands of noises; people behind the doors, voices that could be heard but not understood; doors opening, closing, swinging, bumping; telephones ringing, records, television, dishes, windows, toilets, showers; glass clinking, wood clumping, metal clanging, plastic vumping; everywhere endless sounds from strange machines. She loved it.

It had taken her months to find an apartment that was noise-filled enough to please her. That was another thing that she did not like about Brian. When she had very seriously confided to him how important noises were to her, he had laughed! Roared like a fool and that had been the beginning of the end. Brian was never serious about anything.

Scrape, click, vank, scrape; the door was unlocked and she stepped into her apartment. Home. Thank goodness. Whoom, bum, clack, snap. The door had skimmed with that *whoom* sound over the carpet and then with the quick *bum, clack, snap,* it was closed and Margaret was at last home.

"Aaaik!" McGoo squawked a greeting from the kitchen.

"Aaaik yourself!" she called, relaxing.

Nice. It would be a really nice evening. Just her. By herself. Nobody to bother with. Nothing to do. Shakey's had solved the ordeal of dinner and she wouldn't have to mess with any of that, thank goodness.

Brian never wanted to eat out. He liked to cook, of all things, and would make the most complicated stuff, like Beef Wellington and all sorts of sauces and queer fish things for just the two of them. He would spend hours getting things just the way he liked them and then they would sit on the floor in his apartment above the Strip and they would drink wine and eat and listen to records. Brian had the most sensational records and he would sit close so that he was touching her. She loved for him to touch her. And she loved to touch him. They would eat and touch and lounge around on pillows while they listened to Carlos Montoya and Brian would strum her stomach and legs like she was the guitar and he was Carlos. She loved his touch. And his neck. He had the nicest neck. She loved to kiss his neck. And he loved for her to. And his lips . . . He would hold her and they would touch and eat Beef Wellington and spinach salad and mousse, and kiss.

Margaret turned on the record player and as the sounds of Elton John filled the room, she started to cry. Brian had given her that one. He had given her so many things; crystal decanters, a coin silver pitcher, a Chippendale wing chair. Expensive things. For Christmas she had given him a drawing by Morris Broderson. It had cost more than she should have spent but it was worth it for he had loved it. It was the only "nice" thing that she had ever given him and she had always felt badly about not being more generous.

She went into the bedroom, unconsciously moving to the full sound of sweet Elton. In the corner she saw her knitting. She had tried to make a sweater for Brian but after three months had given up. It was such a mess. And all that stuff about its being simple to learn how to knit from a book was just a lot of lies. She had studied the book until she was practically crazy, had had headaches for weeks. It had almost cost her her job, she had become so irritable. And still the damn thing didn't look like a sweater at all. At least not a sweater for a normal-shaped human. It was a lumpy, lose pile of yarn, pitiful in its deformity. Looking at the lonely thing, touching it, had finally made her so sad that she had stopped working on it.

Brian.

She stepped out of her shoes and kicked them under the bed so that she would not trip over them. Where the hell was Brian anyway? She had been sure that he would be waiting there on the steps. He was always there. Of course she was glad that he wasn't. But still . . .

At least he could have called so that she wouldn't worry. She had expected him to call the office sometime during the afternoon but he had not. Of course she was glad that he hadn't. But still . . .

She unzipped her skirt—she loved the sound of zippers—pulled it over her head. Maybe he wasn't going to call. She paused, her skirt in her hand, and looked at herself in the mirror. Maybe he would never call again. She caught her breath, felt the tears building. There was no easy answer.

She loved him.

And she absolutely hated loving him.

She cried. She knew that it would not help. But she also knew that she could not stop herself.

Charles leaned against the cool tile of the shower and listened as the girl moved about. From his hiding place he could look into the mirror above the lavatory and catch an occasional glimpse of Margaret's reflection as she undressed. He drew the stocking over his face and, with his knife, made a slit that freed his lips. The nylon over his eyes made a pleasant blur of the mirrored image of the girl as she moved in and out of his field of vision.

Margaret put on a short terrycloth robe and unclipped her earrings. Brian had not come. Had he accepted her at her word and ended it? A feeling of terrible loneliness swept over her and she could not control her trembling. Perhaps he would never be waiting on the steps again. Perhaps he . . . The thought was broken by a noise. Several times since she had come into the apartment, she had thought that she heard something. The Elton John album was finished and in the quietness, she listened to the familiar clicks and scrapes as James Taylor's latest dropped onto the turntable. The music filled the room and she gave up trying to figure out what the unknown noise had been. That did not matter. James Taylor was the only thing that mattered. What difference did Brian make? The sounds of the record soothed her. James Taylor. He had such nice lips. Nicer than Brian's. She went toward the bathroom. She would not think about Brian any more. She would think about James Taylor and his lips and the way he moved. He was thin like Brian. No, she was not going to think about Brian.

Margaret put some clothes in the hamper, then from a drawer took her shower cap and, both hands struggling with her hair, tried to put it on. Charles was fascinated by the gracefulness of her movements. She was so close. Not more than two feet away. Easily he could reach out, if he wanted to . . . just reach out and softly touch her shoulder.

But he would not.

Not yet.

There was a terrible scream. The entire apartment seemed to echo with it. Charles gasped and leaned against the tile.

Margaret froze. Definitely there had been a sound. Not the scream. She knew what that was. It came again. That was McGoo. She had forgotten to feed him. It was the other sound that puzzled her. And she was sure that there had been another. Very soft. Still she could almost hear it. Movements. Almost like breathing. Again McGoo shrieked his displeasure.

"All right. All right." As Margaret entered the kitchen, she looked with aggravation toward the squawking bird. From the counter she grabbed a box of bird seed and dumped a generous portion into his cup. "I'm sorry," she said.

But McGoo was not to be so easily mollified. He fluttered about the cage, screaming.

"Look. I said I'm sorry." Margaret gave him some fresh water but he refused to drink. With his wings he splashed it from the container and squawked furiously.

"All right. Don't drink it, I don't care." Margaret started from the room, tired of the bird's continued flapping and shrieking. "Oh, shut up," she piped. She was tired. A headache was beginning. "I'm going to take my shower."

In the living room she turned up the stereo to drown out the piercing shrieks of the myna bird. As she went back into the bathroom, the sounds of James Taylor were so full that even the floors vibrated.

Brian Willoughby parked in front of the apartment house but he did not get out of the car immediately. He was worried and that was unusual, for very few things bothered him. It was Margaret. He no longer understood her. Perhaps he had never understood her. He unwrapped a stick of Juicy Fruit gum, rolled it into a little cylinder and pushed it into his mouth. Juicy Fruit and Teaberry were his favorites. Frustrated, he chewed, sighed.

What the hell was wrong with Maggie anyway? She seemed seriously determined to mess the whole thing up. And for absolutely no reason. Except foolishness. That's what it was. All foolishness. She would understand that sooner or later and everything would be all right. She could not possibly want to end it. Not really.

He walked to the apartment house.

Maggie. He started smiling.

She loved him. He was convinced of it.

At the lavatory, Margaret shook two Excedrins from the bottle and popped them into her mouth. Perhaps they would help but she doubted it. She took her watch off and put it on the make-up table.

Charles watched, his excitement building, as she turned and moved toward him.

Margaret tossed her robe toward the table. The minute it left her hand, she knew what was going to happen. But it was too late. With a sickening sound of breaking, her watch clattered to the floor. She refused to look. It could not be broken. It couldn't be. She knelt to examine the watch, her back to the shower.

Brian stood in the hall, overpowered by the music that came from the apartment. He smiled, unable to stop himself. He always smiled when he thought of Margaret. He started to laugh. The thought of her always made him laugh.

He knocked but there was no reply. He was familiar with the album that was playing, knew it was on the last band on side two. He would have to wait until it was finished, then while the record was changing, she would hear him. He leaned against the wall and listened to the music. James Taylor. He was really fantastic.

Margaret was relieved. The watch was all right. At least the working part of it. But the crystal, that was missing. She felt about the tile floor, found little slivers of glass. Damn. Brian had given it to her and now she had broken it. It was expensive, much too expensive. She and Brian had argued about the amount that he had paid for it. Almost four hundred dollars. For a little watch! She had begged him to take it back to the shop but he had refused, had laughed at her insistence. It was the first gift that he had given her. She had taken such care of it. And now . . . She started to cry. There were bits of glass everywhere.

Slowly Charles eased the plastic curtain back and, as he started to step onto the bathmat, there was a sudden silence. The record had ended and the only sound was Margaret's sobbing. Then he heard someone knocking at the door and he was very still.

Immediately Margaret stopped crying. Brian. It was Brian. It had to be. She grabbed her robe and hurried from the room.

"Who is it?" she called as she reached the door.

Brian laughed. "Who were you expecting?"

It was this exact thing that she despised about him, the fact that he always laughed. The relief that she had felt at his coming was swept away by frustration and anger. "Go away."

Again Brian knocked. "Maggie?"

"Don't make a scene," she hissed through the door as an Aretha Franklin record clattered into place and the music started.

He knocked and shouted above the sound. "Then let me in!"

Grudgingly she opened the door and Brian grinned in triumph as he entered.

"All that knocking and pounding and everything. I have to live here, you know." She closed the door.

"I'm sorry." Brian smiled, contradicting the words.

Margaret stalked over to the record player and turned the music down.

"Why the hell was that thing so loud anyway?" Brian tossed his jacket onto the sofa and loosened his tie.

"The bird," Margaret said.

"Huh?" Brian's concern was now genuine. "What's wrong with McGoo?"

"He's crazy as you are. That's what's wrong with him."

Again he grinned. "Now don't start. I said I was sorry and . . . well, I am sorry."

She lit a cigarette. "Everybody's sorry, Brian."

"And that's not an easy thing for me to say . . ." What did she mean, everybody was sorry? "No, they're not. Some people aren't sorry at all."

She hated it when he trapped her like that. Just like a lawyer. She stared silently at him, assuming an attitude that she considered imperious. "Please. Take your bird and go," she said with dignity.

Brian laughed uncontrollably. The silliness of her delighted him. "An Indian giver I'm not, kiddo."

"Kiddo! You know I hate that kind of Forties talk."

Her face was a puffy little ball of indignation and he wanted to pinch her fat cheeks. "Love ya, Mag," he laughed, giving her a thump on the neck.

"Mag?!"

"Love you. And I've told you that . . ."

"You're hopeless." She started toward the bedroom.

Brian followed. Was she serious? "I've told you that I'll try to improve."

That's what he always said and hearing it once more only served to make her more sullen. "Mag," she mumbled. "Sounds like some fat bug."

Her petulant dippiness beguiled him as always and he was unable to suppress his laughter. "Well?" He pounced on her and began kissing her baby-doll cheeks. "Dut . . . dut . . . Hello, fat bug."

She drew away from him, trembling, outraged. "That's what I hate . . . That . . . That . . ." In anger she scrambled desperately for the words. "That . . . Whatever the hell it is that keeps you . . . that makes you . . . that keeps you from ever being anything but silly." Brian laughed as Margaret's words tumbled on furiously. "You just laugh at everything! And . . . well . . . Everything is not funny! Some things, Brian, are very serious. Dead serious. And calling me something that sounds like a fat bug is one of those things." Brian's laughter had reached a hopeless stage and Margaret turned from him in disgust. "To think I almost married you."

"Bet it would cure that digestive trouble," he whispered and tried to catch her hand but she dodged away.

"This is serious."

Gently he edged her toward the bed. "Of course it is." She sat on the mattress and as she started to cry, he kissed her hands. "Of course it's serious." She continued to sob and he stroked her arms, patted her legs. "It's all right, Baby," he murmured.

Margaret tried to pull away but she could not for he was kissing her. It was pleasant and she enjoyed it although she did not want to enjoy it. She sank back onto the bed, exhausted by her tears. "It is not all right," she whimpered.

Brian smiled. He had known that it would end this way. It always ended this way. He crawled onto the bed beside her and stroked her forehead.

Margaret turned away. She was confused. This was not the way she had planned it. It was true that she did want him but she did not want to want him. His hands were so nice. She loved them. "Brian . . . Brian . . ." She murmured his name without knowing that she did so. He was the most wonderful man. Except for that one thing. That damn silliness. Again she began to sob with frustration.

"What is it, sweetness?"

"You, that's what. You!" Her words were muffled by tears.

"You don't like this?" Gently he untied the belt of her robe, knowing that she loved it.

"It's not that I don't like it. It's that I don't like liking it." Her words came amidst the sobs and he laughed softly, kissed her rounded hips, nibbled on her neck. Margaret shivered with pleasure. "When we went to see *Airport*," she said, "that's when I knew. Really knew. When Dean Martin was trying to bring the plane in, after the crazy man blew it up. Or almost did. And Dean's sweetheart was injured—what's her name, I wonder?" Without seeming to realize it, she was returning some of his kisses. "Wasn't Helen Hayes wonderful?" she sighed. "She wasn't the sweetheart, of course, but wonderful just the same . . . Badly injured, that girl, Dean's girl. Maybe dying for all we knew . . . And there was a hush over that whole big movie theatre . . . Then I heard it . . . That silly giggle." Half-heartedly, she tried to push him away. "And I just closed my eyes. I did. Tight as I could. And curled my toes up in a ball and dug 'em in my shoes."

Clumsily, Brian tried to pull the robe from under her.

"Wait. My arm's caught." Pouting, she took the robe off and while Brian unbuttoned his shirt, she unbuckled his belt and helped him with his trousers. He had the most wonderful body. She loved it. The slenderness of his hips, the muscular cords in his neck and back. As he stretched out beside her, she trembled with love. "Dug 'em in," she mumbled. "My toes in my shoes, I mean. There at *Airport* . . . Just heard that giggle and I thought to myself, 'Lord help us all, here we go for the umpteenth time.' And I was right!" She hit him and hugged him and bit his shoulder. "You. In that theatre. Sitting there, shaking and giggling, tears running down your face like you were watching Flip Wilson do Geraldine or something. And everybody turning around. I knew that minute, oh I knew and I said to myself, I said, 'If you can just stay calm long enough to get out of this movie house without fainting from mortification or having a rigor or pitching over dead from . . . oh . . . If only you can, then you will never go out with this maniac again!' "

He kissed her ear. "But you did go out with me again."

Trying to pull away, she scratched her arm on his watch. Ow . . ." She massaged the wound. "But I didn't mean to!"

"You mean you thought you didn't mean to."

Margaret studied her arm.

"My watch scratch you?"

"I broke mine."

"Huh?"

"My watch. Broke the crystal. Always been so careful with it and I broke it. And yes, yours scratched me!" His beard was scratchy too. "When did you shave?"

Brian loved the simplicity of her mind, the way she strung things together in such an oddly sensible way. He laughed.

"Brian! Stop that!"

He wanted to stop for he knew that his amusement aggravated her but he could not control himself and his laughter increased.

She pushed against him. "You're really insane! I mean it. You laugh all the time. At *Airport*. And, well, right here on the verge of . . . well, intimacy or something." The shaking of his laughter vibrated through her. "I hate to say this, Brian, but you are definitely sick."

He rolled over, taking her with him and held her by the shoulders at arm's length above him. He laughed. "So are you."

Now Margaret was crying again. "Maybe I am. Maybe you're right. But at least I don't laugh all the time." She sobbed. "Now you've really made me cry."

Slowly he lowered her into his arms and caressed her. "Lord Byron said, 'I only laugh to keep from crying.' "

Brian's literary allusions always surprised and confused her. "He did?"

"Something like that." He studied a large tear as it brimmed over and rolled down her cheek. The mammoth size of her tears always amazed him. "Here," he cooed, "I'm gonna bite that bad tear."

"Wonder what he meant by it?" Margaret whimpered. "Lord Byron, I mean."

"Bad, bad tear . . . Aaaar . . ." He attempted to bite the tear but just as he clamped down, Margaret turned her face and he bit her cheek.

"Ow," she squalled. "You bit me!"

Brian laughed. "Byron meant . . . Well . . . He meant . . ."

Margaret rubbed her face. "Bit me and it hurt!"

"I think Byron probably meant that if you don't want to burst out in tears in the middle of a movie and embarrass yourself, then you should start laughing and embarrass other people instead."

She continued rubbing. "Right on the cheek. Where it really hurts." She began to absorb his explanation. "That's stupid. About laughing instead of crying I mean. They didn't even have movies when Lord Byron was laughing."

"I aimed at the tear and you moved." Brian kissed the injured cheek.

But Margaret had forgotten her tears and was thinking of Byron's. ". . . Or crying. Definitely crying! I don't think of Lord Byron laughing. He never laughed . . . Except maybe with that dopey sister or some Turks or something." Brian's laughter was renewed and she pushed him away, furious. "Get up! . . . Just get up and stop that! . . . All that laughing."

Abruptly Brian catapulted from the bed, grabbing her hands as he went. He held tight to them, pretending that she was the one who would not let go, that she was trying to pull him back onto the bed. "No," he cried in artificial protest. "No!"

Confused, Margaret tried to free her hands. "Huh?"

"Margaret. You can just let go because I am going to get up!"

She was livid. "That's what I said!"

He continued to tug at her hands. "I don't care what you say, I'm getting up!"

She cried, struggled to get free. "Brian!"

"No. Not under any circumstance will I agree to get back into that bed."

Margaret wailed, kicked her feet.

Brian gave one last straining tug. "For God's sake, let me go," he cried and released her wrists, pretending that he had finally broken away. As her hands were freed, they flew back and hit the headboard of the bed. She howled as Brian surveyed her with moral uprightness. He spoke in a deliberate, carefully enunciated, Victorian manner. "I am deeply sorry, my dear. I truly am. But this . . ." He nodded toward the rumpled bed. "All of this . . . It's wrong. Us. Writhing around here. In secret." Drawing himself up, he assumed the attitude of the wronged woman. "You can't use me like this, Maggie. Not any more. I'm not good enough for you to marry, am I? . . . No! But plenty good enough for . . ." Again he nodded disdainfully toward the bed. "Well, I'm through!"

Margaret clenched her teeth, her face a mask of tearful fury. "Brian!" she screeched.

"No! I mean it. I'm through! Now you just get dressed. Cover yourself, Margaret." He covered her shoulders with the robe. "Get dressed and get out of here."

Margaret exploded in frenzy. "I live here! Hyena tongue!"

Brian roared with laughter and while she shook with sobs, he sat beside her and stroked her shoulder. "It's all right, Magsy. It's all right."

"It's not," she sobbed.

"It's fine."

"It's awful."

Gently, he rocked her back and forth. "Sssh . . . sssh." Her sobs subsided and he spoke softly. "Now listen, Baby. Just listen." He tilted her face up to him. "We're both maniacs. We're both silly and will be all of our lives."

Exhausted, she choked out one last sob. "You're a bigger one than I am!"

He loved it. "And don't you ever forget it," he said and patted her on the back and kissed her. "Now. Do you know what we're going to do?"

She shook her head, waiting for him to kiss her again.

"Do you?" he whispered.

Again she wagged her head back and forth, indicating that she did not. "No," she whined. "I don't know."

He gently rubbed her cheek. "That's right, you don't."

"What are we going to do?"

He caressed her. "That's what I'm about to tell you," he crooned. "You're going to pack a suitcase. And then we're going to go to the mountains."

"No." But it was not a very definite "no."

He kissed her. "Yes." Still she shook her head in the negative. He smiled as she returned the kiss. "Yes?" he whispered.

She was confused. "Yes," she murmured softly. She wanted him to kiss her again and he did. That was the "yes" that she had meant. She clenched her fists. Nothing was simple. If she wanted him she would have to go with him, would have to accept the fact that he would not change, would never be the serious person that she had always imagined herself marrying. "Where are we going?" she asked.

"Big Bear. We'll go by way of Santa Barbara, spend the night there, then in the morning we'll look over the furniture in the house. Tell you the truth, I've felt very uneasy about leaving it there. We'll select the things we'll want for our house here and get rid of the rest."

"Why can't we get new things instead of all that old stuff that's used and everything?" Without realizing it, she had partially agreed to a shared future.

"No," he said, smiling. And he kissed her. His was a lawyer's mind and he knew that he had won. "There're some very good things. Some of them, signed. We'll sell the French. I never cared much for it."

"I thought you said 'we' would decide. You said 'we' but you've already decided."

"It's not that I've decided. Not definitely. It's just that I happen to like American and English so much better than French."

"I don't like any of it."

"You will once you get used to it."

"I won't."

"You like that wing chair I gave you."

"Yeah. But that doesn't seem old."

"Eighteenth century."

"Really? . . . You mean the seventeen hundreds?"

"That's what I mean."

"How do you know?"

"Look, we don't have time to talk about it now. We have to leave."

Margaret drew away, a little frightened. She felt that if she accepted for the weekend, she was, in a way, accepting for life.

"Well?" He waited.

Still Margaret did not answer.

"Margaret," he said softly, "I'm not going to keep on asking you forever, you know. I love you. And I want you to marry me. But the day will finally come when I won't ever ask you again."

Margaret trembled at the thought of losing him, tears filled her eyes.

"It's not that I want to make all the decisions," he said. "But with things like furniture . . . Well, it's something you don't know about. If you find that you like the French things and want to keep some of them, we'll keep them. But I won't live with a houseful of new furniture, things you can just walk into a department store and buy. In matters like this, matters you know nothing about, you'll have to let me decide. You'll have to accept that because I know more about it than you do." He gave her leg a pat. "Now get packed."

It was the first time that he had ever spoken to her like that, so directly and sensibly. Something about it frightened her. Desperately, she had wanted the affair to end but now that he had hinted at the possibility of it, she was stricken with the forewarning of loneliness. He was looking at her so seriously, his gray eyes unclouded by any hint of humor or laughter. She had never known him to look so handsome, his light brown hair falling over his forehead, his wide generous lips, unsmiling.

Silently he took her hands.

"You meant that about . . . about not asking me any more," she said. "I mean . . . I have to go on and make up my mind?"

Still he did not smile. "I'll never ask again. I've waited as long as I will. We'll start looking for a house next week. If we're not married before the month is out, we will never marry." Then he smiled. "Get packed."

It was an ultimatum and she accepted it. "You go get your things," she said. "By the time you get back, I'll be ready."

"I can wait."

She got up. "That's stupid."

He laughed. He loved it when she pouted.

"Brian, if you laugh, I'm going to . . . well . . . I'm going to . . . just jump out the window. Now go on and pack your things and come back in half an hour."

Smiling, he went to the living room. At the front door, he turned back. "I do love you, Maggie."

Margaret took her suitcase from the closet shelf, then opened a dresser drawer and started rummaging about, her mind such a confusion of feelings that she could not concentrate. Brian was waiting for an answer. He had not said anything else but she knew that he was still there. She could sense it. Well, he would just have to wait.

She was not going to answer. He had been officious and arrogant in his attitude concerning the furniture, treating her as though she knew nothing. Then he had called her Maggie again and he knew how she hated it. Hated it!

She heard the click of the door. He was gone. Relieved, she tossed some things into the suitcase. "Love you, Maggie," that's what he had said, knowing all the time . . . "I just bet," she whispered. "Just bet you love me." The tears started again and she was trembling. Was she having a breakdown? Yes. She was sure that she was. Nerves, they were shattered. A warm shower. Was there time? She would just take time. Brian could wait. Walking into the bathroom, she let her robe fall to the floor.

Charles watched through the narrow space between the curtain and the tile. For a time, he had been sure that he had lost her. Now he knew that she was his. He waited for her to open the curtain.

As Margaret turned to the shower, she noticed the broken watch. It should be put away. After the shower. No. She would be rushed then, for she planned to stay under the warm water as long as possible. Carefully, she picked up the delicate timepiece, her sorrow at the breakage renewed.

Charles's eyes followed her as she left the room, mournfully cradling the watch in her hands. Then very quietly, he stepped from the shower onto the soft mat.

Margaret opened the drawer of the bedside table. She did not want to cry but she could not stop herself. The watch was broken. She sobbed. She had always been so careful with it and now it was broken. She put it in the drawer and then curled up on the bed. She had to get ready but she was so tired. Brian would be back soon and she would look awful, her face red and swollen, her eyes . . . Why would he even want to be seen with her? Why would anyone want to marry her . . . ever? She choked on her tears.

Suddenly she stopped crying. There was something . . . some noise. Earlier she had thought that she had heard things. Now this. This time she was sure. Someone was there. Close behind her. Very close. In the room. Moving, very slowly, carefully. She wanted to turn but she could not. Fear kept her still as the sound moved closer; soft, cautious footfalls as quiet as leaves nestling into tall grass, but she could hear them. Someone was there. Someone . . .

A hand touched her shoulder and as she started to scream, she was firmly turned. The scream froze on her lips.

It was Brian.

He was kneeling there beside the bed.

Shaking, she collapsed against him. "I thought . . ." She tried to get her breath. "I thought . . ."

He caressed her. "You wouldn't answer." Gently, he kissed her. "When I told you I loved you, you wouldn't even answer . . . How could I leave?" Again he kissed her and whispered, "I do love you."

As Brian started the car, Margaret leaned against his shoulder. "I love you too," she said. "I do . . . And I'll . . . I'll try to be better, try not to be so foolish. I know I've been a fool. Crying, whimpering all the time like some fifteen-year-old. But I'll be better, I promise." She struggled to stifle the tears that were beginning again.

He smiled and whispered, "You're fine with me the way you are." And he kissed her hair.

"No," she said, "Something's been wrong. Something, I don't know what." She paused, trying to understand it. "Almost like . . . well, like a kind of breakdown or something . . . Tonight, before you got there, it was almost like I heard things . . . somebody there in the apartment or something."

He kissed her forehead and patted her hand. She was sweet. Helpless and scattered, he loved that about her. She needed someone to take care of her. He relaxed as the car turned onto the freeway.

And, holding hands, they wove their way into the gently moving river of headlights.

CHAPTER NINETEEN

Still trembling, Charles sat on the side of the bed. For that short time when she had come back into the bathroom, he had been sure that she was his. Then she was gone and it was over. He fought against the building anger but nothing could shut it out.

From the kitchen he heard the myna bird, no longer an abrasive scream but a soft sound, almost like gentle laughter.

In quietness the bird stared at him as Charles advanced toward the cage. There was little light in the room and Charles could see only the outline of the metal enclosure.

There was a restless fluttering as the cage was opened, then a loud series of screams, sounds of flapping.

Charles reached through the trap and lifted the struggling bird out. "Really don't like me, do you?" he whispered and smiled.

Standing before the mirror, Charles buttoned his shirt, his mind a confusion of images, frustrations. He checked the pockets of his jacket. The knife was there. And the stocking. He glanced into the glass and smiled as he turned from the reflection of the bed, the tableau that would greet Margaret when she returned from her weekend.

At the front door, he paused, listened. The way was clear. Silently he opened the door and was gone.

The apartment was quiet. In the living room, there was no indication that anyone had been there. But in the bedroom, barely discernible in the shadows, he had left a memento. In the middle of the bed, the slashed, mutilated body of the myna bird was partially hidden within the folds of Margaret's robe.

Charles hurried through the deserted hallway and down the stairs. There was a noise and he stopped. Someone on the main floor had opened a door. He watched as a woman struggling with a garbage container emerged from one of the apartments. Not bothering to close the door, she glanced at him as she passed the stairs, continued on along the hall. Charles waited as she struggled with the back door, finally maneuvering her burden into the darkness.

Immediately, Charles's decision was firm. He hurried down the few remaining steps and disappeared into the apartment. What was she like? He was not sure. He had not really seen her clearly. She would return soon, that was all he knew. But what else did he need to know?

He waited.

Sarah Hammond Watkins struggled with the plastic container of trash. It was heavy and she was tired. Her thin body strained with weariness as she made her way down the cement steps at the back of the building. She rested her burden on the rim of one of the metal cans that was only partially filled. Gathering her strength, she upended the container and watched as the trash cascaded into the can.

This was one of the things that she hated most in life. This and all the other thousand little necessities that went to make up her days. And nights. She clamped the lid tight on the can and took a deep breath.

How the hell had it happened anyway? How? She sighed, wisps of blond hair framing her tired face. If only . . . No. She would not allow herself to start that. It had all happened because of her stupidity, that's how. Her incredible stupidity. She had made many mistakes and now, as the years settled heavily about her, she was intensely aware of them. But for it to end like this. She glanced at the ugly building, turned quickly away.

Divorce. The minute that she had had proof of Jeff's infidelity, she had rushed to the nearest lawyer and freedom was hers. Freedom and a sizable amount of money. How had the money gone so quickly? That always amazed her. If only she had managed better, then . . . No. She would waste no more time with the endless if only's. She had not managed well and here she was in this really impossible situation. She had blindly squandered so much of it during those first months of freedom. Clothes. Travel. But it had been a necessary investment in her future. Her wonderful future. She smiled unevenly. She had been so sure that there would be no difficulty in marrying again. She lit a cigarette, flipping the match away with an angry gesture. Men.

She sat on the cement steps. It was ugly there at the back of the building but at least the night air was nice. Much nicer than the stuffiness of her cramped apartment that was so foolishly jammed with furniture that she would never use, that no one would ever see, admire. Crowded into the kitchen was a Queen Anne highboy, a Sheraton breakfast table, and a Welsh dresser that no one ever saw for no one came to call. And why should they? She had become a drudge and a complainer. She had lost her looks and her money.

Men. She leaned against the bannister. Men had always liked her and she had been so sure that she would have no difficulty in finding the right one. If Jeff wanted to wander, well, let him . . . Could she have pulled it off? She would never know, for she had lost her health before she had found the one that she was looking for. She had had a couple of offers and had turned them down, waiting for The One. One of them who was interested was a doctor she had met on a cruise to Hawaii. That's the one she should have accepted.

Doctors. She despised them, considered them the worst thieves in the country. Her face contorted at the thought of the fortune that they had taken from her during the last five years. Cancer. Well, she had beaten it. At least for a while. One breast gone and half of the inside of her but at least she was alive. Until the next operation. And possibly the one after that. And on and on until finally there would be nothing left of her at all. Then when at last she died, they could dump the little whittled thing that she had become into a Kraft mayonnaise jar and shove it into a hole; save the expense of a funeral. Doctors. The pigs of the world, that's what they were, raking in the loot, bilking and blustering. Her only consolation was that she believed in hell and was convinced that the American Medical Association's final convention would meet there through all eternity.

She flipped away the cigarette butt and lit another, frowning inwardly at the futility of the doctor's orders. What possible difference could smoking make now that there was so little left of her? She shivered in the coolness of the evening air, knowing that she should go in. But she hated the apartment so! Ugly . . . Ugly!

She pictured the house in Brentwood. The rose bushes which she had loved so, had worked so hard to keep. The pool which she had so seldom used because there were always so many things to do. All of it lost. Gone. Completely. Everything. Except the most cherished pieces of furniture that were packed and crowded into these three ugly rooms. Her beautiful house. Her heart trembled with the memory of it. It had been part of her settlement and she had lost it. Lost it to foolishness. To stupid spending. To unexpected illness. But how could she have known? Who would ever have dreamed that it could happen? Could be lost? That she who had always been so sure about everything . . . So untroubled . . . So confident . . . That now, during the years that are, under the best circumstances, difficult . . . That she would actually be in need. She. Sarah Hammond Watkins. It was not possible.

The door opened and she saw that it was Henry Morrow. His bedroom was at the back on the second floor and she was sure that he had seen her from his window and had used the emptying of his garbage as an excuse for a visit. She stood so that he could pass.

He smiled rather sheepishly, "Evening."

Men were so stupid. So obvious. It would be much better if he would just come out and ask her. Did he think that she was a complete fool? Why didn't he just say, "How 'bout it, lady? Wanta give it a go?" She was amused by it, almost laughed and when she spoke, her voice seemed friendly. "How are you?" she said.

"Fine. Just fine, Mrs. Watkins."

"Oh, for God's sake, call me Sarah. I've told you that a hundred times."

"I know. It's just . . . Well, somehow it seems so . . ." He laughed with embarrassment.

"I get tired of all the formality, Henry. At that stupid job I have, it's Mrs. Watkins . . . Mrs. Watkins. It's so boring."

"You're right, I know."

"Boring and unfriendly too. To go all day long with no one ever calling you by your first name." She smiled, finding enjoyment in being the coquette. "It is decidedly unfriendly."

Henry tried to laugh. "Suppose you're right. And if there's one thing in this world I don't want us to be, it's unfriendly."

Was it possible that he did not realize how juvenile he sounded? In silence she studied him, then quietly asked, "What do you want us to be, Henry?"

He fidgeted in confusion. "What do you mean?"

"Us. What you don't want is for us to be unfriendly. You've explained that. All I'm asking is, what do you want?"

A strained laughter bubbled from him. "Well . . . one thing sure. Nobody ever put it to me that way before."

He really was the most absurd man. "What way?" she asked, smiling innocently.

"Well . . . so . . . you know, direct and all." He laughed and looked away.

"You don't like things to be direct, is that it?"

"Well, no. With us . . . you and me . . . I'd like it . . . well, just about any way I could get it." Now he looked at her, a growing assurance on his face.

"Any way you could get what?" Her eyes were a mask of innocence and she listened, unsmiling, as his apologetic laugh came again.

He looked away in discomfort. "Well . . . you know . . ."

"I'm not sure I do."

He moved a little closer. "Come on. You know. You and me."

"You and me what?"

He started to speak but paused and for a long time looked at her in silence. Finally, when he did speak, his voice was very, very quiet, almost a whisper. "You want me to say it? Is that it?"

Now it was her turn for discomfort. "Say what?"

"The words. Say the words. Lots of women want that, at least that's what people say. Not that my experience is that . . . that . . . well, varied. Frankly, I'm fairly uncomplicated in that respect, if it's possible to be uncomplicated when it comes to relationships between men and women. I'm lonely, that's what it is. A simple thing, really. That's all. And you sitting in your apartment, me up there in mine. Both of us by ourselves . . . Why? . . . It's such a waste. All because I don't know how to say, 'Come on up to my place,' without making it sound like a joke. Some bad joke."

Sarah looked away from him with remorse. Why had she led him on like that? She had never been a bitch, had always taken pride in the fact that she tried to deal honestly with people. Even with Jeff. She had not tried to "take" him in the settlement. Now she found herself facing a pleasant man who had become a victim of a game that she never should have started. "Mr. Morrow . . ."

"Henry," he replied quickly. "You said for me to call you Sarah. And I did. Well, you call me Henry. Friendly, like you said."

"I don't know what I've meant by any of the things I've said. I'm tired." She was silent for a moment. "Tired and angry." She smiled. "I know that this will sound foolish . . . but having to do things like taking out the garbage makes me angry . . . And when you came down . . . Well, I shouldn't've acted the way I did."

"You mean that you . . . It was a game?"

"I suppose it was. And all I can say is that I'm sorry."

"No. That's all right. I don't mind. Really I don't. Maybe something good will come from it—like my mother used to say." He laughed. "We don't know, do we?"

"No. We don't know." She started up the steps and he hurried to hold the door for her.

He followed along behind her as she went down the hall. "Just can't tell," he said. "This might be the beginning of . . . well, something that we would both enjoy."

She stopped at the entrance to her apartment, laughed. "You're right about that," she said. "When you say we can't tell. That's the one thing I've learned."

Now at ease, an appealing humor covered his face and for the first time he relaxed. "Soon. Some night soon, you'll have to come up." He laughed. "Like I said, I know it sounds corny . . . But believe me, Sarah, I cook one hell of an Irish stew." He nodded as he started up the stairs.

"Henry," she called.

He turned, his face boyish with expectation.

She glanced toward the plastic container that he held in his hands and smiled. "You forgot to empty your garbage." They both laughed as she disappeared into her apartment.

Sarah closed the door, latched it, double-locked it.

Henry . . . A pleasant man.

She paused at the doorway to the kitchen.

Handsome really. Red hair, still thick. Green eyes. Appealing in the most basic way. The thought of making love again came to her as a surprise, almost an embarrassment, and she laughed aloud.

Irish stew. He had said that he was good at that and she began to speculate on his degree of excellence in other things. Her embarrassment deepened. How would he feel about the operations that she had had? About . . . She could not bear to think about it. She was lonely. She needed . . . company. Someone who . . . Just someone.

Someone.

She sighed and smiled, turned into the kitchen. And as she reached for the light switch, the smile blended into a gasp of desperate pain. Some force had slammed her against the wall. Someone was there, his hand clamped over her mouth. She tried to fight but she could not. The pain was too intense. She knew that she was dying. She gasped as the knife sliced through her. Someone was . . . She tried to scream but the hand was over her mouth and the fury continued.

Someone . . .

Someone help me!

But there was no one. Only the two of them. And she slumped to the floor, awareness a thing forever lost.

Charles leaned against the doorframe, trying to get his breath. He straightened up. She was there on the floor next to him. He looked at her, puzzled. She was old and that surprised him. He held his hands over his face and moved away. At the sink he put his head under the faucet and gradually his breathing steadied.

It would be all right.

Fine.

Everything.

It had turned out well after all.

He looked at her. Old. She was an old woman.

He stepped over her and went into the living room. At the front door, he listened. No one was there.

Gently he opened the door and was gone.

As Charles drove, the confusion of traffic swirled around him, adding to his tension.

Restless.

It had not gone as it should.

There was no satisfaction in the way that it had happened. So quick. There had been no time to plan. No time to . . . He felt a terrible frustration, trembled, ached with it.

The quickening excitement that was always there, had not come and he was left with emptiness, a kind of fear. As he drove through the hills, he thought through it again.

She had come into the kitchen.

And then . . . She was on the floor.

The image in his mind was blurred and refused to focus. He had never seen her clearly. And she had not seen him. Had not really known what was happening. She had struggled. But had she known what she was struggling against? Without that it was meaningless.

He tried to relive the moments as they had happened.

She had stepped into the kitchen, had reached for the light switch . . .

And he . . .

He wanted to isolate the movements, see them as they had been, but he could not. It had been too fast; jumbled, meaningless.

Had she ever even seen him?

She had come through the doorway. And . . .

And that was all.

She had died so quickly. Without knowing . . . Without seeing . . . She had died without even sensing what was happening. That was the source of his frustration and because she had not known, her death was meaningless to him.

For the first time he felt guilt. Not because someone had died, but because he had failed.

Again he tried to picture her. She was old. Of that he was certain. That was not what bothered him. True the others had been young, but age was not an all-important factor. In some odd way, the only ghost of satisfaction interwoven through the memory was the fact that she was old. The newness of it. As it was happening, he had felt the beginnings of pleasure. Then it was over. She was on the floor. Her skirt, pushed up as she fell, revealed thighs that were old. He smiled. But the smile quickly faded.

She had never seen him.

He tightened his grip on the steering wheel. There had not been time for her to know. That was his frustration and it could not be wished away. That necessary moment had been missing; the realization, the acknowledgment of terror, the beginning of eternity.

There had been only two minor rewards—her age and the warm, throbbing wetness that covered his hand as the knife went in. He began to relax. At least there had been that. The wetness. And the loose, hanging skin of her thighs as she lay at his feet.

As the car curved and turned through the quiet midnight streets, his tension left him. He smiled and brushed his hair from his forehead.

Old. Softly, he laughed. There was something nice about her having been old.

He turned into the drive, glad that he was home, eager to close himself into the quietness of his room.

Dammit. He should have taken pictures. Why hadn't he taken them? Should he go back? No. Too late.

Ann awakened. In the darkness she listened. Was he home? She heard the door close softly. Yes. Through the years she had trained herself to come awake with his return. She listened as he came up the stairs, smiled, pleased with the awareness that never failed to alert her. He was coming down the hall. No carpet was so soft as to obscure from her the sound of his footfalls.

"Charlie," she called drowsily, "that you?" Of course she knew that it was. She drew the covers securely around her. He was home. "Charlie?"

"Good night, Mother."

"It's late."

"Good night."

He was home. She turned over, burrowing into the warmth of the pillows. He had not come in to kiss her and for that she was sorry.

But he was home.

Now they were safe.

All of them.

All in their rooms.

All in their beds.

And the doors were locked against whatever unknown things were out there. She closed her eyes.

"Night."

She knew that he could not hear but she loved saying it.

"Love you . . . Love my baby."

She whispered it almost to herself and smiled as she drifted back into the hazy, drug-softened night.

In her room, Elise was awake, listening. The light was out so that he would not know. Never before had she been so aware of sounds. The house was filled with them. And the cars that had passed . . . For hours she had waited, lying still. Finally she had heard him turn into the drive, had gone to the window and watched as he came toward the house. Why had he walked so slowly, paused before he had come in? She had gone back to her bed, listened while her mother called the same old words.

There was a sound. A soft scraping sound and she knew that a drawer had been opened . . . Was it the drawer that she had found? And what was he putting there? Did it mean that . . . No. For if it meant what it must not mean, then everything would be changed. Everything. Her legs were trembling. The pain was building. Then, after a moment, there was the sound of a drawer closing.

She took a deep breath, trying not to make any noise, for to her every sound was magnified. She listened as he moved about the room. There was the ghost sound of soft music. The transistor. He had turned it on. The one there on the table beside his bed. The one they had given him in October for his birthday.

Staring into the shadows, she could see him in her mind as he carefully creased his trousers and hung them up. Tears came to her eyes at the imagined image.

She loved him.

Always she had loved him more than anyone else in her life.

Both she and her mother.

What would they do if . . .

She heard a match strike. He doesn't know that I'm listening, she thought, and was filled with emptiness. She wanted to go to his room, sit beside him on the bed, hold his hand, tell him that she loved him.

She closed her eyes, weary from the tiny, endless sounds of the house. She did not want to listen any more. But she was unable to stop herself.

Comforted by the shadows that softened his room, Charles was lying on the bed. He took a deep drag on his cigarette and slowly exhaled. It had not been as bad as he had thought. True, the night had not gone as planned. But that was all right. There had been the warm wetness as he . . . Gently he traced his fingers across his lips and shivered.

There would be other nights.

A lifetime of nights.

He smiled as he remembered the sagging oldness of her. It had not all been loss.

Idly, he ran his hand over his chest and across his abdomen, moved his toe to the soft, sweet rhythm of the music.

No. Definitely, the night had been more gain than loss.

CHAPTER TWENTY

Carefully Elise inched the spatula under the sputtering eggs and transferred them to the plate without breaking either yolk.

"It's ready," she called.

"Baby Sister." Charles gave her a kiss on the cheek as he sat down at the table. He glanced at the paper which was beside his plate. There were no headlines about the murder. Of course he had not expected that there would be. Probably Monday at the earliest. Perhaps not until the middle of the week. Once eight days had passed before discovery.

He smiled and with a decisive action, sliced his fork through the jiggling yolks. Perfect. Just the way he liked them. He winked his appreciation to Elise.

"You're too good to me," he said, and he started to eat. He was hungry.

Ann's morning medicine was beginning to take effect and the pill hangover with which she inevitably greeted the day was dissipating. She scooped out the last of her soft-boiled egg, slupped it from the spoon and lay back on the pillows, munching a piece of sour-dough toast, content. Within a half hour her morning programs would begin. She picked up the *TV Guide* to check once more the morning movies on 11 and 13.

"Bye, bye, Mama love." Charles's face popped in and out of the doorway before she even had time to see him.

She waited for a moment, expecting him to come back. But he was gone.

"Goodbye kiss?" she called.

There was no reply; and, frowning, she returned to the television schedule, the brightness of the morning a little dulled, the day no longer quite as nice as it had been.

He was gone.

Elise turned off the water, the dishes finished.

She sat at the kitchen table and smoked, postponing as long as possible what she knew must be done.

"Lise."

As she walked through the upper hall, she heard her mother call.

"In a minute, Mother."

She continued past the doorway and turned into Charles's room, carefully shutting the door behind her. The windows were closed, the air still, and she shivered. Then quickly she went to the dresser. The drawer. He had opened it the night before. She had heard him. As she started to kneel, she saw, through the mirror, the unmade bed. Welcoming reprieve, she turned and straightened the covers.

She wanted to leave but she could not. She had to know. Slowly she returned to the dresser, knelt and opened the drawer.

Again she studied the grotesque little displays, the neatly arranged news clippings and stockings.

Then she saw the knife.

It was at the back of the drawer, wrapped in a stocking. Had it been there the day before? No. She was sure that it had not. Was this what he had put in the drawer? She reached out to touch it but drew her hand back. Perhaps it had been there, covered by something—clippings. But even as she thought it, she knew that it was not true.

The drawer. Could the contents be an innocent interest in murder? Could it be simply that . . . But the stockings . . . Why were they with the clippings? . . .

And the knife.

Trembling, she picked up one of the stockings, glanced at the headline that was then unobscured. She lifted the clippings out. Isobel Grove, that was the girl's name. She had been dead for more than a year. Elise studied the girl's face.

Could Charles be the one? She felt that he was and hated herself for that disloyalty.

As she started to return the clippings, she gasped, closed her eyes. There were pictures there, pictures taken in the girl's room. She covered them with the newspaper stories, the stocking; closed the drawer.

Why had she ever opened it? Why had she found it?

And the night before, where had Charles been?

There had been nothing in the morning paper . . . But the later editions? Tomorrow?

Holding to the marble of the dresser top, she stood. The pain in her legs was intense. She waited for the spasm to subside; then she left the room.

"Lise." Ann could hear her passing in the hall. "Why don't you answer?" she called.

Without replying, Elise continued on down the back stairs.

"Lisey!" Ann's voice was shrill with demand. "I need you!"

In the soft spring morning, Elise walked across the yard and down the drive.

"Elise!"

Her mother's voice was a soft, ghost thing coming from that distance and, turning from it, Elise leaned against the gatepost, watched the passing cars.

A Volkswagen stopped in front of the house across the street and the teen-age driver blew the horn impatiently. A young girl hurried from the house carrying a picnic basket and a blanket.

"Hurry up!"

"All right, Duncan." The girl almost dropped the food hamper.

"I'm hurrying fast as I can." As she loaded the paraphernalia into the car, she saw Elise and waved. "Hi."

"Morning, Adrienne."

As Adrienne started to get into the Volks, she paused, feeling that something was wrong. She went around the car and into the street. "Elise?"

"Come on, will you!" The boy's temper was rising.

"Just a minute, okay?" Adrienne's unexpected harshness stunned him for the moment. She turned back to Elise. "What is it?"

There was silence and then Elise tried to smile. "What do you mean?"

"I don't know . . . You look so . . ." Adrienne paused, unsure of the word.

In an attempt to joke the moment away, Elise finished the sentence. "Old?"

But Adrienne was not joking. Always she had liked Elise, and it disturbed her to see this weariness that she had never noticed before. "No . . . You seem . . ." Again she paused.

Elise smiled. "Some days it just takes a little while to get yourself going."

The silence that followed was broken by a blast from the horn. "I'm leaving. And I mean right now!" Duncan revved the motor and put the car in gear.

"All right!" Adrienne went to the car. "Can't I even say hello?"

"Just get in!"

As they took off, Adrienne turned back and called to Elise, "See you later."

Elise smiled. "Alligator," she whispered and snapped her fingers in imitation of teen-age cool. "After while . . ." But the smile faded as she drew a deep, shuddering breath, then turned and looked toward the house.

"Charlie . . . Charlie . . ." Softly she murmured the name and trembled as it echoed through her.

Saturday was Charles's favorite work day.

The offices were quiet. There were no typewriters clattering, no heels clicking, no girls whispering, giggling. He was alone in that part of the building.

He liked working Saturdays, having Mondays off. Solitude. He loved it. Alone he felt the freedom to allow himself to drift and wander at will, with no fear of disturbance.

Los Angeles Public Library. Carefully he stamped the books, his thoughts ranging through endless fantasy. At times he leaned back and closed his eyes, enjoying the dream figures as they wafted by, reliving moments of remembered pleasure.

He smiled with the warmness that they brought.

Elise swirled her hand through the water as it splashed into the tub, making sure that it was not too hot. Her mother liked the bath water warm. But not too warm.

Methodically, Elise had worked her way through the morning, held and protected by established routine. Medicines, the addressing of envelopes, lunch—and the morning was mercifully gone. Finished. Forever. And they were all that much closer to the end. Whatever it would be.

The water seemed right and she turned it off. Getting her mother out of the bed was a difficult but not unfamiliar task. Gently Elise lowered her into the water.

Ann sighed and relaxed into the warmth. She drew a deep breath. It was true. Water was therapy. She let her hands float free, closed her eyes, drifted. "Cigarette," she mumbled. But Elise did not respond. "Lisey!" She wiggled her fingers. "Gimme a cig."

Elise smiled as she put a Lucky between her mother's lips and lit it. She watched as Ann puffed and coughed, drifted and dreamed. She soaped the cloth and started on her mother's back.

"Easy," Ann gasped. "Easy!"

The expected. There was something so comforting about it. "Sorry," she said, her voice trembling. And as gently as possible, she sponged Ann's shoulders.

Ann relaxed onto the pillows. Clean sheets. She loved them. She sighed with exhaustion and, taking the remote control, snapped on the TV.

Immediately she was relieved. The commercial was still on and the afternoon movie had not yet started. She hated it when she missed the beginning.

Alice Faye.

She loved Alice.

While Elise held the tray, she took her two-thirty medicine, the exertion of the bath fading.

As the credits came on the screen, Ann smiled and rooted out a handful of M&M's. She loved them—chocolate and peanuts. And a

Thirties movie that she knew frame by frame. She snuggled under the covers.

Alice.

Great.

And Don Ameche.

Oh, great. Great.

She moved the bag of M&M's closer. What a great afternoon.

Elise stopped, leaned against the building. The pain in her legs was very bad and she knew that she should not have tried to walk so far. Should have taken a cab. To hell with the money. She should have done it. She took a deep breath and continued on down the hill.

She turned the corner and stopped. There they were. The newspaper boxes. There in front of Hughes Market. Through the plastic covering she saw the headline and closed her eyes. The words that she most feared were there.

She inserted a dime, opened the lid, and, trembling, took out a paper.

She would have to sit down.

Why had she walked it? Why had she been so stupid?

Across the street, there was a bus stop. She waited for the light; then made her way to the bench. After a moment she glanced at the headline, her eyes stinging. The sun was warm and she tilted her face to it. Eyes closed, she folded the paper inward so that those incredible words were covered. She would read it when she got home.

She crossed back to the market, went in and got some ice cream. She laughed as she paid for it, not caring that people looked at her oddly. The unimaginable had happened, and she was buying Rocky Road for Mama.

A taxi. God, yes! Why worry about economy now? Why walk up that terrible hill to save two-fifty when two-fifty would not change a thing. Not change a thing! Nothing would change it.

She stood on the corner, waved as a cab came around the curve on Highland. To hell with two-fifty. Again she started to laugh, her eyes filling with tears.

Three o'clock.

The alarm sounded. Charles snapped it off and put on his jacket, smiling with satisfaction. A nice day.

As he opened the door at the end of the hall that led to the main lobby, the soft murmuring that was always there greeted him. He turned into the reading room and glanced through the papers, his eyes calm, his hands steady.

She had been found.

Watkins, that was her name. Sarah Hammond Watkins.

He should have taken pictures. He should. Why had he been so stupid?

Quickly he skimmed the story.

Nothing, no clues.

Smiling, he crossed through the lobby.

On the way home he would get the papers.

Ann scraped the last of the ice cream from the dish and laughed at the antics of the MC on the afternoon show. Rocky Road. Sweet of Elise. But a taxi! Why would she do anything so extravagant? She looked over at her daughter's untouched work table. She had not addressed any envelopes all afternoon.

Money. The desperation that came from not having it. She tried to close it from her mind but she could not.

If only she had saved. Some of the others had. They had looked ahead and they were living in splendor still. It would have been so easy. If she had just . . . But she had not and nothing could change it. The recognition of her stupidity, her blindness, always surprised her. She realized how silly she had been and it embarrassed her, how dense to think that those days would go on forever.

Alan's family had had money, but they had never liked her. No. It was stronger than that. They had actively disliked her. Still, after so many years, that knowledge was painful to her.

Why had they hated her so? Why? She closed her eyes, tightened her hands on the Kleenex box. Why?

True, she had been foolish in her pretensions. She knew that now, had known it then really. But it was only a pose. They must have known that. The tangle of memories from those days came flooding back and she sighed, clenched her teeth, the humiliation of that defeat was forever close, inescapable. Of course, hers had been an attitude that was artificial, a kind of studied theatricality. But that had been a protection. They had known that. They must have.

She leaned forward and looked at the picture of her husband. It was in a silver frame on her dresser. She kept it there, always close. Often she would glance at it. She had loved him. And if her attitude in those years of rushing about, laughing, seeing, being seen, had been superficial, what she had felt for him had been genuine—the one truthful thing, the one complete thing in the midst of all the pretense. Always she had been old-fashioned in that. Her husband. Her children. From the beginning she had been constant . . . And Alan's mother. Ann was sure that the woman had known that. But finally it had not mattered. They had never liked her, had been unable to forgive her for what she was. Abruptly, Ann threw the covers back. The memory was suffocating. She loosened the string in the yoke of her gown.

"She won't do."

That's what she had heard Alan's father say.

He had repeated it. "Just won't do," his voice soft, sorrowful.

It was when Alan had first taken her to Detroit to meet them. She was on the stairs and they had not known that she was there. Perhaps if she had handled it differently, had not let them know that she had heard.

But how could she?

Nothing that he could have said would have cut more deeply. She had walked immediately into the silence of that room and had faced the three of them. What he had said had represented the failure of all the things for which she had fought so desperately.

"Won't do."

Well, who the hell were they to pass judgment? Detroit. Detroit, Michigan! God!

Her toes curled against the sheet as she remembered the foolish things that she had said to them. But why wouldn't she "do"? That is what she had not understood. Still did not understand. She had been pretty. Successful. Bright enough. Had read all the books that they had read. Knew which was the salad fork, how to dress. So what was it? And from those people. People from Detroit, for God's sake, that city of money and trash. Not to be received in Detroit! Charleston perhaps. Macon or Montgomery. But Detroit!

She had told them what she felt and they had never forgiven her.

After Alan had died—in that needless way . . . Needless!—she had never heard from them again. They had not even wanted to see the children. Finally their money had gone to Alan's brothers and his sister, who was a hopeless, sloppy drunk. Ann smiled. Always she had loved the fact that those ashen, bloodless people had produced an only daughter whose drunkenness, whose pitiful vulgarity, had turned their final years into mournful things.

"Let them have the money." That's how she had felt at the time. And because of pride she had not contested the will.

She lit a cigarette and looked about the room. If only she had it to do over again. If only she . . . Her lawyer had told her to take it to court and she should have done it. She flicked her cigarette in the general direction of the ashtray. Well, she hadn't. Pride . . . She had done nothing, and the possibility of wealth had been lost.

Pride. She closed her eyes, frowned.

How could she have known that her career would fall apart? That so quickly everything would end? How could anyone have known that? Even considered it possible? She had been rising. The good years, the best years, the real parts, Greatness; ahead. And the whole damn thing had fallen apart. All of it. Incredible! Within three years. Gone.

She stamped out the cigarette and with a vicious snap of her thumb, flicked on the television. She did not want to think. She could not stand it.

"God . . . oh, God . . ." Here they were. The three of them. Hanging on. Twenty-five years later and still hanging on.

She looked about the room. The house. At least she had held onto that. She sighed and reached for an M&M, glanced at the Perry Mason rerun. The house. She lived in a mansion. Nothing would ever change that. Nothing.

She chomped down on a chocolate-covered peanut.

Detroit! She hoped that they would have another riot.

Elise heard the car.

She went to the window of Charles's room where she had been waiting and watched as he walked toward the house. She heard the door close and went and sat on the bed, not knowing what she would say to him when he came into the room.

"'Lo, Mama." From his voice, Elise knew that he was in good humor.

"Gonna gimme a kiss?" Elise heard her mother call. But Charles had not stopped, was coming on toward his room.

She heard him laugh. "After while maybe." How many times, she wondered, had she heard the exchange?

He was smiling when he came into the room and he closed the

door without noticing that Elise was there. He glanced at the newspaper that he was carrying, turned to the dresser.

He stopped, caught his breath. The drawer. It was open.

Then through the mirror he saw Elise and whirled around to face her.

For a long moment neither of them spoke. Finally Elise nodded. "I see we both have the papers," she said.

Charles leaned against the dresser, trembling. "You were spying. You've been watching me."

"I found out by accident. I was cleaning the room and . . ."

"That morning in the kitchen," he said. "When was it? That morning I was looking at the paper. And you came in. Jane Atkins. You looked at me. That morning. I knew that you were watching me."

"I wasn't watching you, Charles," she said, and nodded toward the drawer. "I wish I hadn't seen it." She turned from him. "I didn't know what to do . . . Don't know what to do." Elise looked up at him as he moved slowly toward the bed. "It will kill Mama," she said. "It will kill her."

Her words were meaningless to Charles. His mind was tumbling, trying to adjust to the danger that surrounded him. "Don't tell," he whispered. "Don't!"

"People will know, Charles. Finally. You'll be caught."

He reached for her hands in silent pleading but she rose and moved away from him.

She wanted to turn back to him but she could not. She stopped before the window, looked out over the lawn. "Why?"

"Please, Elise."

Reflected in the window glass like a pale ghost, she could see the faint outline of the drawer.

Charles went to her, touched her shoulder. "You don't understand."

She turned to him. "You really expect me to do nothing?"

"Lise . . ."

She looked at the drawer. "When I saw that I could hardly breathe. I just wanted to be dead . . . I think that's . . ." She could not find the words. "I don't know . . . the loneliest thing I've ever seen." She studied his face, expecting to find remorse but she found only quietness there. She walked past him into the middle of the room. "All those girls. Alone . . . Did they know you? Did they care for you?" She turned back to him. "Or did they not even know that you were there . . . until . . ."

"Lisey." Ann was calling and for a moment they were quiet.

Elise continued to search his face, tears welling in her eyes. "I wish we could die," she said. "All three of us. Right now. Now!"

As she started to cry, Charles went to her, put his arms around her. And after a moment she leaned against him.

"Lise," Ann called again. "Somebody."

"We can't talk here," Charles whispered, and he guided her toward the door.

Elise stood in the hallway outside her mother's room while Charles adjusted the television set which was a confusion of rolling images.

Ann was in a petulant mood. "I called and called," she whined. Then as the distortion in the picture was corrected, she was slightly mollified.

"Taking Lise to the A&P," Charles said and threw her a kiss as he left the room.

"Charlie, wait," she called. But he was gone. "Lise. Get me some Luckies!"

CHAPTER TWENTY-ONE

As the car moved with increasing speed through the hills, Elise was mesmerized by the onrushing road. The wheels sang as they rounded the curves. They almost went over the edge and she looked in fear to Charles, realized his intention. She relaxed. Finally they would crash through the guardrail at one of the turns.

Relieved that the initiative had been taken from her, she moved closer to him. "Go on," she whispered. "Go on, Charlie." She knew that they were about to die and she welcomed it, looked forward to the moment when the steel would twist and slice through them, when flames would cover them both.

"Now," she murmured. "It's all right. Now."

Again the car swerved and barely missed going over the edge. Finally they came to a stop on the dusty shoulder of the road. Still clutching the steering wheel, Charles leaned his head against his hands.

"You shouldn't have stopped, Charlie." Elise waited for him to turn to her and when he didn't, she looked away. She had thought that the necessity to decide, to act, had been taken from her. "It's the hardest thing," she said and reached over, touched his hands.

For a long moment they sat in silence. Then Charles got out of the car and looked over the hills. A yellowish gray film of smog covered the city. He walked along the rock formation that jutted out over the desolate ravine. In the quietness, he turned back to his sister and held out his hand. "Lise."

She studied the beckoning hand, then very calmly stepped from the car and started along the uneven path. She almost tripped on the loose stones but regained her balance and cautiously made her way to the steadying hand that was waiting.

Together they went farther onto the giant rocks. Charles stepped behind her and held her shoulders as they looked to the city and the hills beyond.

Elise trembled as he touched her. "All these years," she said. "How many years, Charlie, I wonder? Us sitting up there in Mama's room waiting for you." She almost smiled. " 'Charlie's home! He's home!' . . . We'd do our silly numbers. Both of us." She leaned away from him. "Now I know about you." Her voice was quiet in the stillness and the words seemed to float there. "That's the hardest thing, Charlie. The hardest thing in the world to say." She looked over the edge to the rocks below.

Charles held her against him and whispered, his lips almost touching her hair. "You don't have to tell."

Elise closed her eyes and slowly shook her head. Without resistance she allowed herself to be guided still closer to the edge.

Charles eased her forward and drew his hands away from her shoulders. He watched as she stood there unsteadily. He waited but she did not move. He knew that with the most gentle easing, she would be gone.

He wanted to do it. But he could not.

Elise held her breath, relaxed forward.

As she was about to fall, Charles caught her to him and pulled her away from the edge. After a silent moment she turned away from him and sat on the rocks, welcoming the warmth of them. Still she did not look at him.

"You should've done it," she said.

Charles looked across the city. How far to the hills on the other side, he wondered. "But you're not the one," he whispered and smiled.

The statement was a mystery, a puzzle that she did not want to understand. "All right," she said and stood up. "You can't kill me, I'll kill us all. It'll only take one phone call." She started back toward the car.

"Lise." He wanted her to understand. She stopped but did not turn back. "Listen to me," he said.

After the barest hesitation, she continued on toward the car.

"No." He hurried to her, grabbed her hand. "I want you to understand." She turned to him and he smiled. "Is it so awful?" His voice was soft, whispering. "Is it?" He waited but she did not speak. "And anyway, what does this have to do with us?"

The smile, the inflections were so familiar. It was part of the charm that he had always used to get his way. She knew that if she looked back his eyes would hold complete assurance. For as long as she could remember she had done what he wanted. He expected it.

When she did not turn to him, impatience edged into his voice. "Who were they?" he said.

Stunned by the harshness of it, she looked toward him but he seemed a stranger.

Then he smiled and went to her, knowing that he would win. "Who were they?" he whispered and turned her so that once more they were looking out over the haze-covered city. "Look. The world's still there." She was no longer trembling. Definitely, he would win. "I love you. And if you . . ."

"I love us all," she said. "And what is that?"

"But not enough. Not enough to leave it alone . . . Is that so much?" She did not answer. Why wouldn't she understand? "It's nothing to do with you . . . Me." His voice was rising. "Me! . . . What will they do to me? . . . You want that? You'd do that? Turn on me like that?"

Of course it was not what she wanted. What she wanted was for none of it to have happened. But it had happened and there was nothing that could change it. "It's turned on all of us, Charlie. I can't understand it. But whatever it is . . . this . . . whatever . . . It's over."

In silence they looked at each other and Charles knew that he had lost. His reaction was puzzlement rather than anger. "You're going to do it," he said. It was not a question.

"Yes."

"And nothing will change your mind . . ."

Elise nodded toward the cliff. "You had your chance at that."

Charles watched her as she went to the car, moving carefully on the uneven ground. Softly, he laughed. "Surprise, surprise," he said. "The Gymp's a strong lady."

After a moment he followed.

Slowly the car curved down out of the hills.

"I'll tell Mother after dinner," Elise said. That was the part that she most dreaded.

Charles laughed, a lazy, pleasant sound. "It's almost worth it."

Elise turned to him, puzzled.

"To see her face, I mean," Charles said and smiled. "Really think you can do it, huh?" He winked. "Well, forward!" He turned into the traffic of the broad avenue at the foot of the hills. "I may have a few surprises of my own."

Elise waited for him to explain but he only smiled.

They pulled into the drive and stopped. Twilight had faded and after a moment Elise got out of the car and went through the darkness toward the house. She expected Charles to follow and, when he did not, she turned back to him.

"I love you, Charlie," she called softly. "You know that already. You've always known it. But I needed to say it . . ." Then she turned and walked away.

"Hey, Lise." Charles got out of the car, went to her. "Whatever happened to the M-G-M finish?" He smiled.

"It finally faded," she said. For a long time they looked at each other in silence. Then they went on toward the house.

Charles took her hand. "Like old soldiers."

"Like old lies," Elise said as they went up the steps, holding hands as they had when they were children.

There was something that he had missed. There had to be. Ben's frustration had almost reached breaking point. Carefully he had gone over his notes; had relived, point by point, the development of the case trying to reassure himself that there was no avenue that he had not explored.

The girl, Elizabeth. She was the link.

There was something that she was not telling. He was sure of it. He did not know what it was. But something. He had seen it in her face. That night. After her encounter in the theatre.

The streets were quiet as he walked toward the apartment building. Something. There must be something that he had overlooked.

"But she's upset," Avis said. "Surely you can realize that."

"Of course I realize it. I'm not subhuman." He had given up trying to understand the woman. He was sickened by her, by everything that had contrived to block him in the case. Turning from her, he went in the direction of Elizabeth's bedroom.

Avis stepped in front of him. "But there's nothing more she can tell you."

"That's something we don't know yet, right?" Without waiting for an answer, he tapped on the door. "Elizabeth," he called softly. And when there was no answer, he gently opened the door and went in.

Elizabeth did not want to be questioned further about it. She did not want to have to think about it any more. She was sitting in the bed, resting against the pillows, the covers pulled up about her although it was not cold. "It's exactly like I said." Her voice was hesitant. "I don't know anything more."

With triumph, Avis looked toward the detective. "She's already told you all that she . . ."

Ben turned on her, interrupting. "No," he said, his voice as cold as his eyes. "You are not going to stop me in this and I mean it." He tensed, waiting for her to challenge him and when she did not, he leaned toward the girl, spoke in a softer tone. "I want to hear it again, Elizabeth. Everything." And he sat in the straight-back chair that was in front of her study table.

Avis watched, fighting for control. He was insulting and arrogant and she intended to report him. She wanted to order him out of the apartment. But there was something about him—something of menace—and she hesitated. But why, she demanded of herself. Why should she be intimidated in her own home? All the things that were said about the police were true! She started to speak.

Ben had been waiting and when he saw her brow tense in anticipation of voicing her thoughts, he cut through the silence. "You're going to report me, right?" He wanted to laugh when he saw the startled look cover her face. "Well, for God's sake go on and do it," he said. "Do it. Now! Go on and make your call. Do whatever you like, just stay out of this." He turned back to Elizabeth, speaking calmly. "Now the fact that I've heard it all before doesn't . . ."

"This is my house!" Avis's anger boiled over. "Mine! And if I . . ."

Ben sighed as he hunched over the table. His voice was quiet, hurried, and it seemed almost that he was talking to himself. "From the beginning you've been unco-operative in this," he said. "Of course that's not unusual. We run into it a lot. But this is a very complicated, an extremely important case and I'm going to do what I think is necessary and right whether you like it or not. So report me. I don't care if you do. A lot of people report me. A lot of people don't like me. I don't care." He turned to her. "This case is the only thing I care about right now and you're not stopping me." In silence he studied her pinched face.

Avis wanted to answer his arrogance but she could not. Her anger had built to a point near tears and she did not trust her voice.

"That first night," he said, and nodded toward the living room. "In there. You tried to postpone the questioning until the next day. You don't like me. We've been over that. Liking, not liking; it doesn't matter, not to me." He paused and all three were aware of the stillness of the room. "You say Elizabeth is upset. Well, something tells me that Elizabeth is not quite as sensitive as you think she is. In fact I think that, all considered, she's tough. And in my book that's a compliment."

Elizabeth studied his profile, thinking what a nice face he had. In the dim light, he seemed younger, the lines of weariness, dissolved. She was grateful to him for he had taken her hand in the car when she had needed someone. He had sensed that.

"I wouldn't do anything to hurt you," he said.

For a long time he looked at her and Elizabeth felt herself relaxing. She was glad that he was there, wanted him never to leave.

Ben looked about the room. There was little of vanity in it and he was saddened by that. The girl was pretty in a very special way and she did not know it. It was wrong that she should be unaware of something so important to a young girl. If she were his daughter, she would know that she was pretty. He would not want her arrogant with it, but he would see to it that she knew. The ghost of a smile edged his eyes.

Avis was fascinated by his unpredictability. She leaned against the doorframe, no longer wanting to fight him. She waited for him to continue. He was a mystery now and she wanted to understand him.

"I realize that you want to shield your daughter," he said. "I understand that and I sympathize." He picked up a pencil and began tapping on the table top, still not looking up. "But the fact is that Elizabeth is the only person known to have had contact with this man and lived."

He dropped the pencil and they were both a little shaken by the quick, sharp sound. They waited, both of them enjoying a sense of closeness with the man.

"Of course a lot of others saw him. But they didn't live. You knew one of them. You've probably read about most of the others. But what do you know really? I mean about the things he did. About those girls and the things that . . ." Leaving the sentence unfinished, he rolled the pencil from hand to hand across the painted top of the table, the staccato click-click-click filling the silence.

He stood, walked slowly to the window, looked out. The quiet of the night shadows seemed to steal into the room and he touched his fingers to the glass as he stared into the darkness.

"I want the same thing you want, Mrs. Mitchell," he said softly. "I want to protect her." He turned to Avis. "And I want the man."

His voice was calm and deadly and Avis shivered, for she knew that for him killing was not only a duty but a pleasure.

Elizabeth watched as he moved toward the bed. She knew that he would protect her, trembled as she studied his hands. He came into the light; and when she saw the lines that creased his forehead, she wanted to smooth them out. His eyes, a faded dust blue, seemed weary and she wanted him to look at her. *Look at me*, she willed. *Now. Look at me.* And when he did, she caught her breath. How had he known what she was thinking? She wanted to look away but she could not. She was afraid that if for one moment she broke contact, she might never find it again. He cared for her. He did. It was in his eyes. He wanted to protect her. And for that she loved him. Wanted to please him. Wanted . . .

"I want to hear the whole thing again," he said. "All of it. The fact that you've been over it before doesn't matter. Just take your time. Start from the beginning." He sat on the bed and leaned toward her. "You're in the telephone booth . . ."

When Elizabeth spoke, her voice was quiet but strong. She was surprised by the steadiness. "I had just finished talking to Mother," she said. "I hung up the receiver . . . and . . . and he was there." She looked away as memory came back, chilled her. "He was holding me," she said and still her voice was firm. "Pulling me against him. He gave me the phone so that it would look like I was still talking. He showed me the pictures. Three of them." She did not want to go on, but the dust-blue eyes that were older than her father's were there, waiting. She was held by them and she could not turn back. "Then . . ." As she stared into the eyes, her voice began to shake but she did not stop. "He held me . . . Close . . . Very close." Suddenly the words were tumbling over each other, none of them finished, all sliced short. "His hands, they were strong, very strong, and, and they were, I had on earrings and his hands, he put them here, like this . . ." She covered her ears with her hands. ". . . and it was like this . . ." Slowly she pulled her hands down over her breasts to her waist. ". . . and he kissed me, whispering all the time, and his hands were, he was holding me, I could see his reflection in the glass, holding me, his hands . . . And I thought . . . I thought . . ."

The dusty eyes held her as firmly as any hands could and she lowered her voice to a whisper. "He was strong, and he was . . . there was some . . . I don't know . . . not pleasure, certainly not that, but . . . but something . . . You see nobody ever held me before. I haven't thought about this, I mean I've tried not to think about it. I could see his eyes; they were reflected in the glass. He wanted me to look at them and I did and he was . . . His face seemed handsome to me then. I couldn't look away . . . there was something that . . . I wanted him to . . . He was still holding me, you see. I could feel him. He was close against me and without wanting to, I wanted him to . . . No. I mustn't. I know I mustn't say these things; but you said everything, you wanted everything and this is what happened, without my wanting it to happen, within me, I mean, and I wanted . . ."

"Where are they?" Ben's words cut through the quietness of her voice, an urgent command.

Elizabeth looked at him, not understanding.

Ben stood, breathless. "The earrings . . . You said you were wearing earrings."

Elizabeth opened the jewelry box and the earrings were there, resting on the velvet. She reached for them.

"No. Don't touch them." Ben's voice was as abrupt as the snap of a finger. "Which ones are they?"

"There." Elizabeth nodded. "The ones with gold disks."

Spearing them with the pencil, Ben transferred them into an envelope.

Elizabeth watched as he left the room. She heard the front door close. He was gone, so claimed by urgency that he had not said goodbye. She turned and when she saw her mother, tears filled her eyes and she began to sob.

"It's all right," Avis said. "It's all right, Baby."

But she knew that it was not all right.

They both knew.

CHAPTER TWENTY-TWO

"A lot you care," Ann said. "Either one of you." She was shaking with anger. Where had they been? Leaving her alone for so long. Thoughtless, that's what they were. Thoughtless . . . Inconsiderate . . .

Elise stood by the bed, preparing her mother's medicine while Charles watched, a controlled smile of pleasure playing through his eyes.

Ann was on the verge of tears. "You know I'm afraid to be by myself, Lise." Her chin was quivering. "You, too," she said to Charles as she started crying. "Here all by myself . . ." Again she accused Elise, this time with the ultimate in guilt provocation. "And my five-thirty! What about that? I missed it!"

Elise had the medicine ready. Carefully she held the brimming teaspoon toward her mother. "Don't spill it."

"Don't care at all. Either one of you!" She gagged on the awful taste, reached for the water and gulped it down. Exhausted, she collapsed onto the pillows. "Tonight I'll be the one that'll have to pay," she whimpered.

They watched as she cried and pouted, neither of them moving to comfort her.

Ann was stunned. Why were they acting like that, both of them standing there, so silent, watching. Then softly Charles began to laugh and Ann snapped her head toward him, her temper flaring. "That's right," she said, "go on and laugh." And, cradling her aching hands in her lap, she rocked back and forth, turned to Elise for sympathy. "I was scared, Lisey. Scared!"

Elise stroked her forehead. "It's all right."

"She'll be fine." Charles smiled coolly as he leaned toward his mother. "She's tougher than we know."

Ann pulled away from him, confused.

"Aren't you, huh?" Charles said. "Tough!" And he pinched her arm as though it were a game.

"Stop!" Ann slapped at him; and when he laughed, she edged toward Elise, desperate for comfort. "Already dark," she whispered. "It's awful here when it's dark. And you're by yourself." She struggled to sit higher on the pillows.

Elise took her arm. "Let me help you."

"That's a joke." In fury Ann hit at her daughter's hands. "Now you're going to help me." She gave a harsh laugh of derision. "Well, when you go down to the kitchen, it's all messed up." Gently she ran her fingers over her arm. "I burned myself." And again she started crying.

"I'll fix something," Elise said and started to leave. But she paused, turned back when she saw Charles sit on the bed.

"Did her hurt her hand?" he lilted in baby tones.

"Don't!" Ann pulled away when he reached out to pat her.

Charles smiled, laughed.

"Smile!" she said. "Go ahead. Laugh . . . Okay. Ha! Right back to you, ha!" Her anger rose to a point of desperation and she sobbed and choked on the tears.

Elise went back to the table, shook two tablets out of a bottle and held them out to Ann. "Here, Mama."

"No!" In a fit of temper, she knocked the medicine from her daughter's hand and clutched the spread in misery. "I won't take them! I won't!" She lifted her trembling hands. "I hurt."

Charles stroked her shoulder, still taunting with baby talk as he pretended to soothe. "She hurt?"

Confused, Ann struggled desperately for an answer. "Elise?" she said, her voice thin and breathless. "Lisey!"

Charles patted her. "We got a surprise for you."

"Don't!" said Elise, sickened by the abuse.

Charles smiled at his mother. "A real surprise," he whispered.

Surprise? What surprise? Ann was curious but she did not want him to know. "I don't care about any surprise," she said and sniffed.

Charles put his arm around her and for the first time seemed sincerely to offer comfort. "Know what we're going to do?" he cooed. "We're going to eat in the dining room. Think of that!" He smiled, confident that he could lure her back.

But Ann turned away. She was not ready to forgive.

Still Charles knew that he would win. It was a game that he enjoyed. He stood up. "We're going to sit down at the table," he said. "Like real grown-up people." Ann looked up and he smiled his most charming smile, lowered his voice. "We're going to chew our bread. And chew our potatoes. And tell each other the truth." He winked. "Won't that be fun?" he whispered; and he wanted to laugh at the petulant, spoiled-child expression that covered his mother's swollen face.

And while Ann tried to understand, he nodded with that ghost of courtliness that she loved so and left the room.

Like some turn-of-the-century judicial chamber, the walls of the dining room were covered with walnut wainscoting. It was a dark place, seldom used, not cared for. The paint on the ceiling was peeling and the crewel draperies, heavy with dust, were frayed. Dominating the room was a Hepplewhite banquet table, the only good piece of furniture in the house. Elise had taken special care to set it with their best—serving bowls that she had almost forgotten, silver that had been closed in plastic bags or stored in the cupboard with camphor squares to keep it from tarnishing. It was obvious that she had attempted to make everything "nice."

Charles was lighting the candles as Elise helped Ann into the room. "Surprise," he called and smiled as he blew out the match. He wanted to laugh. The power was with him and he knew it, felt the slow building of it. The storm was beginning. But quietly, not as it usually did. Tonight it would end, she would know and he would see her moment of knowing. Then, after she knew . . . He did not know what would follow. The moment would dictate that. But the power was with him. That he did know. And that was all that he needed to know.

Ann's face was radiant with pleasure. Then she remembered that she was angry. They had abused her. Both of them, making her wait. Alone. Now she had them where she wanted them for it was obvious that they were eager to make amends. Well, now it was their turn to wait. Her lips turned sullen. She tugged at her robe, retied the sash. It was her best. And if it was a little tattered, the cuffs a little soiled, that in no way reduced her assurance that it was a garment of a certain splendor. She felt a marvelous sense of importance. They had treated her badly. Now they were contrite. And of course she would accept this gesture of apology. But not right away. Finally, she would. But they would have to earn it.

Her eyes roved over the table. Candles. In the flickering light everything looked so beautiful. The Georgian cake basket. Alan's aunt had given it to them when they married. She was surprised to see it, thought that it had been sold long ago. Her heart quickened at the sight of it. If the need should arise—as it always did—there was an easy seventy-five dollars that could be had with one telephone call. She knew that the dealer on La Cienega to whom she had sold most of the things, resold them for five times what he had paid. But that could not be helped. Seventy-five was better than nothing.

She saw that Charles and Elise were waiting for her reaction and she covered her feelings. "If you think I'm going to forgive you this easy," she said, "you're wrong."

Charles laughed, excited by the fact that his mother did not know the game that was about to be played, enjoyed seeing her indulge herself with the same old sullen tricks that she had used so clumsily for as long as he could remember.

"Madam," he said. And with an excessive display of galantry, he held her chair.

She was tempted, but signaled him away. "I don't want your help." She pulled away from Elise. "Either one of you." And with a posture of pride, unaided, she took her seat.

Charles leaned close and whispered, "Not even going to give me a kiss?"

"No. Of course not." She refused to look at him. It was a minor triumph and she enjoyed it.

His lips brushed her cheek. "Come on."

"I said no."

Smiling, Charles went to his place at the head of the table. In a slow, deliberate charade of Victorian manners, he seated himself. "I'll be Daddy," he said, and winked at Elise.

Delicately, Ann rearranged the folds of her robe, careful not to forget the famous pain in her hands. She was afraid that the conversation would dissolve into other areas and she did not want the little skirmish to end. "I told you I'm not going to make it easy," she teased. "And I'm not."

Charles nodded with a show of defeat, assumed a remorseful attitude knowing that she would consider it victory. In silence he took the lids from the serving dishes. The steam from the creamed chicken wafted its aroma through the musky room. He began serving, aware that his mother was waiting for the next thrust. He was ready but he did not look at her, for he preferred to work slowly.

"You'll be sorry you didn't kiss me," he said.

Ann was not sure. Behind the soft, usual tone of his voice there seemed to lie a threat. But she could not be certain. Finally she decided to ignore it, barked a derisive, "Ha!"

An uneasy silence settled over the table. Charles looked away, continued serving. "Remember that," he repeated and smiled. "Remember. I offered to kiss you."

Ann was puzzled. He was not playing the game as he usually did and that disturbed her. But she ignored the warning. "Mr. Irresistible. Ha!"

Now his voice was predictable again with an underlying playfulness. "You're the one that'll be sorry."

"I will not!" Ann laughed and turned to Elise. "Hey, Lise, look at him. Mr. Marvelous!"

Charles bowed and nodded as though to acknowledge Ann's "win."

Again silence came and Elise was fearful of what it might bring. "Charles . . . Don't you think . . ."

Charles interrupted. "You're right, Lise. It's time." He turned to Ann. "Elise has something to tell you, Mama." And he handed Elise her plate.

"Charles!" Elise was alarmed.

"Well whatever it is," Ann said primly, "I don't care to hear it." She smiled, certain that she could beat him at any game he chose. After all, she was his mother. She toyed coyly with her fork, but

finally curiosity won the round. "What is it?" she asked and watched
as a smile spread over his face. She should not have asked. Definitely
a blunder. But the mistake was made and, whatever the surprise
was, she wanted to know. Elise was looking away and that was an
aggravation. Always that had been the most provoking of her daughter's hesitant habits—that tendency to look down, the inability to
steadily hold her own, eye to eye with the world. As a child Elise
had walked with her eyes to the ground and still the habit persisted,
as though she did not want to be seen. Ann's frustration grew, she
could hold it no longer. "Charlie!"

He exploded with laughter.

"All right. So I'm curious."

". . . *Yellow*," Charles cried. "Starring a bunch of naked Swedes."
He moved his shoulders in imitation of a teen-age dance. "Look,
Ma. No clothes!"

Ann was vaguely soured. She did not subscribe to nudity in films,
considered it a foreign perversion. "You said that Elise had something to tell me," she snapped, no longer attempting to conceal her
annoyance.

He studied his mother's petulant face. It was all there. All the
things that he hated most—her selfishness, the childish demands, that
willful insistence that everything be as she wanted it, and interwoven through it all, the love that she felt for him. He was glad for
that vulnerability, knowing that it made her his. She stretched her
hands and it seemed to Charles that she was reaching for him.

He knew that when finally he told her, that face would crumble,
change forever. His heart quickened and he smiled.

"Charles. Are you going to tell me?"

"Not yet."

In the quietness, Ann's disgust began to build. Softly Charles
laughed and she turned away, sullen. She hated to lose.

"Charles," Elise whispered. "Don't do this."

"Do what?" he asked as he dipped the serving spoon into the
steaming chicken and, with controlled malice, flipped the gravy-
laden meat over the rice. With his fingers he fished about the bowl
for other morsels to add to Ann's plate. "Wings and necks and backs
and thighs . . ." he said and winked at her. "Tell you after did-din,
Mama." From the gravy he pulled a dripping wing tip. "Oop . . .
How disgusting." He held the offending member toward his mother.

"Colonel Sanders' little thing." He tossed the wing onto her plate. "Don't say I never did you a favor."

Distastefully, Ann dumped the wing back into the bowl. "Awful, the way you treat me," she said. "Awful. And don't you think I'll forget it. Because I won't. Not in a million years!"

Charles began eating with exaggerated gusto; smacking his lips, licking his fingers. "Love chicken . . . Uh . . . Uh-huh!"

Ann's distaste was complete. "That's disgusting!"

"What?" Charles's face was that of an innocent surprised.

"You're sickening. Table nice," she reached out and touched the crystal goblet. "Everything so nice. And you acting like this."

With a show of puzzlement, Charles let the chicken fall to his plate. "Like what?"

"Like . . ."

Charles grabbed the serving spoon and, leaning over, loaded another dripping portion of the creamed chicken onto Ann's plate. "Like this?" he shouted. And trembling with temper, he began to laugh. "That what you mean?" Again he emptied the contents of the spoon onto her already overladen plate.

"Now, go on, Mama," he said. "Go on. Gobble and gorge and belch out loud. Then whimper and whine, 'I hurt, Lisey. I hurt.' . . . 'Come on, Lise. I'll help you change the sheets and clean her up.'"

His fury gone, he smiled with quiet sweetness, leaned toward her. "Love you, Mama," he whispered. "Love our mama . . . Right, Lise?" Then after a moment he turned back to his mother and, in silence, studied her. "Tonight it's going to end," he said softly and almost smiled. "That's a promise. Tonight it is going to end." Suddenly his voice was big, vigorous. Laughter was building. "Show and Tell, old Witch of the West. Time to Show and Tell."

Elise stretched her hand across the table but could not reach her mother. "Don't listen," she said.

Ann was trying to understand. She blinked her eyes as she looked from one to the other. Something had gone wrong. Badly wrong . . . But what? It was beyond her.

Like a dutiful son of thirty years before, Charles sat erect and folded his hands. "I'm Fauntleroy," he said. "And l'il ol' Fauntleroy loves his Dearest."

Elise could not stand any more of it. "Unforgivable, Charles!"

As he turned to his sister, all pretense was gone and he spoke quietly, "But memorable."

Something was happening—something that Ann could not follow. "What is it?" she asked, her voice urgent, her breath catching.

For a moment Charles considered ending it, but decided against it. It was too soon.

"What is it!" she repeated.

He smiled. "It's *A Song to Remember*, starring Cornel Wilde. And . . ." He waited for Ann to answer, to play her part in the game. When she did not reply, he hurried on. "You don't want to play? . . . Merle Oberon!" He continued eating, his voice now conversational, friendly. "How's Merle, I wonder?" He reached for an imaginary telephone, segueing into that game. "Hello, Merle?" he purred. "How's the season in Mexico?" He leaned toward Ann, smiling, coaxing, as though nothing had gone before. "Come on . . . You like games. You know you do." His face was radiant, inviting her to share the fun. "Come on, Mama. You're going to play."

"I'm not!"

Charles laughed with genuine pleasure. "Oh yeah. You know you are. It's fun."

Ann was still frightened. Everything, even the most familiar game seemed dangerous to her now. "Not fun," she said and tried to lift the goblet but she was trembling and could not do it.

"For you it is . . . Fun forever." Charles's eyes were now guileless, his voice a smile. "*It's a Woman's World*, starring June Allyson. And . . ." He waited and when she did not answer, he laughed. "Little Junie Allyson. And?" He smiled, knowing that the smile would bring victory. It was a charming smile. Always charm had been his power. He was sure that it would succeed. "And?" he coaxed.

"Arlene Dahl. And I'm not playing!"

Charles's laughter filled the room. "Too late. You're a *Designing Woman*, starring . . ."

In frenzy, Ann gave herself to the game, eager to retreat from whatever the mysterious thing was that had almost happened. She was convinced that she had been in danger although she had no hint of what that danger meant, what caused it. With an almost violent commitment, she played the role that was demanded of her. "Lauren Bacall! And?" She turned quickly to Elise.

Elise found a horrible fascination in it. The game. Her mother's face. The watery, aging eyes were smiling with desperation. "Gregory Peck." She turned to Charles. "And?"

Charles's power was complete, and it brought him such satisfaction that he could hardly still his trembling. "Dolores Gray," he said, and immediately his smile faltered. Was it Dolores? Was she the other woman in the picture? He was not sure. It did not seem exactly right. "Or . . . Wait a minute . . . Was it Monica Lewis?" He did not know which one it was and his confidence dissolved into indecision.

Ann leaned back in her chair and folded her arms. Now the smile was hers. "Which one?" she asked quietly.

"It was . . . It was . . ."

Now steady, Ann took a sip of water, enjoying the moment more than she had enjoyed anything for a long time.

Elise cupped her chin in her hands. "Which one, Charlie?"

Monica? Or Dolores? A fifty-fifty chance. He could not think. "Designing Woman," he said. "Greg. 'Betty' Bacall . . . And . . ." He shrugged, picked up the imaginary telephone. "Hello? . . ." Even though he was not looking at them, he could feel the tension of their waiting. With difficulty his voice assumed an intimate, casual tone. "Hello . . . Monica?"

"Sorry!" Ann cried, grabbing an imaginary receiver. "Wrong number!" And she gave a triumphant bark of laughter. "You lose!"

Although Charles was shaken, on the surface he remained calm. Smiling, he shrugged his shoulders and dipped his head as though to acknowledge a meaningless mistake. "The condemned . . ."

Flushed with triumph, Ann immediately interrupted, wanting to prolong her moment with an extention of the game. ". . . of Altoona!"

Charles dipped his fingers into the bowl of chicken and popped them into his mouth. ". . . Ate a finger-lickin' meal."

Ann's excitement settled in readiness for another round. "Starring Sophia Loren. And? . . ."

It was Elise's turn and she spoke so softly that they could hardly hear her. "Maximilian Schell. And?" She could not look at Charles.

Charles relaxed in the silence. This was not a game that mattered. He would win finally. There was no escaping it. He smiled. "Some oldies from the gas chamber."

Ann laughed and gurgled, drunk with accomplishment. It was the only time in all the years that they had been playing that she had ever scored a double win against him. "I won! I won!" she cried and her head bobbed and danced crazily. Her eyes blurred with victor's tears.

Charles's voice was very soft. "Think so, huh?"

Ann answered immediately, laughing. "I know so!" She watched as Charles picked up a drumstick and started eating. He pretended as he nibbled that it did not matter. Well, she knew him better than that. She knew everything about him. She knew that above all, he hated losing to Mama. Watching his ridiculous attempt at pretense, she snickered. She knew that she should not prolong the moment—that it was wrong to crow so loudly—but she could not stop herself. Not after the awful way that she had been treated!

And what was wrong with crowing a little anyway? It was only a game. And she had won. Won twice! So why not laugh and give a few cock-a-doodle-doo's? She reached over and tickled his chin. "Won twice, Charlie. Twice!"

She enjoyed the release of laughter. Now everything would be all right. Charles had abused her and he was paying for that abuse. Everything would be fine.

"Ooooh, he's mad," she said, her voice a baby coo. "Look at that, Lise. Charlie's 'bout to get mad." She pinched him, ready now to end it. "Can't you let poor ol' Mama win one sometime?" She chuckled and shook her head. "Baby . . . Such a baby." It was over. They were even. It would be a nice night.

Charles dropped a bone onto his plate and with a loud smacking, licked his fingers, rolling his tongue from one to the next as he cleaned the thick gravy from them.

Ann was revolted. She knew that he was only doing it to aggravate her and he had succeeded. "I hate it when you do that." With studied care, she took a few delicate bites, pleased that her show of manners would irritate him. Without realizing it, she spilled a gravy-saturated morsel of chicken on her dressing gown.

Charles laughed; and when she looked up, he nodded to the stains that had dribbled down the front of her robe. "You were saying?" he inquired casually as he took another piece of chicken from the bowl and quickly sucked the meat from the bone. Then he turned back to her and again inspected the stains that her clumsiness had caused. "Look at that," he said, and let the bone fall to his plate. "Talk about disgusting."

Attempting to carry it off, Ann continued eating. But she was trembling. Carefully, she balanced a small portion of rice on her fork and raised it to her lips. Having managed it successfully without spilling anything, she chewed delicately, taking care not to glance at Charles. If he chose to eat like an animal, that was his decision. But by the same token, she had choice. And she chose not to acknowledge his piggishness. She took another bite, chewed.

Charles dipped his bread into the gravy, stuffed it into his mouth, his anger at Ann's performance growing. He watched as with her knife and fork she separated a sliver of chicken from the bone. "Why the hell don't you pick it up?" he shouted. "What's all that . . . that . . . 'lady at an afternoon tea'?" Prissily, he imitated her movements. "Here!" He scooped a piece of chicken from the bowl and slapped it into her trembling hand. "Pick it up, for God's sake. It's a little late for manners, isn't it? After all these eternities."

Ann was bewildered and silent. The assurance that she had felt earlier that some danger was there, returned. In the excitement of winning, she had forgotten. Danger. She was convinced of it. But she did not know what it was. She tried to smile.

Watching her quivering lips curl into a grotesque mask of pleasant pleading, Charles felt only revulsion. "Go on, dammit. Eat the stuff," he said. "Slop it all over yourself. Think we care?"

Elise had to stop it. "You can't treat her . . ."

He would not let her finish. "Just because I say, eat?"

"But why, Charlie?" If Ann could understand it, then perhaps she could control it.

He studied her with weary disgust. "All those finicky little movements. The whole damn charade." He imitated her, showing how ludicrous she had looked. "Elegant." He laughed. "Learn that in Georgia?" Carefully he watched and saw with pleasure that the words were taking her back home. "That the way the red-necks eat their chicken? I didn't know that. Your daddy, in the mill, he eat with those little bitty bites?" Her eyes filled with tears, and he could hardly control the joy that it gave him. "And your mama. From that famous dirt farm we've heard so much about. How'd she like her chicken? I mean after she'd killed it and picked it and cleaned it and fried it? Did she eat with those prissy little bites?" He waited, hoping that she would speak, but she said nothing. He smiled and softly added, "Guess I just take after the old man."

"No."

Ann had spoken so quietly that he had hardly heard her. He

leaned forward, wanting her to say more, ready to answer. "What's that?" he asked.

She fought for control. "I said no. No, you're nothing like your father. Always, I thought that you were, but I was wrong."

He indicated the stains on her robe, his lips curled in disgust. "Look at that. All over you." With an abrupt move, he sprang from the chair, stood behind her and, holding her head, tried to spoon globs of rice and chicken into her mouth. "Here! Slop it all over yourself!"

Ann tried to break free as the food fell onto her robe.

"Good?" Charles asked. "Is it good?" And dropping the spoon onto the table, he returned to his seat, took a sip of water as though nothing had happened.

In the terrible quietness that followed, Ann looked desperately from one child to the other. "I don't understand," she said, trying to stop the tears that were threatening. "What did I do?" She waited for an answer but none came. "Elise? Tell me."

"You've done nothing." Elise wanted to offer comfort but knew that there was no way to heal the wounds.

Ann turned to Charles. "Have I?" She needed to know. "If it's something that I've done . . ." Again she waited but he said nothing, only smiled. "Well, tell me! I want to understand it."

Elise turned away, unable to continue watching her mother's desperation. "It's all right," she said.

"Sometimes . . ." Ann paused, searching for words.

"Sometimes, what?" Charles's tone was conversational.

"Sometimes I don't understand."

With his fork, Charles drew roadways through the rice and, smiling slightly, he began the explanation. "We planned something nice for you," he said. "Why ruin it? And you are the one that's ruining it, you know. Always have been."

Ann lowered her head, no longer able to control the tears.

"Look how you're acting. Sniveling and whimpering." He leaned across the table and lowered his voice almost to a whisper. "Go on, Mama," he coaxed. "Sweet Mama. Pick up your food. Pick it up and eat it. Just eat it in your hands. What difference does it make? It's nobody but us." Gently he put a piece of chicken in her hand and guided it to her mouth. Charles laughed softly as, trembling and tortured, she no longer resisted. "Easy," he whispered. "See how easy? We know how you live and we'll clean it up like we always do. Always have. We'll take care of you. Do it all the time, don't we? Up there in your room. In that place with all that filth that you like around you . . ." He smiled. "Don't we take care of you? Do this. Do that. We run and do. Fetch and carry. Change those sheets." He turned to his sister. "How many sheets you think we've changed, Lise?"

He waited for an answer but no one spoke.

Ann pushed her chair a little back from the table. Her defeat was total and she wanted only to leave. She spoke very softly. "I shouldn't have tried . . ."

"What?" Charles leaned toward her.

Still Ann spoke in whispers. "I should not . . ."

Again he interrupted. "Can't hear you."

Ann's pain was so deep that she no longer realized that she was crying. "I should not have tried to come down here," she said.

"No? Then what should you do?"

"I'm not able . . ."

Charles laughed. "Oh, you're able all right. That's one thing you are for sure." He indicated the tears. "That's right, sweet Mama thing, turn on the water works." The tears did not stop and the sight of them released a verbal fury. In frenzy, his words tumbled over one another. "Lie in that bed and whack out the orders. Right, Sarge? Lie up there in that filth. Pee all over yourself . . ."

Elise could stand no more. "Don't!"

Charles continued without pausing. ". . . and all over the bed while we . . ."

Elise clutched his arm. "I said don't!"

"Don't what?" He pulled free and turned back to Ann. "And we're always there to change the sheets and scrub you up." He directed his attention to Elise. "Don't what?"

"Don't say those things."

Ann covered her face. "Even if they're true."

Viewing her mother's humiliation had shaken Elise completely. "Especially if they're true!"

Ann's hands were throbbing. She was in pain. "I'm not well."

Charles was amused by her predictability. "Play it again, Samantha."

"I'm not. Not well! And I can't help it if . . ." She could not say the words.

Charles pressed her. "Can't help what?"

"Can't help it if I . . . If I . . ." She could not say it. They never talked about those things—the fact that at times she could not control her body functions. At night sometimes, when she was under sedation. The mention of it bowed her with shame. But why? Why was he doing it? Why would anyone? It was a mystery.

"If you what?" he insisted.

"If I . . ." She searched his face, hoping to find some explanation. It was the face that she had known and loved for so long. But different somehow. "I nursed you," she said. "Well, now it's full circle. But why would you say it? We serve each other. We belong to each other. What else do we have? . . . Each other. That's all there is."

"Is it? This awful place. This is all there is?"

Awful? Did he really think that? Ann was no longer sure of anything. She looked to Elise for reassurance.

Quietly Elise faced her brother. "If it's so awful, why do you live here? If it's so terrible, why have you stayed?"

"If I'm so 'filthy,' " Ann whispered, "why is it Charlie always runs home to Mama?" There was silence. "Why?" she repeated, calm settling over her. It was a tantrum, nothing more. Like those that he had had as a child. She smiled reassuringly to him. "You do, you know. Always have. Charlie always runs home to Mama."

He watched the smile as it touched her lips and it filled him with loneliness. It was that that had always defeated him, for he loved her smile. He closed his eyes against it. "Think you got me hooked," he said, "don't you?" His voice was a whisper.

Elise spoke quietly. "We're all hooked, Charlie."

Ann's smile dissolved into laughter. Everything would be all right after all. "All of us," she lilted. "And Mama's your fix and that's the truth, Little Baby."

Her laughter shook him. "That you will never be."

"That I have always been. Mama's been your fix from the very beginning, Baby Love. And you're mine." She held out her hand and after a moment he took it.

"You said it. I didn't." He inspected her hand, spotted with age, swollen with pain.

"That's it," she said. "Why say any of it?" And she tightened her grip on him, enjoying the shivers of hurt that sped through her.

Charles pulled his hand away. "You'll live," he said. "Until you die." And he smiled.

She wanted to caress his face. Hold him. Love him. Tell him that she loved him. "Yes," she whispered, "because I know you love me. Whatever you say, you love me. However you treat me, you love me. And that is the one thing that I know." She started to rise. "Lise." She held out her hand. "Help me back upstairs."

He watched, fascinated by her strength, sickened by it. But held steady by the knowledge that he would destroy her. "Wait a minute," he called. But she did not turn back.

Supported by Elise, she made her way to the door.

"Hold it, lady!" His voice was a command. "The surprise!"

She stopped. "No. No more surprises." Still not looking at Charles, she leaned against the doorframe, trying to get her breath. If only she could reach her bed. There everything would be all right again. She would be safe. The security that years of loving had given her was bleeding away. And she was frightened. If that assurance deserted her completely . . . If she lost that . . . No. Loving. Being loved. Nothing must ever disturb that. For that was the only reality. Everything else was games, foolishness, memory, dreams.

Charles took a stocking from his pocket and pulled it over his face. Soft laughter filled him as he took the knife and slit the material. "Mama," he whispered, his lips working free. "Aren't you even going to look?" His voice was now a promise of playful, secret things; sweet things.

"Charles, I've had all I'm going to . . ." She turned and when she saw him, she was silent; frightened. A game? No. It was too chilling. It was . . . Something terrible was about to happen. She felt it.

With cat-quiet steps, he went toward her, his finger to his lips. "Sssh," he whispered. "The surprise . . ."

Elise stepped between them. "I won't let you do this!"

His smile, distorted by the mask, was grotesque. "Not so strong now, uh?"

"You can't. Not this way."

"You said after dinner."

The mystery had gone beyond Ann's ability to follow. "Lise . . . What is it? What are you saying?"

"Don't." Elise grabbed Charles's hand. "Don't do it."

"Story," Charles said. "Once upon a time, as the saying goes . . ."

Fingers of fear closed inside Ann's chest and she gasped for breath. "I don't want to hear."

He laughed. "Once upon a time there was a boy named Charlie . . ."

Desperate, Ann turned to her daughter. "Lise!"

"Stop, Charles!" But Elise knew that he would not.

Charles kissed his sister on the cheek. "I told you that it would be worth it," he whispered. "And it is." Pulling the stocking from his head, he went to Ann. "I want to show you something . . . In my room." And, smiling, he held out his hand.

She took it, not wanting to, not meaning to. "I don't want to see," she said. But she was drawn to him. His voice was so quiet. His eyes, so soft. His smile, a promise.

"A drawer full of keepsakes," he whispered.

"Wait!" Elise caught Charles's shoulder. "You wanted it secret. We'll leave it that way."

There was silence and Elise thought for a moment that he was going to agree. Then he smiled, and before he spoke she knew that she had lost.

"Too late," he said, and put his arm around Ann. "Come on, Mama. Up we go!" He guided her toward the hall.

"No!" Violently, Ann broke away. The assurance that something terrible was about to happen returned. She did not want him to come with her.

Elise tried to hold him. "Charles. Please. I promise!"

Ignoring her, Charles reached for his mother, whispered softly, his voice a seduction, "Something I've saved for you. It's taken years." He edged her forward. "Now the drawer is full and it's time to give them to you . . . Come on. Lean on me." Ann tried to pull away but he would not let her go. "Remember what I said earlier? That you'd be sorry that you didn't kiss me. Remember?"

Ann's hands throbbed with pain. "I don't understand what you're doing," she said.

"All sorts of things to show you."

She shivered with fear. And, not wanting to understand this new and terrible game, she broke free. "I don't want to go with you." She was desperate. "Lise!"

"It's all right, Mama," Elise said, taking her hand.

Charles was not disturbed by the interruption. He was glad to have the moment prolonged. "Where else can you go?" he asked.

Her lips trembled as the tears began. "I can't stand it when you . . ."

"You can stand it."

"No."

"Oh, yes." His voice was a quiet insistence.

Rocking back and forth in misery, Ann held her arms out. "I'm burning," she said. "Oh, God, I'm burning!"

Elise held her, tried to comfort her. "Let me help."

"On fire, Lise. All of me."

"It's all right," Elise whispered.

But it was not Elise's comfort that Ann needed. She raised her eyes to Charles. "It kills me, Charlie . . . Kills me when you . . ."

Charles interrupted. "That's it," he said softly and smiled.

She choked on her tears. "Breaks my heart."

Charles's voice was so quiet and sweet that it seemed almost a lullaby. "See. You do understand," he said, and putting his arm around her shoulder, led her into the hall. "Almost home."

"No." Ann pulled away. "I don't want to . . . I don't know what you're trying to do." Confusion was all about her and she needed to be alone. "I'm tired, Charles. Tired and I'm going upstairs." He held his hand out but Ann turned from him. "I don't want you to help me. Either one of you," she said and she started toward the stairs. "Tired and my hands are burning . . ."

Charles watched as she slowly climbed the steps. Then he smiled at Elise as he went back into the dining room. He took a piece of chicken from his plate and laughed. "One thing I'll say for you, Lise . . . You can cook."

"I don't know you," she said as he reached for another piece of chicken. "Sitting there. Watching you. And Mama's face. I don't know you."

"Thought you were the one who did," he said and smiled as he moved toward her. "Come on." He nodded to the stairs. "Want to watch?"

"Don't. Don't tell her. You'll destroy her."

"Promise?" he whispered.

"I won't let you."

He laughed. "The Gymp's strong. But not that strong."

Elise grabbed his hand. "Wait . . . I don't know . . . Don't know what to do. You can't do this."

Charles smiled. "Baby Sister is such a baby." He embraced her. "Just want it not to be true, don't you? . . . Well, it is true."

Elise hid her face against his shoulder. "I love you, Charlie."

"All of it is true. And there's nothing we can do about it. Either one of us."

"Do you love me?" she asked. But there was no answer. "Tell me that you do."

The smile was gone, replaced by a kind of puzzlement. "Love Baby Sister?" It was a question. Then he laughed. And as he slipped the stocking back over his face, he brushed her forehead with a kiss.

Later she was never sure exactly how it had happened. Certainly she did not plan to do it, was as surprised as he. The knife was on the table. As she turned from him she saw it. Then . . . She did not mean to pick it up. But it was so close. And she took it. It was a dissociative action, just as what followed was. And later. When she thought the whole thing through. Again and again. She could never exactly understand.

With one swift movement, she drove the knife into the soft vulnerable area beneath the rib cage.

Always she would remember the pain in his face, the surprise.

She stepped away from him.

"No . . ." He reached out for her but she did not move to help him and he sank to his knees. Desperately he wanted to see her, to touch her but through the gauze-like stocking, she was only a blur, and fading. "No . . ." He could not breathe.

Elise watched as he fought for breath. She could not move. "Forgive me," she whispered. She had not meant to do it. Had never wanted to hurt him. She loved him. She loved him and wanted him never to be hurt. She had only wanted to stop him.

Struggling for breath, he put his hand over the wound. "No . . ."

"Say it, Charlie," she pleaded. "Say that you forgive."

"I . . . I . . ." He fought, his body shuddering. He could not breathe. There was no air. And then he was on the floor, thrashing, his feet slamming against the table, the floor, as he gasped for life. Air. There was no air.

She wanted to look away but she could not. How had it happened? How?

His lips became a terrible distortion and he clawed at the stocking that covered his face. Frantically, his powerful hands reached up for air. But he was lost. The power was going from him . . . Mama . . . He was small, no longer a giant, and he was falling. He wanted to touch something, hold something, but the world was moving away . . . Mama! . . . Why couldn't he touch something? The air! His hands fought for it. But it was not there. He tried to rise, then fell back, his body convulsing . . . Mama. Where was she? Why wasn't she there!? . . . And as he turned, writhing and kicking, the knife was twisted, further ripping the tissue of his lungs, then his heart.

Finally the sounds of struggle ceased and he was still.

"Forgive," Elise whispered. "Forgive!"

She knelt beside him, touched his hand.

"Why wouldn't you say it, Charlie?"

Gently she ran her fingers over his lips.

"Why?"

CHAPTER TWENTY-THREE

In the fingerprint lab, Ben watched as the technician dusted the gold disk of the earring. "Come on," he muttered, frustrated by the man's deliberate, clinical manner.

Finally the dust was blown away and it was there.

A perfect print.

"It's a beauty," Ben whispered and began laughing, for to him the swirls and ridges that comprised the fingerprint were more than beautiful. They were proof that his life was well spent.

"We've got him," he said. "Now we've got him."

Elise sat alone at the table. It was over. She had not meant to do it but that no longer mattered. It was done. He was dead. And what would follow?

The desperation that closed about her was so complete that she could not think. But she had to think. What could she do? A plan. She would have to have a plan . . . But what? Thoughts had become evasive, thin things, and she could not hold them.

She looked at Charles and her mind became a haunted place, too filled with memories to think of the present. Small, forgotten things threatened to become her reality—things that had happened years before when she and Charles were children.

He was dead. She knew that. She had killed him and she would

have to have some plan . . . some way to save them from questions
. . . from the terror that would come with her mother's knowing.

A plan.

But she could not think clearly. Her mind was a storm and she
could not even force herself to move from the room. She wanted to
cry but could not. Her emotions were gone. There was no feeling.
He was dead. She was looking at him. And she felt nothing.

A cigarette. She wanted a cigarette. Hers were upstairs but she
could not go up there. If she did she would have to talk to her
mother. She could not do that. Not yet.

Charles had cigarettes.

Fascinated by the gauze-covered face, she walked slowly around
the table, knelt beside her brother.

Charles.

She touched his lips, allowing the coolness of them to travel
through her fingers. The confusion of the last few days settled about
her and she leaned over and kissed him. "Why wouldn't you say you
love me?" she whispered.

She took the pack of cigarettes and matches from his shirt pocket
and, sitting close so that they were touching, she smoked.

A plan.

She would have to have a plan.

Gently she rocked back and forth, the rhythm of movement comforting her. Think . . . Think! She knew that she must, but she
could not force herself to it. She reached out, took Charles's hand.
And she watched the smoke as it floated gently in the stillness.

Smoke . . . That was all that she could think of.

Ann's room was dark. She did not want the light.

The house was too quiet and in that silence, she lay still, the covers pulled up to her chin. She knew that soon Charles would come
up the stairs and she listened for his step.

She did not understand what had happened there at the table,
knew only that it was of staggering importance—so serious that perhaps the relationships in the house had been changed forever.

Forever.

She shivered with the terror of the word and the isolation of her
early years came back to her, seemed to drift through the room,
reach out and touch her.

Lonely.

She closed her eyes to escape the shadows that waited in the corners.

No. It was not as serious as she feared. It could not be. It was a game. And soon Charles would come into the room. He would smile and it would be over. Forgotten. Lost forever in memories that would never return and they would be as they had always been. But she knew that it was not true. It would never be forgotten, completely. The memory would always be there, waiting. And because of it their lives would be different.

The chill of the evening settled about her as she listened for his step on the stairs; and the loneliness, the hollow years of her childhood, were suddenly in the room, closing about her and she wanted to cry. She trembled, knowing that the slow, hard-fought passage of time had not freed her. She was still alone, just as she had been at the beginning. The ceaseless struggle had led finally to nothing and she was alone. The flight that her life had been was, after all, a failure. She was afraid.

In the stillness she listened. Someone was moving in the hall below. She held her breath, concentrating on the sound. There were footfalls on the stairs. Charles? She listened. No, not Charles. It was Elise. She relaxed . . . waited . . . Elise . . . Elise would help her, protect her. But it was not Elise that she wanted. She wanted the night not to have happened. Only that. And how had it happened? It was a mystery to her. How? What had started it? She had been cross. They had left her alone and she had been cross. Well, there was no fault there. Surely they understood that. Always she had hated being alone. Even as a child, she had hated it. And when finally they had come in, she had wanted to make them pay. Was that wrong? All right, perhaps it was. Perhaps she had been wrong. She would tell them that and then things would be right again. It would be forgotten and everything would be as it had been. Slowly the door opened. Elise would understand. She would make things right.

"Mother?" Elise stepped into the darkened room. "Are you all right?"

"I don't understand it. Not anything that happened really. I've been lying here trying to understand."

At the bedside table, Elise poured a glass of water, started measuring her mother's medicine. "There're some things we'll never understand," she said.

Ann turned away. "You don't know how it hurts me, Lise. When he says things like that."

"He didn't mean those things."

The beginning of a laugh trembled on Ann's lips. "He meant them," she said. "Oh, he meant them all right." Her voice was thick with tears. "I'll convince myself later that he didn't. But now, this minute, I know that he meant everything. And perhaps more. Terrible things. Things that he didn't say . . . But why? That's what I can't understand. I've been lying here, in the quiet, trying to make it come right. But it won't. None of it will, Lise. It just won't come right." She leaned forward, whispered, "Is he still there?"

"He's gone." Elise held the medicine out.

"I didn't hear the car."

"Here." She handed Ann the glass of water. "He's gone."

In the darkened entrance hall, Elise sat on the stairs. At last her mother was asleep. She had waited in the room until the medication had taken effect, knowing that she would need the night to herself, for whatever was going to be done must be done before the morning.

But what could she do? She must decide but that seemed an impossibility, for her mind would no longer function. Had her mother noticed? No. She had been too caught up in her own fears.

Charles. He was still there beyond the door that led to the dining room.

Charles.

She relived those moments. feeling the knife as it went so easily into his body, seeing him fall—so slowly—his hands reaching toward her, the surprise on his lips.

And he had refused to say that he loved her. "Love Baby Sister?" he had said. But it had been a question. The inflection in his voice had made that inescapable.

Had he understood? Had he known as he fell that no other choice was open to her? That the quick movement of her hand had been an action that was not planned, not questioned, not even understood?

She looked to the door.

Charles. It had to be finished.

Steadying herself on the bannister, she went slowly down the stairs, not knowning what she would do.

For a long moment she looked at the body and suddenly the room was filled with ghost memory. Charles child-self seemed to linger in the musty air. She could see him as he had been all those years before and she was shaken, filled with the love that she had always felt.

There seemed to be a stirring in the room. Or was it only within her? That child that Charles had been, was he in the room? Somewhere hidden between the gauze-fine layers of air that could not be seen? She felt that he was and she trembled.

No one must ever know. But how could that be done?

He must never be found. But how could she manage?

She took his hands and pulled him along the floor toward the kitchen. It was the only way. There had been an argument. He had left.

Left and never come back.

The memory of the night would soften with time and Ann would wait for him, knowing that some mild California evening he would come up the stairs, tap on her door and smile . . . "Love my mama . . ."

She would never know what his life had been, what he had been.

With time, with the constant reliving of those moments at the table, it would become simply a misunderstanding.

And Ann would wait for him.

No one would ever know the truth.

In the laundry room, Elise lowered the body into the tub and leaned against the wall, exhausted. But she knew that it was only the beginning, that she could not allow herself the time-wasting luxury of rest. Abruptly, she turned and went into the kitchen.

It was decided. The plan was firm.

She needed a cigarette but there was not time.

She stood at the sink, knowing that she must start but she could not force herself to do it.

The table. The thought was a reprieve. She would clear the table. And then she would finish what she had started.

At the sink she dried the last of the plates, neatly folded the towel and hung it up.

She could postpone it no longer. She went to the laundry room.

Charles's head was resting against the rim of the tub, rolled to one side in an attitude of slumber. Water from the faucet dripped onto his neck and glistened there, a reminder of life.

Elise trembled as she started unbuttoning his shirt.

It was what she had to do.

Ann stood by the window, looking out. A match flared in the darkness as she lit a cigarette. For a moment she studied her reflection in the glass, fascinated by the image that waited there—that frail, witchlike woman. Was it possible that she was that old? How could she be? And where had it gone? The energy and dreams? The determination that had brought her so far from home?

Charles.

She blew out the match and turned away as the reflection faded to black. Where was Charles? She had not heard the car. Had he walked? Was he so eager to escape that he had walked down the hill?

She sat on the side of the bed. Would he forgive?

But forgive what? What had she done?

She lay across the covers, softly caressing her hands. The pain was stronger than it had ever been before. So strong that she could not sleep. Even after taking as much medicine as she had.

"Charlie," she whispered. "Oh, Charlie . . ."

She folded her arms across her breasts and held her shoulders, not caring about the pain. "Forgive me . . ." Would he? "For whatever it is, forgive me."

Like a child she gently rocked from side to side.

Elise had not realized that it would be so difficult. She knelt beside the tub, the implements nestled among Charles's clothes which were beside her on the floor. The knives had been sharpened but still the task was more exhausting than she had thought. She had finally cut through the sockets where the arms were joined to the shoulders.

She trembled with fatigue as she carved along the crease at the top of his thigh. Her mind was claimed by memory, by images and sounds. All were from the past, from the days when they were children, when there was no thought of terror beyond the terrible loneliness that held them so close one to the other.

She cut through the flesh, sawed where the bones were joined. But she did not hear the sound of the blade against the bone. Instead she heard his voice calling as he had when they were children.

"Here I am, Charlie," she whispered in reply and saw herself running toward him across the yard.

With her hands she twisted the leg back and there was a sound of breaking. And the sound brought her back to an immediate awareness. She rested her forehead against the rim of the tub, certain that she was going to be sick. But there was not time to be sick. She must finish.

She took the cleaver and, turning her face away, brought it down in a powerful stroke. There was silence and she looked at what she had done.

Then as she cut the tendrils of flesh and severed the leg from the trunk, the doorbell rang.

Elise stood in the front hall, her heart racing; her mind, confusion. She fought to control her breathing, knowing that she must not make a sound.

There was a knock.

With careful, quiet steps she approached the door, leaned against it, welcomed the coolness of the wood.

"Who is it?" she whispered.

Again the knock came and, as she reached to open the door, she saw that her hands were covered with blood. She looked at her blouse. Bits of flesh were caught there like fragments of light. They seemed to glisten.

The bell rang again. "Lise," she heard someone call and she unlatched the small brass covering and looked through.

It was Billy. "Brought the leftovers," he said. And smiling, he held up a neatly tied pastry box, swung it back and forth, his face a vapid promise of fun times.

"Well, come on. Let me in," he lilted, his stance a pose of coy impatience.

"I can't."

"Something's the matter." Suddenly the fun was gone, replaced by a moment of death. "It's Ann," he said and his eyes filled with terror.

"She's tired."

"Tell me the truth!"

"I am, Billy. She's sleeping."

"You're sure that's all? You're telling the truth?"

"I already gave her her medicine."

He was relieved. "Then let me in," he said. "Just stay a second. Quiet as can be." Again he swayed the pastry box. "We're in luck tonight. There were mocha cakes left. Five of them. Napoleons too."

Elise watched as his smiled faded. "Just leave them there," she said.

Billy's heart caught. "Then something is the matter," he insisted, his voice again hollow with fear. "It's Annie."

"No, Billy. No." She did not want to talk to him. Could not stand looking at him. His terrible aging, woman face filled her with disquiet and she wanted him to go. "It's nothing," she said, but he did not leave. He continued standing there, looking so foolish in his silly, tight waiter's jacket. Why wouldn't he leave? There was so much that she had to do.

"But don't you want the mochas?" he pouted.

"Leave them," she said. "Just leave them there and come back tomorrow." And she closed the tiny brass door and, with a snap, latched it.

Billy stood in the darkness of the porch. What should he do? Something was wrong. Definitely. There must be. Otherwise, why would she refuse to open the door to him? Charles was there. His car was in the back. If Annie was sleeping, the three of them could visit, eat the mochas and drink coffee. No! Something was wrong. And he did not know what to do. Should he call someone? But who would he call?

After a moment he went into the yard and looked up to the windows of Ann's room. There was a light—the dim one that was left on when she was sleeping. Perhaps Elise was telling the truth.

But . . . that did not explain her behavior. Definitely something had happened. He went back onto the porch, determined to find out what it was.

Elise had not moved. She was waiting there, her face close to the door. Billy was moving about on the porch. She could hear him. Why didn't he leave? The sounds of movement stopped and she knew that he was standing very near.

Again Billy reached out toward the bell, but stopped himself. If Ann was asleep, that might awaken her. He started to knock. But what would he say when Elise came back? He clamped down on his dentures, wiggled them about. He did not know what to do.

Then within him something happened, something that he did not understand. A chill passed over him and he shivered with the sudden certainty that his fear was justified. Elise was on the other side of the door, listening. Billy was sure of it. She was standing very still, being careful not to make a sound. There was only quietness but still he knew that he was right. She was there. Waiting. And something terrible had happened.

He knelt down, put the box of pastries on the top step and walked across the lawn. The silence of night was everywhere and his steps were so light that he might have been moving through space where sound was an unknown thing.

Then he heard it.

A quiet scraping.

The small brass covering was being opened and he knew that Elise was watching, waiting for him to leave.

He continued on across the grass. She needed to be certain that he was gone. But why? He did not look back. Why was she watching? Why did she not want him there?

He reached the car and as he closed the door, put the key in the ignition, he began to tremble, a terrible cold fear touching him. What was it? He started the engine, slowly drove down the winding drive. As he turned into the street, his trembling became so extreme that he could hardly control himself.

"But why?" he said aloud.

He did not understand it.

The pages of the scrapbook were old and yellowed, the photographs, faded. Ann was seated on the floor, the contents of the cedar chest scattered about her. The light, filtering through the Tiffany lamp shade, cast tinted shadows over the pictures. She leaned close to examine one of the photographs, touched it lovingly. It was Charles, standing alone in the yard, a very serious little boy in a 1935 Buster Brown collar. His face was eager, trying to smile, wanting to please as he waved to the camera, a toy clutched in his hand.

"Bring it here," Ann whispered. "Mama said bring it here."

She smiled, fascinated by the soft, multicolored fragments of light that fell across the picture. "That's right," she said and gently circling the face with her fingers, she laughed quietly. These were the possessions that she most cared for, the memories frozen on the photographer's paper and in her mind—nothing else mattered as deeply.

Charles. He had said terrible things. Terrible. She shivered.

Elise stood in the doorway of the laundry room. There was too much to do and she was so tired.

The face. She was glad that it was covered by the stocking for she knew that she could not stand to see his eyes.

She tried to plan but it was difficult. The rib cage. If she could peel the skin back . . . If she could catch the ribs, pull outward . . . break them . . .

As she knelt by the tub, the body—what was left of it—moved; slipped on the liquid-slick tile and the head came to rest in such a way that the dark pools beneath the nylon that were Charles's eyes, seemed to be watching her.

There was a sound.

Ann lifted her eyes from the photograph and gazed about the room. There were only shadows but she was sure that she had heard something.

"Charlie?" she whispered, her voice hoarse and rasping. She listened for a moment but there was nothing but silence. She stood and looked into the shadowy corners. "Baby," she said, expecting him to come out of the darkness.

Had it been her imagination? No. She was certain that she had heard something. Reflected in the mirror, she saw herself and slowly moved to the image. She smiled. And studying herself with innocent wonder, she touched her fingers to the creases that bordered her lips.

What had the sound been? Definitely, she had heard something. She gave a soft, ghost laugh.

"Thought it was you, Charlie boy," she said and the laugh froze on her lips. Someone was there. Through the glass, she looked about the room. There was something. There in the shadows.

Quickly she turned, upsetting a bottle of cologne which spilled over the dresser top.

"Is it you?" she whispered. She could see nothing but she felt that some presence was with her. There was a sound and she looked to the window.

A rush of wind billowed past the curtains and she was unable to move. A presence had entered. She was sure of it. Although nothing could be seen, there was a sudden coolness to the air and she was chilled.

"Charlie?" she whispered, and waited. But there was no sound.

The cool air brushed past her and she caught her breath.

"Is it you?"

It was done.

Elise stood at the sink, the warm, comforting water splashing over her hands.

That part of it was finished.

The head. That had been the most difficult. Touching it . . . the slippery material of the stocking . . . It had . . . No! She would not think about it. She fought to keep thoughts that were now buried within her mind from surfacing. She would not think about them. There was too much that must be done.

There was a sound and she turned, leaving the water running. The air seemed to stir and a coolness settled into the room.

What was it? Elise stood very still, the water dripping from her hands onto the floor.

It was nothing.

But there had been a noise—some rustling—she was sure of it.

She turned the water off, forcing her mind to emptiness. There was nothing there. Nothing. No sound. No movement. Nothing.

It was over.

Thank God.

It was finished . . . That part.

And no one would ever know.

Ann was seated at the window, watching as the first streaks of day began to lighten the sky.

"Charlie," she whispered. And, her face weary and sorrowful, she turned from the last of the darkness that was beyond the window. "I hate the dark," she said.

Elise took her hand. "Come to bed, Mama."

"Always hated it."

"It's almost morning."

As Elise helped her to the bed, Ann tried to speak, but could not. She was confused and wanted to cry. "Charles," she said finally. "He'll be here."

Elise pulled the covers over her mother. "No."

"He didn't mean those things." Ann tried to laugh. "Foolish . . . He'll be here, Lise. By the time I wake up, he'll be standing right there. Right where you are."

"Go to sleep," Elise said. She could not stand to watch the childish, eager face.

"I'm sorry, that's what he'll say. And that quickly, everything will be all right."

"He may not come back, Mama. Not for a long time." Elise wanted to curl up on the bed beside her mother. She wanted to be held and comforted, rocked back and forth and gently kissed.

Ann watched her daughter, trying to understand what she had said, what the words had meant. She turned away from the mystery of it.

"It may be a long time," Elise whispered. "A very long time."

There was silence and then Ann smiled. "Look, Lise," she said and held her hands out. Her lips trembled as the smile became a ghost.

"Look . . ." Her voice was frail, filled with wonder. "I'm all on fire."

The morning grayness of the California autumn invaded Charles's room with dampness. Elise knelt before the bureau and opened the drawer. For the last time she inspected the trophies that were hidden there. Carefully she gathered them up and took them to the fireplace. Already the logs were burning. The clothes that Charles had been wearing—and those that she had worn—were waiting on the hearth. She tossed his blood-stained shirt into the flames and watched as the fire ran its quick, greedy fingers over it.

She forced her mind away from memory.

The shirt was only a shirt. Not his. Not Charles's.

Ann awakened, tried to focus on the day. But her mind was blurred by pain and medication and she could not grasp things.

The scrapbook was lying on the floor. Why was it there? She gasped with the pain that was in her hands and for a moment seemed lost.

"Lise," she whispered and, leaning over to the medicine table, searched for the tablets that would soothe her. She found the plastic cylinder and struggled to open it.

Her hands shook and the tablets spilled onto the floor. She needed something for the pain. Desperately, she wanted the tablets and they were gone. In confusion, she stumbled across the room.

"Lise," she called.

Elise looked up as Ann opened the door. She had just put the last of the news clippings and photographs into the fire. Only the stockings remained.

"No," she said, as her mother came into the room.

"Need you, Lise."

"Go back!"

Memories of the previous evening began to intrude on Ann. She moved toward the fire. "What is it?"

Elise stood. "Don't look . . . Don't."

Ann turned to her, confused and frightened.

"Go back, Mother." Elise's voice was soft, urgent. Slowly Ann backed from the room.

Elise was hiding something. What was it? No! She did not want to know.

Ann closed the door and stood alone in the hall. She turned and walked slowly back to her room.

Where was Charles? Why didn't he come home?

"Mother . . ."

Elise stood by Ann's bed, the breakfast tray in her hands.

Slowly Ann awakened. She stared about the room, shielding her eyes against the brightness.

Elise placed the tray before her, handed her morning medicine to her.

"Know what, Lise?" Ann looked toward the windows. "I'm afraid," she said and leaned back against the pillows. "I don't know why, but I am." Her voice was a whisper and she closed her eyes against the day.

CHAPTER TWENTY-FOUR

The room—walls, floor, air, everything—seemed alive, vibrating with mechanized sound.

Impatiently, Ben waited as the giant banks of machinery made their dispassionate selections. Programed to reject all cards that did not belong to the same group as the print found on the girl's earring, they did their work with speed and efficiency.

In rhythm to the ceaseless whirring, Ben reviewed his actions; checking them off, point by point. Everything had been done. Everything.

And if the man's prints were on file anywhere, he would be found. It would be over.

They were almost there. Ben could feel it.

"We've got you," he whispered, his voice cold and eager.

"Yes, sir," he said. And one by one he cracked his knuckles and bit his lip, in beat with the vibrations of the room.

"Yes sir!"

Elise clutched the telephone, her face creased with frustration. "No," she said. "I have to have immediate delivery. That's the point!" Her voice edged toward anger. "Yes, we have an account. I've already given you the number." How many times did she have to explain? "No! This morning! I want it this morning! I'll be glad to pay extra if . . ." Her voice trailed off as the stranger on the other end of the line interrupted. "Yes, I understand that. But you must understand that I have to have it before noon. Noon at the absolute latest. So if you'll personally see that it gets on the morning delivery, I'll appreciate it." She listened, relaxing. "Thank you. Thank you," she said. "I can't thank you enough."

She hung up the receiver and for a long time stood where she was.

It was almost over.

It would be on the morning delivery. They had promised.

By midafternoon it would be finished.

Elise sat on the back steps, waiting for the truck. She stared across the lawn which held so many memories. Everywhere they were waiting. She could almost hear the voices from the past as ghost images flooded through her mind.

They were both there, her father and Charles. Their hands, their way of moving, the warmth of their eyes came back to her more strongly than the emptiness that was real. She saw her father as he had been on some long-ago afternoon. He smiled and held out his hand. She wanted to go to him but she could not move. Then she saw Charles. He was beckoning. But it was the Charlie of memory, for he was a child. She wanted to call out, but she could not. She watched as he went to their father.

And, their backs to her, they walked into the shadows beneath the trees.

She longed to follow but she knew that she could not.

With difficulty she stood and started back up the cement steps. The yard was now a haunted place and she could not stay there.

She reached for the screen door . . . Her hand trembled on the knob. She did not want to open it for she was afraid of the house. Suddenly the rooms beyond the door were more terrible than the yard.

She clenched the metal knob so tightly that pain stabbed through her hand. She welcomed it. Pain was real. The rest was imagination, memory, regret. She would not bow to it. There were still things that had to be done.

Quickly she went into the house, letting the door slam and rattle behind her.

Surely they would deliver it before the morning ended.

They had to.

They had promised.

"That's it!"

The delivery man slapped his hand down onto the shiny enamel that encased the new machine which he and his fellow worker had just installed.

It was a compactor, designed to press material into compact, tightly pressed blocks.

"Fill it up." He dumped the contents of the garbage can into the machine. "Shut this." He slammed the small lid with its glass window. "Flip it on." He snapped the button, leaned back. "And now just watch it work." He folded his arms, smiling at the efficiency of the machine.

Elise watched through the glass window of the lid as a blunt metal lever hovered over the center of the interior of the machine. Slowly the lever pressed down, crushing the tin cans and other refuse that was within. This completed, the lever returned to its start position, awaiting another activation.

His face aglow with satisfaction, the delivery man opened the lid and took out the bag of garbage that had been compacted into a small, neat package.

"Yes, ma'am," he said. "Best thing for the job ever invented." He held up a flat metal disk that had been a tin can. "See?" he bragged and patted the machine with rough affection. "This baby can take three garbage cans of stuff and mash 'em down into one little sackful." His weathered face became a winning smile. "Yes, ma'am," he said.

Elise was almost finished.

It had gone more quickly than she had thought it would. At first there had been some difficulty and she had been forced to cut some of the larger sections into smaller pieces. But after that . . .

She felt a terrible urge to laugh. The garbage disposal, a lot of it had been taken care of there. It was already almost three and she was exhausted.

But definitely she would finish in time.

Time. Three. Time for Ann's midafternoon medicine.

Quickly she washed her hands and hurried from the room.

In quietness, the men worked.

There was a row of desks and seated at each was a man trained in fingerprint analysis. The cards that the computer had selected were examined, compared to the suspect's print. It was a frustrating job and an air of tension hovered.

Ben knew that his presence there was wasted, perhaps even aggravating to the men who were working, and that he should go to his office and wait. But he could not. They were close to the end. He felt it. And he wanted to be there.

One of the men arose. And, taking with him the card that he had been examining, he went to his superior. For a moment they conferred. Then, as they walked toward Ben, he knew that it was over.

"Here's your man," the officer said as he held out the card.

Ben looked at the name, the address. "What's he on file for?"

"Driver's license application."

Ben nodded to Logan. "Let's go."

Ann sat before the flickering television set, her attention once more captured by the magic of the small screen. There was a noise in the hallway. "Lise?" she called.

Elise came in and carefully measured her mother's medicine, forcing herself not to hurry. But there was so little time. Twenty minutes at the most.

Ann did not shift her gaze from the dancing stars of the afternoon movie. She smiled at the familiar couple on the screen. "Ginger and Fred," she said.

The pedestrian predictability of the comment stunned Elise. She turned to the set where the two celebrated figures tapped and whirled across a shining floor. Elise trembled as she watched Ginger and Fred dip and float through a chorus of smiling, shuffling girls of the Thirties.

Elise could not control herself. Tears streamed down her face, a torrent of laughter broke from her. She could not stop it. She did not try. Balancing crazily between laughter and tears, she knelt beside her mother.

Ann was startled. "What is it?"

Frenzied and shaking, Elise buried her head in her mother's pillow. "Ginger and Fred," she said. "It's Ginger and Fred."

For a moment Ann was almost frightened. Then, without realizing that she was doing so, nor understanding why, she too began to laugh. "Ginger and Fred," she exclaimed and pointed to the screen.

While the two women laughed, Ginger and Fred tapped and spun. The laughter edged closer and closer to hysteria as the staccato taps became more frantic.

"Ginger and Fred." They laughed and shrieked. "It's Ginger. Ginger and Fred!"

As Elise hurried into the kitchen, she glanced at her watch. Yes. She would make it. Ten minutes. That long at least.

She disappeared into the laundry room and emerged carrying the last reminder of what had happened. She opened the lid of the compactor and deposited the stocking-clad globe into the waiting compartment, closed the lid and switched on the machine.

For a moment the lever hovered over the mesh-covered sphere. She wanted to turn away but she could not. She was fascinated. "It's over," she whispered as the lever pressed steadily downward.

"Now it's over."

Ben leaned forward as the car wove its way through the freeway traffic. Why had he let Logan drive? It had been a stupid decision.

If he had been behind the wheel, he could have made much better time. He was sure of it.

"Which off-ramp?" Logan asked.

"Gower. Then Franklin to Highland. Then into the hills." Ben nodded to an opening in the stream of cars. "Into the right lane," he said. "Now!"

The truck was coming. Elise could hear the grind of gears as it labored up the hill. She could not see it but she knew that at any moment it would round the curve and stop at the drive.

She hurried across the lawn, straining as she clutched the last of the heavy bags. Just in time. Trembling with exhaustion she ran as fast as she could. She stumbled, almost fell. A terrible pain surged through her leg and she stopped. Stupid. She leaned against the trunk of a tree. Stupid to hurry so. Now . . . Now when it was almost finished. If she had fallen . . . fallen and dropped the bag . . . Well, she had not fallen. She had planned and planned well. She had finished in time and now it would be over.

No one would ever know.

The garbage truck was waiting at the gate. One of the men approached with the cans from across the street. He saw Elise and nodded as she came toward him. He was emptying a can into the steel jaws of the mechanized truck when Elise put the bag next to the others that were waiting there, her arms shaking with the strain.

"I'll take those." The man grabbed them and smiled at her as he tossed them into the truck.

Elise's eyes held his. "Thank you." The words were a sigh, barely audible, and she willed him not to look toward the grinding mouth of the machine.

"Anytime." He checked her over. Not bad, he thought and his smile broadened as he emptied the contents of another can into the truck. Hurrying across the street, he tossed the cans back where he had found them. Then he turned to her and smiled brilliantly. "Not bad at all," the smile said. "For a cripple."

"Ho!" With a roar he signaled for the truck to proceed, hopping on the side as it passed.

Elise strained, looking for any sign that might bring discovery. Was there blood? That had been her fear. She did not see any. No. Whatever evidence might have been there had been obliterated by the contents of the cans from across the street.

The garbage man turned and gave one last wave as the truck disappeared around a curve.

For a long time Elise stood where she was. Then she turned and went slowly back toward the house.

It was all done.

Finished.

They were safe.

In a week or so she would notify Missing Persons and strangers would come to the house, conduct their interviews.

Charles would become a name in a file. That would be his headstone. That and the images that she carried from the night before would be all that was left of him.

She paused at the tree where she had almost fallen. If she had not caught herself . . . If her foot had turned a little more this way or that . . . Then she would have been lost, the contents of the bag scattered over the lawn where they could have been seen . . . Was that what it was with Charles? Something as small as that? A stumbling somewhere long ago? She did not know. She only knew that he was gone. And all that would remain would be a file in some closed drawer and the endless, slow, graceful action of the knives and cleaver cutting deeper and deeper into the folds of her mind.

She continued on across the grass. A file in a drawer. That was all. He would exist nowhere else. No. She stopped. There was one other thing. Her mother. The love that they had both felt for him. That too would remain. That would last forever.

Billy's pastry box, neatly tied and filled with last night's leftovers, was waiting on the top step. She picked it up as she went onto the porch.

Softly she closed the door behind her and stood in the silence. The afternoon movie was over and most likely her mother was napping. Soon she would awaken and it would be time for dinner.

She turned, walked into the living room. It was an ugly place, dust-laden and never used. For years she had cleaned it twice every week, despite the fact that no one ever went in there. Then as she became weaker, as the pain in her legs increased, she had given up, let it go. What difference did it make?

She sat in one of the wing chairs, dust rising from the frayed cut velvet. Her legs were throbbing, her hands trembling, her mind dissolving.

"What will happen?" she whispered. Nothing. Nothing would ever happen. "To me," she said. "What will happen to me?"

Fear possessed her, claimed her completely.

Nothing would happen.

Always she had depended on Charles, had known that in the end it would be the two of them. That finally Ann would die. Had secretly waited for the day when Mama would die. Then it would be Charles and Elise. Forever.

But now? What was there now? Her mind seemed to float, then surge away, caught by undertow. Now all that remained was . . . Desperately she searched, knowing that there must be something . . . All that remained was . . . was . . . Ginger and Fred. She shook with quiet laughter. Ginger and Fred. She was made breathless by the loneliness of it.

That was all.

Ann and Elise. And Ginger and Fred.

She heard the sound of a car turning into the drive. Billy, she thought. Come back to eat his mocha cakes. And she went to the window. Billy. He would always be there as well.

But it was not Billy.

She did not recognize the car. Nor the men. They were walking toward the house.

The bell rang and she went into the hall. As she started to open the door, she was shaken by a terrible trembling. There was blood . . . there where she had rested her hands the night before.

Again the bell rang.

"Who is it?" she asked.

But before the answer came, she knew.

Boldly she opened the door, determined that she would not be defeated.

The officer greeted her with his badge. "Ben Hamilton, Los Angeles Police Department. We're looking for Charles Johnston."

"Charlie?" Elise said. "He just left."

And after only the slightest pause, she almost smiled.